AF

The D Word

First came ABC then came D.

Joanna Warrington

Printed by Createspace
First published 2014
01

http://www.joannawarringtonauthor-allthingsd.co.uk

ISBN: 1502778904
ISBN 13: 9781502778901

1
Clifford

September 2007

It is impossible to relate Clifford's tragic story without a liberal salt and pepper sprinkling of expletives. Imagine an autobiography by Russell Brand or Gordon Ramsey de boned, stripped bare of expletives. Clifford liked a good rant. It was part of his nature. He found it cathartic. The 'F' word, the 'B' word and the 'S' word and occasionally the vulgar 'C' word were all used to good and potent effect. Whereas a chimney spewed smoke Clifford spewed words. Words turned heads, made people sit up and listen. Words could hurt, heal, damage or slay in an instant. He had the mouth of the Blackwall Tunnel and the looks and stature of a common garden gnome.

He could clearly recall his finest hour - the first time he used the 'F' word - not long after his eighth birthday; a defining moment in his early life. He had an accident at school in which he shamefully messed his pants. The teacher wrapped his soiled clothing in brown paper and sent him on his way. His classmates teased and tormented him down the busy North London street to the bus stop. Turning round and telling them to 'fuck off' had been the biggest buzz ever. Years later he described it as a rush of ecstasy to the brain. Instantly he was inches taller and stronger. He was proud of himself. From that day on he practiced the word regularly.

It was curious that a journalist - a scribe once upon a time for the BBC - believed swear words to be the best in the English dictionary. A single swear word could replace twenty empty sounding words. Not even his 84 year old mother could shame Clifford into stopping - especially not on the morning of the 14th of September 2007 - the day he was flying to China.

'Mum, it's six in the fucking morning. I've got a flight to catch from Heathrow in a few hours. You know what the queues are like on the M25 - and you're panicking about a little queue forming outside the Northern Rock.'

'I might lose my entire savings. Everything your father left me.'

'Stop fretting. It won't come to that. Don't withdraw the money. Are you listening to me? You don't understand the first thing about economics. I bet you've not eaten breakfast. Go and make yourself a decent bowl of porridge. I'll call round when I'm back from China and if there's still only half a jar of peanut butter in the fridge I'm going to *have* to place an order for Wiltshire Meals. I know you don't like the idea but lots of old folk have them.'

Clifford put his phone back in his pocket. Worrying about his elderly mother was the last thing he needed right now. There were so many other important things going on. He was trying to win a new business contract in China – the reason for his trip over there. Tension mounted as it always did before deals were secured. He had the long flight to unwind with Tom Clancy's 'Hunt for Red October' and a double gin; small pleasures in his hectic life.

Annie

Annie hadn't eaten porridge in weeks. Clifford was always telling her to eat porridge. These days she had no appetite. She waited for the kettle to boil, poured a cup of tea and returned to the TV - her eyes fixed on the queues at Northern Rock. It seemed unreal, in modern Britain. The last time she had seen such long queues was in the Great Depression. She just about remembered her dad queuing at the Labour Exchange, day after day waiting for a job to turn up and the look of anguish he would try and hide when he came back early with still no job.

She was the type of person to see a queue and join it even if she didn't know why people were queuing. At 8am - ignoring Clifford's advice not to worry - she gathered her bank book, passport and a council tax bill in case they needed identity and hurried off down the hill to her local branch of the Northern Rock. At 4pm she was trudging back up the hill, thousands of pounds fluttering around in old Tesco carriers.

At 6pm as she ate a peanut butter sandwich for her tea she felt happier that the money was safe. Shutting the curtains on the world outside she was relieved that the money was now locked away in her grandfather's old wardrobe, the rusty key in her chipped Charles and Diana teapot under the kitchen sink, hidden between the bleach and the Harpic.

The news reports had terrified her. It seemed safer to keep the money at home; to use the wardrobe as an ATM. Bank cards and pin numbers were confusing and the staff were always asking her if she could 'access the web' whatever that meant. Nobody seemed to take cheques anymore. Life had become complicated. And she could never remember her pin number. At first she wrote it on a scrap of paper and kept it folded in her purse but Clifford shouted at her when he found out.

The postmistress was the only person who knew her number. She trusted the postmistress and if she forgot the number she could pop in to be reminded. But lately even the postmistress had started to complain; saying she could lose her job if anyone found out. Annie wondered why people made a fuss over small favours.

It was easier not to ask people for help or tell them too much. And whenever she asked Clifford for help – maybe to change a light bulb, or the washer on a tap or ask his help with filling in a form he was always sharp and in a rush.

'I'll do it next week' he'd say, or 'can't you do that yourself.' His swearing scared her. Made her heart jump to her throat. To be scared of your own son was a terrible thing. He seemed angry with her and with life and wondered where that had come from.

As she sat on her Ercol chair waiting for the weather forecast, picking at the peanut butter sandwich, she thought about their lives and the past. So much had happened. Could she still trust him? She wasn't sure anymore.

A thought started to prey on her mind, like a worm burrowing into a rotting carcass. It was a dark and sinister thought. It was something she had rarely talked about over the years; a pain buried in the hope it would ease with time. Recently though it had risen to the surface - along with all the other mounting troubles swelling inside her head. She'd wait until he returned from China and ask him some pertinent questions – questions that should have been asked a long time ago.

That night she woke, disorientated. A dog was barking. The radiators were making a gentle bubbling hum. She sat up. Eased her feet into slippers. She felt clammy. Her nighty was sticking to her chest. The room was bathed in full moonlight for it was a clear night.

She felt her breasts. They weren't engorged as she had thought. She had been sure they were pumping and heavy with milk. She looked at the bottom of the bed. There was no cot. Only a blanket box covered in her clothing from the previous day. For one awful moment she thought her baby had been snatched. Her heart thudded in her chest. Then reality trickled through as it slowly dawned on her that her dream had become a part of her. Her confused state melted away. Grief suddenly weighed heavy. Her baby had been gone for many years. All around her the silence of the night seemed at once oppressive. She longed for the cry of a baby. She put her hands to her breasts again and remembered she'd had a mastectomy. She looked down, turned towards the moonlight and saw the scars.

She went into the kitchen. Remembered the money in the wardrobe. It was a lot of money to store in her flat. Anxiety niggled. She needed to find a way of keeping a track of it. Taking a notebook from the drawer she began to draw columns working out a system to manage it. Then she tore a piece from the back and wrote a list of reminders:

1. Ask Clifford about Simon.
2. Pay milkman.
3. Pawn broker calling Wednesday.
4. £300 - plumber to fix leaking tap.
5. £200 - odd job man putting curtain rail back up.

Life was going to be so much easier, more convenient now that her money was easily accessible for paying all the odd job people who frequently knocked, offering to help her with various jobs and services. And of course it avoided having to trouble Clifford. He was far too busy to help. She'd show him. She could cope perfectly well. He'd always told her not to answer the door to strangers. But these were nice, pleasant people who popped in for a cuppa and a chat and it saved time trawling through the Yellow Pages.

Annie checked her diary after breakfast. It was the 20th of September, the day Clifford was returning from China. Unless she'd made a diary entry she would have completely forgotten he was going there or when he was returning. He went on so many business trips. She couldn't keep up.

It was only five in the morning but she prepared two teacups, a milk jug, a teapot and a plate of biscuits under a cellophane wrap and set it on her hostess trolley with a doily - ready for later when he called by. She had forgotten to ask what time he'd be calling so she sat next to the window for most of the day looking up and down the road until finally she saw his car pull up at 5pm.

Clifford fidgeted in the chair. He'd glanced at the clock on the mantelpiece four times during the past twenty minutes as they talked. Looked at his watch twice. Checked his mobile three times. She knew he didn't want to be there, in her flat. That was clear. Why bother visiting, she thought. She'd spent the day waiting and looking forward to him coming and he was now checking his mobile for the fourth time.

'What's it like out?' She glanced out of the window.

'Mild. For September.'

'Where did you park?'

'By the garages.' There was then a brief silence.

'What airport have you been to?'

'Heathrow.'

Annie looked out of the window again. Clifford took a sip of tea.

'What's it like out?'

'Mild.'

'Where did you park the car?'

'By the garages.'

'Sorry. Have I already asked - what airport did you say?'

'Heathrow. I always go from Heathrow. You know that.' He gave a spectacular huff.

'Much happening in Eastenders lately mum? And Emmerdale?' He sighed again.

'Erm. The usual arguments. People having affairs, babies.' And then she remembered.

'Well...' He eased his bottom to the edge of the settee and shuffled to get up. The familiar creak of his old leather jacket and the jangle of money in his pockets as he put it back on made her heart tug. There wouldn't be any other visitors that week. Not until the plumber called.

'I suppose I'll have to get home. Unpack, put the washing machine on.'

Annie watched him adjust his jeans, pulling his belt tighter as he always did when he stood up.

He returned his cup to the kitchen, rinsed it and set it to dry on the draining board. She waited in the doorway wondering how to begin. It had been so long since they had talked about Simon's death. He'd ask *why now?* And she wouldn't know. Blood pricked and thumped in her head. She leant against the door frame for support.

She followed him into the hall, her slippers squeaking on the lino. He reached for the door handle and as she touched his hand she caught a *what now* look plastered across his face. He sighed.

'How's Simon?'

His face hardened. Body stiffened.

'Simon? Don't you mean Ben? He's fine. Mum you're getting muddled these days.'

'Ben. Simon.' She hesitated. 'What happened the night Simon died?' She gripped his arm, gently pleading. He jerked it away as if her touch burned like electricity.

'That was years ago.' His flustered look had been replaced with incredulity.

'How did he die? Clifford. How did he *really* die? I need to know. You...'

'Yes? What are you saying mum? He stopped breathing. You know he did. It was a cot death.' The look had been replaced with a hint of sarcasm.

'You never wanted a brother. You were jealous of him.'

'What's this about? For fuck sake.'

He stepped closer, his hand on her shoulder. She shuddered.

A radiator groaned to life behind them. A door banged in the flat above.

His fingers pressed tightly on her shoulder, the grip sending waves through her upper body as if it were a wizard's staff. She stepped back, alarm coursing through her and waited. Maybe he would remember. His face had darkened. He sighed. She could taste the strain in his breath. He looked at the left wall. Then the right wall as if the answer was painted across the hallway.

'You think I murdered him don't you?' The word was out. Black ink splattered before them staining their relationship forever.

'You think I would kill my own brother? I was eleven years old mum. I was still a kid myself.'

'You never wanted him. Did you pick him up? Hit his head maybe in a fit of anger? You changed when he was born. You became moody, irritable. I remember that much.' She persisted.

'It was a shock. You were what? Forty? Pregnant at forty? Christ mum. What were you both thinking of? We had no space. If you hadn't invited my dreadful grandparents to live with us then maybe, just maybe things might have worked out differently. None of it made sense. Why didn't you prepare me, tell me you were pregnant? What kind of parents would keep something like that from their child?'

She didn't know how to reply. Hadn't planned a reply.

'Don't make me feel ashamed.'

But the truth was she had felt ashamed. Simon had been a mistake. The doctor had warned that the pregnancy would be risky. She remembered the wonderful feeling of holding him and feeding him, kissing his soft downy head. Everything else was now a blur.

'I wanted you to have a brother or sister.'

'The gap would have been too big.'

'You were in the room. Peering into his cot. Maybe you smothered him and tried to blot out the memory? What happened? I need to know.' She persisted.

'What do you take me for? I've lived with the pain of this for 40 odd years... the memory of dad shouting at me for days after, saying ' happy now?' And that look he always had that told me *you are as guilty as sin.*'

'Stop shouting.' She covered her ears with her hands, cowering backward to the wall.

'I've got to go. I've only just flown back from China. My body's in a different time zone.'

'Yes you've never got time. Always in a rush.'

Annie closed the door, wrapped her dressing gown tightly around her waist against the evening chill and the thoughts that disturbed her. As she returned to her sitting room, settling back on her comfy chair she was more convinced than she had ever been. She felt uneasy. Her son was a murderer. What would he do next?

2
Clifford

March 2008

It had been a long day in the office. Had been dark for hours. Clifford had worked through a raging hunger but was now beyond eating. Being diabetic he knew this wasn't good but in the frantic week before the mag was 'put to bed' it was always like this.

He hated returning to his new rental each evening – a daily reminder that he'd been kicked out of the marital home. He turned the key in the front door desperate for the second gin and tonic of the day he knew he shouldn't have. He looked at the mail lying on the bristly mat, his stomach knotting when he saw the familiar black ink on the cream envelope – another demand he was sure from his ex wife's solicitor for payment of spousal maintenance or a request for a statement of earnings. Fuck, he thought. When would that bitch ever give up? I've worked my arse off for decades. For what? Lawyers at my heels like a pack of hounds. I'm on the verge of losing what I've spent a lifetime building up. He began to climb the stairs, tore open the envelope, cast his eyes across the letter then tossed it over the bannister.

As he reached the fifth step he stopped. He remembered that he was going to pour a G & T. He didn't want one anymore. He rested his arm on the glossy handrail and looked up. It seemed a long way to the top. His legs felt like they would give way. His arm felt heavy against the handrail. His head swam. He sat down waiting for the feeling to pass. At 54 what did he expect? He was a burned out wreck living his life in the fast lane as if he were 26. Was this the strain of a hectic lifestyle working 24/7 worrying constantly about profit margins and balance sheets?

Thanks to the bitch - his ex - the dream of early retirement lay shattered. She'd squandered so much money leaving them broke and was now using greedy £400 an hour lawyers to settle the divorce. As he leant against the wall he wondered when his personal Iraqi conflict would draw to a close. They were about to lose the marital home and he'd be working forever to rebuild his life. He had to keep going but dreaded looking over the hills into the valley of old age and inevitable poverty.

It had been a cold day. The house was chilly. So why was he sweating? He inched to the seventh step, wiped the beads of sweat from his brow and rested against the icy wall hoping it would cool his back. Maybe he had flu. After a few moments he turned onto his knees and gradually, as if moving through porridge he climbed the remaining stairs like a drunk, resting at the top before crawling into his bedroom. His legs felt heavier than ever.

Something wasn't right. Warning bells were ringing. He sat on the bed, his shirt clinging to his body and suddenly he saw the parody of his life in the lyrics of his favourite song by the Eagles; 'I didn't see the stop sign,' 'I was caught up in the race.'

And then he gripped the bedside table as waves of sour tasting nausea rose. Acid burned his throat. A projectile of flecked vomit spilt out. He let it gush. He was drained, had no energy to go to the bathroom to look for a cloth. The carpet could wait. His head throbbed. He needed to lie down. Then he remembered that his blood glucose readings had been unusually high that morning. Maybe there was a link. But as he rested his head on the pillow a thought wormed into his mind. Fuck. *Is this how I'm going to end my days?*

He'd read enough. He knew the signs. He'd watched his father go through this. These were mild signs but because of possible nerve damage due to his diabetes they were only ever going to be mild symptoms but if he ignored them it could be fatal. Part of him wanted to dismiss his anxiety and go to bed, forget it and wake up in the morning refreshed.

But he wasn't going to take the chance. He reached for the landline mustering as much strength as his body would allow. As the publisher and editor of an international magazine on the car tyre industry everything depended on him. He was the boss. The business couldn't run itself. He was Clifford the technology writer, the globe trotter who scoured the world with his two bags; containing his clothes and his laptop and all the other crap needed to ply his trade looking for stories of other nations' scientific prowess and nearly always travelling economy. It was a lucrative niche in a crazy world where journalism was fast disappearing in a sea of press releases published verbatim by cut and paste hacks. He couldn't afford to be ill. He mustn't be ill he thought as he pressed the digit nine three times and waited for the answer.

'Emergency. Which service do you require? Fire, ambulance or police?'

'Ambulance. I think I'm having a heart attack. I'm diabetic.'

He didn't move while he waited. Felt woozy. He wondered if he'd pass out. The wait seemed long, though in reality not. It was a relief that the front door was still unlocked.

Several pairs of feet pounded the stairs. Someone called. Another was talking to base. They ran through a series of questions. In no time at all they had diagnosed a mild heart attack explaining how the equipment - a twelve lead electrocardiogram worked. He heard the words ST elevation and myocardial infarction.

Blue streaks flashed across the lawn as they carried him into the ambulance on a stretcher and on the journey explained that he'd probably had a mild heart attack. A blood test at the hospital would detect the presence of specific types of proteins released into the blood from the damage in the heart due to the attack. Once confirmed that he had suffered a mild attack he'd be given an angiogram to find out the exact location and the seriousness of the blocks in the coronary artery. Clifford wasn't taking it all in.

His mind was whirling worrying mainly about his 23 year old son, Ben. He couldn't leave him in the shit. How would he finish his veterinary course without his financial support? And he worried about work. There was no one else to write the articles and coordinate the team. And to a lesser extent he was concerned for his mum. There were whispers of batty behaviour. Who would organise a care home when the time came?

And he thought of his dad all those years ago dying from a heart attack. Maybe he'd always known he'd suffer the same fate.

He woke the next morning in hospital plugged up to monitors. A nurse came round to take his bloods. He looked around. Everyone else was much older. Some looked like living corpses waiting for their last breath. He shouldn't be here. He felt fine.

He knew he couldn't take his health for granted any longer. Was this the wake up call he needed? It was odd but for the first time in his life he actually felt lucky to be alive. He'd long ignored the warning indicators on the dashboard: raised blood pressure, high cholesterol.

Over the next few days as he rested in hospital the feeling of relief at having pulled through started to change. Once more he felt negative about his life. Diabetes was a slow road to death. He'd always been aware of that. Sooner or later he was bound to develop other debilitating complications of diabetes: nerve damage, neuropathy and retinopathy.

The doctor came to discharge him and Ben arrived to give him a lift home. He hadn't seen the lad in a while. Ben was always too busy in London studying.

'You've been lucky. This time. I'm going to prescribe a spray in case you develop more chest pain.' The doctor explained.

' It widens the blood vessels to help the flow of blood and oxygen to the heart. I'm also going to prescribe beta blockers to lower your blood pressure and warfarin to thin the blood and another medicine to reduce the lipid content in the blood. You need to keep your blood sugar levels under control – obviously with the Metformin you have been taking but we'll add an extra drug, Gliclazide. It's quite a cocktail I know. I'm not happy with your blood sugar readings. You need to get the bloods under control. I'll book you in to see a dietician and some regular exercise will also help but for the moment I'd say just some gentle walks each day.'

'Dad thinks he can hammer his body like an old company car.' Ben joked to the doctor.

Clifford felt mounting irritation.

'Oh fuck off. I only hear from you when I forget to pay your college fees. You've only been here five minutes and already you're having a go. Well this whole mess is down to your fucking mother causing me stress with her lawyers, destroying everything, stalling the house sale and screwing me for a grand a month in bloody spousal maintenance. How many women unless they are wives of celebrities claim maintenance for themselves? It's outrageous. If I snuff it don't think she's going to support you through your course. '

Ben rubbed his stubbly chin. His straw coloured hair looked like it hadn't been brushed or cut in a while. Clifford noticed how tired he was looking. And he thought he could smell a whiff of beer on his breath. There was something a bit tramp like about him.

'Calm down Dad. You'll have another heart attack at this rate. You bang on about the divorce every time we speak. I'm sick of it. Get over it.' He looked at the sweater Ben was wearing. Jack Will's. Obviously too much money to waste, Clifford thought.

Ben looked directly at the doctor in a concerned but authoritative way. Suddenly Clifford could see him in his veterinary role and he felt a brief flush of pride for his son.

'He needs a proper regime?'

'Keep out of it Ben. I'll ask the questions.'

'Yes.' The doctor answered. ' I'll leave you with some leaflets.'

Clifford looked around the sterile ward and over to the elderly patients lying opposite, then to the doctor.

'I don't need to read any bloody leaflets. I'm not a kid. And exercise? Do behave. Where would I find time for that? I'm working and travelling 24/7. Some of us have businesses to run.'

'Ditch the car and walk... sometimes.' The doctor ignored his rudeness, made an upside down smile and shrugged.

'You don't want to be back in here. This can be managed very well but you need to do your bit too.' The doctor added.

' I'm car reliant.'

'Well, I'm sure with the help of the dietician and a few changes in what you eat you could get your weight down to a more healthy level.'

Clifford sat up.

'Have you ever lived the life of a fucking diabetic jet setting businessman? Have you any idea? The time differences, lack of choice on the plane. What should I do? Pack sandwiches in cellophane like a school boy on a trip to the museum? Food the world over has become Americanised. Everything's laden in fat and sugar. I can't do diets. I eat out regularly with clients, have late night drinks at fancy restaurants. I can't sit there with water. What would be the point in living? I know I'm on the road to a slow death.'

'The fast road if you're not careful. If you calm down a minute maybe we can make a plan for you.' The doctor offered.

'A diet plan that would suit a retired person with nothing better to do.'

The only plan Clifford had was a double gin and tonic in The Castle Inn.

'Dad. Man up for fuck's sake. When I came in here yesterday you were taking it all really seriously.'

In a patronizing tone he added 'as you should.'

Ben straightened. Clifford watched him tighten the belt around his waist. He thought how thin his face was looking and wondered if he'd lost weight. He looked gaunt. The lad was an extra worry he didn't need.

'So what's happened in the past few hours? You're like a storm cloud. Why are you back to being complacent about your health?' Ben gave his arm a friendly nib.

Clifford knew he'd been complacent about his health but never admitted that to anyone. Today he felt differently. The luck he had felt had dissipated. He needed to get out of hospital. He swiveled his feet to the ground focusing on today - the here and now making mental lists of all things that needed doing in the office. All he could think of was making money. He had to rebuild his life, post divorce. He thought of his week ahead. For sure he'd go back to his old ways because he always did. He had no choice. Life went on, heart attack or no heart attack.

They were quiet in the car on the way home. The gulf between father and son felt wider than ever.

'You ok?' He asked as Ben filtered into the left lane in front of the pier. 'You don't look it.'

'Thanks Dad.' Ben reached for the radio. Flicked it on. Turned up the volume.

'Well you *don't* look it. What's going on?'

'I'm just tired. My mind races all night sometimes. I'm not sleeping very well.'

'You worry me. You can't fail another year.'

'You're just thinking about more tuition fees.' Ben rammed the stick into second.

'S'pose. You've seen what's just happened. My health is against me. I can't support you forever.'

'I went to Berlin last weekend to see a band.' Ben made a quick switch of conversation.

'Berlin? You didn't tell me. I don't know anything that's going on in your life these days. Who with?'

'New girlfriend. Abena.'

'Girlfriend?' He rolled the word off his tongue digesting the news. What sort of name is that? Sounds like Ribena. She Polish? Slovakian?'

'No Nigerian.'

'Fuck! She's black. You're going out with a black bitch? Did you tell her your dad's Alf Garnett!'

'Oh fuck off. I'll dump you right here if you're going to be racist. Grow up Dad.'

'I'm not saying a thing.' He shook his head like a weeble and went quiet. His eyes followed the steely sea as they drove along the coastal road. It felt like he was sitting next to a stranger.

'Who paid for the trip? I don't pay you ten grand a year to go swanning round the world,' he asked as they approached Peacehaven.

'Money again. You're obsessed. Mum paid as it happens.'

'The bitch gave you money for a weekend away? Her latest statement of earnings said she'd earned nothing. Where's the money coming from? At the end of the day it's my money. My hard earned money she stole through her reckless spending.'

'Just drop it. I've had enough. Can't you just be nice for a while. I'm sick of all your bitterness, remorse, regret.' His hands tightened around the steering wheel.

A week after his discharge Clifford woke thinking of sex. He hadn't thought about sex in days. That wasn't like him. He lifted the sheet. Looked down. But there was no hard on. It was like watching the filament in a light bulb fizzing out. Were things now on the slide he wondered? Was this the beginning of the end? Was this what generally happened to men in their mid fifties? First to be screwed financially by your ex wife and then screwed by your best friend down below. If his dick had been a cruise missile he'd consider decommissioning it.

He sat up. Looked down again. In the good old days it was a missile; he'd cum too quickly but now it was like flicking a switch waiting for something to happen, but the solenoid in his genitals was failing to respond. He wanted his best mate back. The train had been cancelled. He tried accessing the coital memory folder. That usually worked. He scanned the folder of the '100 Great Fucks' of his past but the tape had been erased.

Maybe he had an 'intermittent' dick. There was nothing worse than kit you couldn't be sure of. It was the unpredictability of it. If he met a woman how would he know how it would behave? There was no rhyme or reason. He wracked his brain but couldn't find one. 'It' and 'him' had become separate entities, two estranged friends no longer working to the same agenda. In short, his dick was behaving like a Morris 1100 in Basil Fawlty's life – the sketch where he ended up thrashing the car with a tree branch.

It wasn't going to perform to order like a street entertainer. It was like driving a car with soggy suspension or a faulty electrical circuit. Maybe it wasn't important for the moment for there were no women currently in his life, or none he wanted to enter into a sexual liaison with.

He got up, went to have a shower, trying to place the niggling problem of his failing dick to the back of his mind, as junk tends to be thrown under the bed or up in the loft.

3
Clifford

June 2008

Clifford had no idea as he chucked his bags in the back of his Audi A4 that the actions he was about to take would have disastrous ripple effects on his life.

He slammed the boot lid down with force, glanced at his watch as he approached the traffic lights. There was enough time to call in on his mother en route before heading up the M23 towards Heathrow on another business trip even allowing for traffic queues. He was off to Bangkok. He loved the city. It was teeming with everything forbidden. He was looking forward to the nightly pleasures. He'd refreshed all the useful Thai phrases: *how much? Is that for the whole night?* But it would be depend upon his intermittent friend; cock banging in Bang-kok might be hoping for too much.

It was always quite a performance waiting for his mother to answer her door. As he waited he hoped she wasn't going to mention Simon again.

She seemed to take longer than normal and when she unlatched the inner door looked flustered. He took her arm noticing that she was a little unsteady on her feet and guided her back to her comfy armchair where a mohair blanket rested on the arm.

‘ Clifford I've lost the key.'

She was close to tears. Her body sank into the chair.

‘What key? To the front door? You need to get me a key. You're an idiot not to have done that already.'

'No not that one.'

'What key then?' Irritation fluttered in his stomach. 'There aren't any others.' He looked round as if a key were about to magically appear.

'The key to the big wardrobe in the bedroom. I've been looking all over the flat but can't find it anywhere. I need to open it.' She raised her bony fingers to her mottled cheeks with a look of despair.

This was all he needed but the key had to be found. He couldn't leave her in an agitated state.

They started to look – her handbag, jewellery box, kitchen drawer – all the obvious places. Maybe it was in her coat pocket, dressing gown, blouse pocket, any damn pocket.

'Look can't you just wear some of the clothes in your drawer instead. I'll sort it out when I get back.' Clifford stole a look at his watch.

'I can't find it.'

'I know that mum.' He restrained a huff. It was like looking at a daft old dog in a basket for a clue.

'I'm keeping you aren't I? You never have time. How do you think it is for me, without your father?'

'Don't start mum. I have a flight to get. This has taken half an hour so far.'

'You go then.' With a stroke of her hand she waved him away.

'Look do you want this sodding wardrobe opened or not?'

' I *do* need it open,' she pleaded.

His conscience played havoc, swinging precariously between thoughts of passport control queues to a need to support his mother. She looked so anxious and he knew he had to do something in the precious minutes left available to him.

An inner voice told him to leave well alone and go. How would it look if the neighbour dropped by for a cuppa and saw the smashed wardrobe door? Or they heard him smashing the door with the hammer? The whole thing didn't feel right, but on the other hand he knew he had to get on with the task; open the damn door. It was the only way he was going to make an exit.

And it was at that point that despair turned to anger like a chameleon moving into new territory.

'For God's sake mother.' He was aware he sounded like Norman Bates in Psycho.

'Don't swear at me.' Her voice was quivering.

'You're going to give me another heart attack at this rate. What am I supposed to do? Take a fucking hammer to the wardrobe?' Anger spilled from every pore.

'The heart attack was your own fault. You eat all the wrong foods. I've always told you that ever since you were a small boy.'

He pushed past her into the small hallway where she kept a few basic tools in a cupboard. Under the glow of a bare light bulb he fished into an untidy plastic box, pulled out a hammer, hurriedly returned to the bedroom.

He stood a little way back momentarily admiring the tones of wood, the tall wardrobe he remembered so well from childhood. Fleeting memories of hiding among the fur coats and pretending to be in Narnia came flooding back and in one firm strike of the hammer it felt like he was fracturing his very childhood, splintering the already cracked and fragile relationship that had long existed between them.

He could smell his mother's floral scent at his neck, her warm milky breath upon him, the rattle of her gasp and then her piercing scream. As he prised the door from its' hinges he was aware of the sobs close to his ear of 'no,' 'no,' no' coming in fits and starts.

And then he saw it and fell to his knees, hands clasping his face. His mind froze. Time stood still. He felt trance like, unable to move. He stared as notes, lots of them, came fluttering out like feathers from a chicken coop. He reached forward unable to comprehend the blanket of money piling at his knees.

'What the hell is this about?' His voice was growing steadily weaker. He felt the blood draining from his head, his stomach swimming.

'My savings, my pension.' She was crying now.

'But it looks like you've robbed a bank mum. It should *be* in a bank locked away safe. Nobody keeps this much in a wardrobe.'

'You wouldn't listen to me. I had no choice. It wasn't safe at The Northern Rock,' she pleaded over and over.

'It can't stay here.' He rose; cramp in his feet and swiftly came back from the kitchen with a bundle of bin liners.

'Leave it where it is,' she shrieked watching him scoop the money into a bag.

She made a feeble attempt to tug the bag, her nail making a tiny tear. The bag was cheap and thin. He pulled the bundle up to his stomach away from her safe and high, worried the tear would get bigger as he hurried to leave, ignoring her protestations, her clawing hands and closed the door behind him.

As he flew down the path he nearly collided into two hefty dustmen. He didn't want to stop or exchange pleasantries. His head was bent low as he passed them.

'Hey sling 'em in the truck mate,' one of them called after him.

' Fuck off.' Clifford called back.

'Only trying to be helpful mate. Won't bother next time.'

'There won't be a next time.'

Clifford slung the bag on the back seat, his mind a whirl. He didn't know what to do. He didn't have time to stop at the bank. In any case they were sure to ask questions. His mind raced like an uncontrollable horse. Question after question galloping along. How could she be so stupid? Was he missing something here? He thought back to Christmas when she had spent three entire days sniping at him. She seemed so wound up all the time. If she'd been a younger woman he would have told her she was on her period.

On occasions she had been plain nasty, making snide comments about his marriage and complaining about the food he cooked - turkey, the vegetables. The turkey was too dry; the vegetables too soggy. She even complained about the present he'd bought her. And she always grumbled that he'd forced her to move to Sussex. She never dropped that gripe; ever bitter on that score.

He decided to drop the bag at home. He had a safe - the best place for it until his return.

He headed out of town. The camera flashed at Preston Park; his mind not on his speed. He thought about the state of her flat. When he'd opened the fridge door he'd seen a couple of floppy carrots and wilting broccoli, smelt sour milk. He was so focused on finding the key at the time that he hadn't quite registered the scene around him. Guilt sat like lead in his stomach. He'd thought nothing of it at the time but the toilet was stained. Normally he choked on the intoxicating smell of bleach when he went for a quick pee. And he had noticed some breakfast on her blouse. Normally she was so immaculately dressed. He asked himself over and over *am I missing something here*?

But what he didn't predict was the implications of what he'd just done.

4
Clifford

June 2008

He woke dreaming of retirement sitting on a sandy beach. Then he saw his luggage on the carpet beside the bed and his suit draped over the chair. There was so much to do.

'Fuck.'

He remembered he'd missed his flight to Bangkok. He fumbled for his phone. Called his travel counselor to rearrange his flights, then the office to ask them to rejig his Bangkok appointments.

What a burden his mother was becoming. About a year ago she had expressed an interest in a Jewish care home in North London. She knew people there. Seemed to like the idea of the care home. Maybe that was the answer.

As he swiveled his legs over the edge of the bed there was a hard knock at the door. Someone was determined to catch him in. This wasn't the tentative knock of the Jehovah's Witness or British Gas.

'Mr Clifford Chancer? There's been a bit of a disturbance.' Two police officers stood on the doorstep.

Suddenly he felt light headed as if his body had moved to the ceiling and was now floating weightless, looking down on a situation he didn't understand and wasn't a part of as they explained the allegation of theft his mother had made. Through the fug of questions he denied it explaining what had happened. They didn't seem to believe him. Wanted him in for questioning.

Why on earth was his mother this confused? He just needed to see her to explain that the money was safe. This was his mother for Christ sake - not a complete stranger. The officers couldn't see how ludicrous this was. But the more he objected the worse it seemed to get and the next minute he was in the back of their police car, handcuffed on his way to Hollingbury Custody Suite accused of theft.

The reception area at Hollingbury was rather like a set from Star Trek and he was an alien being processed within this spacecraft. A team immediately took control and then he felt he had journeyed from Dr Who or Star Trek to the Halls of Justice in Mad Max and the 'main force patrol' set about stripping his identity, extracting his mind and filleting all sense of logic and reason, casting him aside into the general trash heap of society's scum – the real thieves, burglars, muggers that roamed the streets of Brighton by the day and night, making old peoples' lives hell, intimidating and threatening. He had done nothing; just tried to help his mother.

He was ordered to empty his pockets. They were filled with coins from several currencies. Why did that surprise them? They were the cast of Star Trek finding out as much as they could about this new time traveller. But it was a tedious exercise.

He really wanted to say '*look cunt, that's a gold card. That's a platinum business card. Something your bank will never grant you, on your crap salary working here, in this God awful place'*. But he'd kicked up enough stink by refusing to accept the allegation of theft. He needed to just go through the motions, get himself out of there onto the plane. This was a waste of time. The total incongruity of the ordeal reminded him of being back at school when the teachers persisted in accusing him of doing something he hadn't and no matter what he said they just weren't going to believe him.

He was asked if he wanted to make a call to anyone. 'I have no one,' he snapped back.

He was put in a cell until the formal interview; locked away, a danger to society, a danger to his family. Sitting in that cell made reality kick in. A confused old woman wasn't going to wreck his life. He stared at the wall ahead of him tracing a crack down to the floor. The crack represented his broken family with its' fractured relationships: marriage, his faltering relationship with his son, the shattered bond between mother and son that never really was. A further jagged hairline crack in the flooring represented Simon who loomed so large over everything through the brief fleeting time he'd graced the earth and his long absence. How could a tiny human continue to have a rippling effect upon so many lives? He needed a brother more than ever right at that moment.

In the interview room he was no longer that ghost hovering on the ceiling. He sat up. Took control.

'*Right PC Plod*' he'd wanted to chide. '*Shut up and run the tape and I'll tell you what happened.*' But he knew that would get him nowhere. A prickling heat rose, firing him along. He imagined himself back in the office -behind his desk at the helm. His Titanic. Steering away from that iceberg again. The police were a bunch of nobodies - ignorant institutionalized shitheads simply following protocol. What crap to call the police force 'criminal intelligence,' Clifford thought.

Gradually he got his story through to them. He walked away that day on police bail with conditions attached: he wasn't to contact his mother and had to periodically report to the station until the CPS had made their decision.

Annie
July 2008

Annie put her coat on. She checked her hair in the mantel mirror. Her eyes moved across the pictures of her family on the dusty mantelpiece. She wiped away a tear. Picked up the picture of baby Simon. Stroked his face with her finger, placing it in the middle - pride of place. She studied the picture of Clifford and Roda at their wedding. Roda was smiling, dressed in a Lady Diana style sailor suit with a big white collar. She could see the doubts cast across Clifford's face even then. She slammed the picture face down with a tut.

She arrived at the solicitor on time.

'There you are.' The young solicitor passed the new document across the table with a pen ready to sign.

'If you sign here please,' the solicitor tapped her long finger nail on the section she had marked with a pencil cross and then leaned back to adjust her glasses behind her ears. Annie took the pen aware that the simple carefully sculptured signature would be her goodbye wave spoken with resentment from the depths of her grave. Her bony hand hovered over the x.

'All previous wills you've made are now null and void. This one takes precedence now.' The solicitor explained.

'You understand. Don't you?' Annie asked.

'It's not for me to judge Annie. This has to be your decision. But I can see your reasons and they are good enough. You've been through a lot. I'm happy to make the changes if you are. Maybe it's what your husband would also have wanted? We'll take care of everything for you. You don't need to worry.'

'If Clifford hadn't dragged me to the doctor I'd still have a breast you know.'

'He wanted you to get better.'

'I didn't want to go to the doctor. He has no idea what I went through. The pain, the swelling. It was a ghastly illness.'

'I'm so sorry you suffered.' The solicitor smiled sympathetically.

'And while I was in the middle of treatment he dragged me down to see you to sort out a will and a power of attorney. Makes you wonder if he's only after my money. He's quicker than me. These days my brain doesn't work fast enough. Sometimes it's easier to go along with Clifford rather than disagree. Otherwise he starts shouting and swearing and talking too fast. He's got no patience you know. I can't bear it. He makes me feel dizzy. I feel like sleeping for a week after I've seen him.'

Annie sighed. 'He's so controlling. Christmas was dreadful. He took me back to my cold empty flat half way through the afternoon in a foul temper. I'd barely finished my tea and cake and I was ordered to put my coat on. I don't know what's wrong with him. Sometimes I'm ashamed to call him my son.'

5
Clifford

August 2008

'The case has been dropped?' Relief washed over him. 'I could have told the Social Services she had dementia weeks ago. It took this to happen before they finally looked into her case. I've been through hell and back. They're a bloody waste of space.'

He leant against the kitchen counter relief washing over him.

'I knew she was on the last knockings of lucidity. The officer who interviewed wouldn't take my word for it. So what's going to happen now?'

'The social services will be in touch with you. You'll need to think about her on going support and care. A plan will be put in place,' the officer explained.

He still felt like a criminal. A man cast aside for a crime he hadn't committed. Now that he could contact his mother he felt awkward about it. How could their relationship ever be the same? There was no going back. The accusation of theft was a bitter pill to swallow.

A week after the police phoned Ben rang.

'Grandma asked the Social Services to ring me.'

'Why?' He was confused. 'Don't you have enough on your plate?' He reeled with shock.

'Dad don't shoot the messenger. I didn't ask to be involved. She wanted me to find a care home.'

'I'm her son but she doesn't want me involved. How do you think that makes me feel? After everything I've fucking well done. It was me not you who called the surgery months ago to organize for district nurses to visit once a week.'

'And she didn't like it Dad. She hated that regime.'

'What would you have done? I'm trying to run a bloody business. I couldn't look after her as well.'

'You know what she was like though. She moaned about the different nurses *parading* through her flat. She said it was like they owned the place. They were hard work, talking too quickly, rushing from room to room. She couldn't keep up with them or their complicated questions. I didn't cancel them. You didn't either. She did. She wanted control back in her life. You can understand where she was coming from.'

'She should have let me get a cleaner and order Wiltshire meals.'

'Don't worry anymore Dad. She's safe now.'

'Should have been me sorting it.'

'I did spend lots of time with her when I was growing up. Maybe she trusts me.'

'That's only because your pig ignorant mother insisted on working and dumped you on your willing grandma.'

'Do we have to go through all this again? Her care's sorted. That's what I rang to tell you.'

'I suppose she wants to move to that Jewish care home in London? She was never satisfied that I'd brought her to live by the sea. Looking back I shouldn't have bothered.'

Clifford could still hear his mother's voice. *I was happy in London, until you dragged me down to the coast. I had friends up there, places I could visit.*

'Well. I hope she'll be very happy. If anyone bothers to take her out she'll soon see the dump that North London's become: full of black faces, scum on every street corner. It's a shit hole. I rescued her from all that. Thought she'd appreciate the sea air here and watching her grand son grow up. It's all been such a waste. Still. Not my problem any more.'

Clifford stared at the phone wondering whether to call the care home and check she'd settled in. He wondered how she would react if she knew he'd called.

A Greek nurse answered and said she was a bit unsettled and maybe it would help if he visited.

'You people don't know a thing,' he hit back. 'She accused me of stealing her money when I was trying to help. How do you think I feel? She's in God's waiting room now and I don't want to take that journey downhill with her, watching her slide into an abyss in which she eventually doesn't recognise me.'

He needed a stiff gin. It was as if a black raven cloak covered their whole relationship choking it to death. There was no future and the past had happened. Inside he was already trying to say goodbye. An inner voice screamed for her life to end. Who was his mother? He didn't know anymore. Had he ever known? She was now trapped inside the prison walls of dementia that used to be her mind, now in organic deterioration incarcerated in a room full of broken and lost souls, condemned by the court of time. And the more he dwelt on that thought the more it bought into focus his own mortality.

He also wondered how long it would be before he had a second more serious heart attack. He didn't want to be thrown out like trash to the junkyard of old wrecks. Better to be dead than that to look forward to. It was hard to see a future at all except pain, despair and anguish.

6
Clifford

February 2009

Clifford was on a factory tour in India.

' I'm not so bad for 54.' He told his reflection in the hotel mirror.

He'd recovered well from the heart attack. He took his cocktail of drugs each day and didn't give it too much thought. He'd entered wispy hair land, his belly was getting noticeably fatter, but he was a bloke so what did it matter? It was different for women. They were the flowers for bees to be pollinated: no attraction, no pollination.

The predictable repetition of bland hotel chains across the world had become his life and he loathed it all: light switches were the most irritating things never located in obvious places and when you turned them all off to get into bed there was always one left on and it took ages to find the switch. He never used the radio alarm. They were way too complicated and the air con was always a piss off. The TVs were usually huge with 100 channels of shit. The beds were vast with a great collection of pillows but nobody to share it with.

It never took him long to trash a hotel room. He liked to behave like a rock star – behaving a complete slob. Dumping his toilet bag and a mountain of medication in the bathroom he made a quick check of the suite: no floaters blocking the toilet or stray pubic hairs in the bath. Nothing *yet* to complain about.

Wandering down to the ground floor he passed Lord Ganesha – and silently begged him not to put a curse on his sensitive bowel.

He pushed through the revolving doors into the oppressive heat of Hyderabad; watched the taxis pulling in, wiped beads of sweat from his forehead. Beyond the fine granite forecourt and brick pathway surrounding this five star grandeur was no man's land - a dustbowl of red rock, in which rubbish and fine grit swirled in the light breeze. In the distance, set against the backdrop of derelict buildings and rapid building programmes were scraggy tarpaulin tents which dotted the landscape. He could see bare footed children running around their parents, cooking on open fires and taking showers next to the roadside.

It was the weekend. He hated weekends away. He pushed through the revolving doors back into the cool air conditioned foyer. He swiped a sweet as he passed the bowl on the reception counter flicking the wrapper onto the floor unashamedly in front of the smiling receptionist. The lift propelled him back to the solitary confinement of his hotel cell where the only pleasures in store were another dump and a wank over internet porn until the working week began again.

What was he supposed to do on weekends away? Ajoy Datta, his Indian Mr Fixit; owner of the factory he had just visited hadn't the social skills or grace to provide entertainment of any kind.

The corridor was quiet. Two maids chatted next to a laundry trolley. He'd visited the one and only tourist attraction, a hill fort. He didn't want to wander aimlessly round a market either, getting hassled by street traders.

Shutting himself in his hotel room he soon forgot the poverty and squalor of the world outside; blissfully protected by the crispness of the white cotton sheets of his bed and the smell of fresh shampoo in the bathroom. Life outside seemed so cheap: a daily brush with death and chance -small children fending for themselves, crouching by the roadside at night, their eyes bright in the headlights of passing cars. There were beggars on every street corner and cripples too. Women with babies that seemed comatose and all the rest of sad humanity in the city where, in all probability his bank's call centre was located.

It was hard to believe looking out of his window that this country was being slowly transformed into a world superpower.

He flicked on his laptop, sat at the desk, still feeling bloated from breakfast. It was too early to be tempted by a mini bar break in of Pringles or Toblerone.

He got up. Went to the loo while the laptop booted. He wished at this point in the day that he was in Japan - sitting on a warm 'Toto' with all the high tech advanced features of bottom washing and deodorisers. They were the next best thing to an orgasm after a magnificent bowel movement. The experience always left him with a post defecatory smile. Straining on the toilet he considered that taking a dump was rather like horse racing. You never quite knew who the winner would be. Would it be Red Rum? Or Brown Humpback? or Tiddly Turd? Who could he place his bet on today?

With his sphincter still contracting he returned to the desk to check emails, wondering whose bare bottom had sat on the seat before his. Then he clicked the 'favourites' bar. The moans of Ben Dover's team of luscious happy ladies being fucked and licked by well endowed black men soon filled the room. He liked to watch a good orgy - one in each orifice; a good spitroast, reducing her to a crazed wreck. They always seemed to have such wonderful happy faces -unlike the women he'd been with in brothels – having to turn them over for a doggy to avoid looking at their miserable faces. He loved to watch these women's faces, with cum spilling over their lips.

'Bring it on,' he whispered in a smutty voice moving his hand into his trousers to cradle the warmth of his balls.

But it was useless. *Stupid intermittent unreliable dick.*

'Ben Dover never has this problem.'

He looked down at the pathetic flaccid thing coiled between his legs. Seeing such huge black cocks on the screen made him feel a mixture of shame and inadequacy. Not being able to ride a bike or swim had bought him enough shame when he was fourteen years old and a bucketful of bitterness towards his mother and father for never having taught him. But that was nothing compared to this.

He had always been embarrassed and ashamed of its size, going way back to changing for PE at school or lining up at the urinals taking a sideways kurt glance at all the other boys. But this was a different issue entirely. Mr. Small Cock had become Mr. Super Unreliable Cock. If only they could invent a plug in charger, a gadget to clamp to the balls to recharge the limpet.

'Who's master? You or me?' He asked his friend. 'How am I going to be ever able to have another relationship?' He flicked it with his finger. It was a friend with issues.

As if to add insult to injury he could hear the deep moans of a couple having sex in the room next door. Jesus. This was all he needed. He turned up the sound of Ben Dover's team.

The noise had subsided, both from next door and from the team – who were splayed out in all sorts of erotic positions on a heavily stained bed.

He leaned back in the chair returning to a fresh google search. This time he logged into his usual dating site. There might be an intelligent woman: one with a mind and a body but with a fresh, wet pussy not a shriveled up dried old prune. He wanted the perfect combination of 'mind' and 'meat.' He could see a new name for a dating site using those two words.

In an ideal world that woman would be life partner material. There had to be a real connection. She'd be informed about current affairs, the economy and science to hold an interesting discussion. Clifford doubted there were many women of that calibre out there. Most were dull, shallow, vain; only interested in their hair and clothes. That type of woman would drive him crazy. The only thing you could realistically do was fuck 'em and forget them.

He had discovered the possibilities of internet dating within days of leaving his ex wife. But he knew that love wasn't going to solve all the shitty problems in his life.

Internet dating in the beginning had been exciting. It was one giant meat market within his living room - like bursting through a wormhole in the fabric of space into another universe.

Since his initial discovery of this whole new world he usually had a couple of women that he chatted to on line. Only a couple had actually materialised into dates. Stick insect Penny- with the dried up fanny being one. And Kim, the cellulite blob being the other. He'd seen all manner of human life hidden behind those passport style pictures: the desperately lonely, the desperately broke, the desperate for sex, the depressed, (like himself) the dumped, the divorced, the bereaved. The list went on. The saddest 'cases' he came across were women who were trapped in the most tragic of situations caring for very sick and elderly parents... the fun in their life over as they put duty first. And worst – women who were caring for sick and dying partners or watching their partners decline in mental health – incarcerated within the walls of early onset dementia. Their relationships all but over they were crying out - not exactly for an escape route but a form of solace.

He began a fresh search for ladies within the age range 40 to 60.

Within minutes of fishing a daily shoal of wrinkly old troats had plopped into his virtual net. Half he tossed over board. Many lacked the imagination to write anything other than cliches. Others hadn't even bothered with that.

Most of the profiles contained somewhere the phrase 'I'm looking for a soul mate to cuddle up to on the sofa with a bottle of wine and a DVD.' He wondered if Blockbusters and DFS were secret sponsors of the dating site. And what was a 'soul mate?' Some illusive airy fairy term that women used.

Predictably they invariably said 'I'm looking for a man with a good sense of humour.' Clifford always wanted to reply 'well find a comedian then.'

'I also like to go to the pub, have meals out (Italian, Chinese, Indian) go to the cinema, go for a walk, cook a meal at home, go on holiday and I like shopping.' What the hell, he thought. The profiles were just shopping lists. They might as well have added to the list 'go to the toilet, take a dump, breath.'

He was looking for just one, single, solitary sentence that would do more than make his intestines contract. He was looking for that elusive pique of interest.

And it was just when he was about to return to Ben Dover that he saw her. He noticed her hair before he read her opening gambit. One side of her dainty frame stood in the shade of a Cypress tree in the graveyard of an ancient village church. The people milling in the distance told him this was a wedding. Light illuminated part of her dark hair -tones of red and ember, like a blanket of fallen autumn leaves, glossy and gleaming. It was freshly washed and styled in curled layers; blended well with the shimmery burnt orange she was wearing. This woman had class. Her warm shy half smile beckoned him in.

She described herself as the girl next door.

'My mum says that I'm the most interesting person she's ever met... but bless her, she doesn't get out much.'

And then his eyes caught the words *radio four* and *politics*.

Maybe she was the rare gem he was searching for – someone with class and brains. But would she ping a return email?

7
Gina

March 2009

Wayne's bloated lips were inches from Gina's. Her heart thudded. Cheeks burned. His breath was upon her; raven eyes boring into her soul like an owl on a perch watching its' prey. There was nowhere to escape. His frame filled her exit route, blocked out the light. She spied the straggly grey hair around the base of his neck. It badly needed a trim. When they had been together she hadn't put up with little things like that.

'Ave you left the Sharon?' He looked up the corridor. His jowls flopped as his head moved. Gina squirmed. What had possessed her to sleep with him all those years ago?

'Sharon? What the hell are you talking about?' But she knew what he meant.

'I can hear water dripping.'

'The *shower* is dripping. But it's not your flat. I'll be sorting it.'

Over his shoulder she could see Carrie watching Angelina Ballerina curled up on the settee pulling fluff from her blanket as if she were a white slave in a carding mill.

'Erm? Erm?' He forgot the shower, peered at her through slitted eyes, pleading once more. She looked at her watch. She had a train to catch.

'I still like you, you know.' He put his finger on her cheek, traced a line. She pushed it away. How could she not know after all these years?

' You look nice today. Why don't we go to your bedroom for a while? Erm?' He continued to plead. ' You always used to like it.'

He tried to whisper but Wayne didn't know how to whisper or do anything quietly.

Gina moved further into the space between the front door and her computer desk toppling the wooden chair over with a jerky twist of her body. She wanted to grab his faded paint splattered t -shirt, coil it into a knot then slam him hard against the wall like swatting a fly. Every time he picked up or dropped off Carrie she was reminded of the sordid act that had taken place in the car park of a Little Chef on the M23 in the back of his swimming pool blue Micra in 2003. She could still see the image of his hairy bottom pounding away on top of her, the front tyre bouncing in the pothole, the car knocking against the bins and the gormless expression on his square face. If only she could wipe the slate of the past.

His face was now closer. He had egg on his chin - always had egg on his chin even when he hadn't eaten egg. Runny bright smears and clumps of yellow crusted into his stumble. Her stomach was doing somersaults.

'We've been over for months. Why don't you look for someone else?'

Gina wondered what it would take for him to finally get the message. She wanted to tell him to just take Carrie and go but she knew what he'd say. She could hear his baby tantrum in her head. She struggled to be assertive.

'You're so 'orrible to me. I don't deserve to be treated like this Gina.'

It was easier to go through the motions. Let him work through a tantrum.

'Stop it. We're over. I've always been clear about that.'

'You came round me first. Made the first move. I thought you were happily married. Are you ill?'

'Oh please. Because I don't want you I must be ill! Wayne you're pathetic. You were a mistake. Hey we all make mistakes.' She flung her arms up in despair. 'I should have made my marriage work.' It was strange to hear herself say that.

'It was already over with Nick.' He was right. But that wasn't the point.

'Having an affair made things worse. I'd never do that again. You should have respected the institution of marriage.'

'I didn't enter into it.'

'You were at our wedding. A witness in effect.'

'So you're saying you regret your daughter?'

'Don't twist things around. If that's the case I'd regret Saria and Joss too because marrying Nick turned out to be a mistake.'

Gina remembered so clearly the turning point in her marriage - the day Nick called on her mobile during prayers in a church service. He didn't care. His needs had always come first. The ring tone had bounced across the cold walls and up to heights of the steeple. She had pushed her way hurriedly along the pews, her heels click clacking on the stone slabs squinting as she adjusted to natural daylight to see Nick's face, a picture of thunder under the kissing gate.

'Hurry up, we'll be late. Get the kids from the crèche. Get into the fucking car. Now,' he had screamed; the word echoing across the yard and probably heard in the silence of the church by the whole congregation. She could still see his bright red face in her memory desperate to get to his golf tournament, frantic they were going to be late to meet his friends, wound up that he'd been deprived of a shag that morning. Sex had been his daily tonic together with the wine and cider that had creept up in measures by the week.

At first Nick had seen the funny side.

'One of these days I think I'll die from lack of sex.' Or *'a drop of spunk will soon cure that.'*

But as his patience waned a furious temper had taken over.

'You frigid whore. You have other holes I can ram it into.'

He'd exchanged the loving nickname sweet angel for dozy bitch. He had days of silence and childish moods escaping to the pub, returning hours later swaying on the doorstep. In bed he would get out his dick, thrusting it in her face.

'Do you want to put this around your lips?'

She remembered the feeling of dread when his hard dick had rubbed against her back as she breast fed Saria and Joss at two in the morning, or his hands cupped around her breasts demanding a 'titty fondle' as she stood at the sink scrubbing at greasy pots and pans while the children ate their breakfast in the room next door. He'd had the sexual appetite of a twenty year old and had remained ferocious from the day they had met.

In the early days of her marriage to Nick they had made love all night. It had been fun back then.

But then the marriage changed. Night after night she would wake to the bed shaking as he tossed off under the covers hearing his final muffled whimper and then the tug of the sheet, an unspoken 'fuck off' to her rigid body lying there in the darkness. By then he'd long given up pulling her hand across, stretching her limp fingers around his shaft.

'Where are they?' Wayne voice was upon her. Gina's thoughts snapped back to the present.

'Nick's just picked them up. He was on time as dads should be. He never comes in and lingers like you do.'

But the moment she said that she regretted it. The words were out.

'Get back with him then. Never mind the way he treated you. He's obviously Mr. Goddamn Perfect. Pays maintenance on time. Picks up on time.'

Wayne began pulling baby faces and flung his arms around. Sometimes when he was like this he'd kick something – anything, like the time he kicked his mobile across the street when it didn't work or the time he jumped on his sat nav. She waited. Looked around. Stared down at his dirty shoes and the laces that were always undone. Without warning he flung his foot into the skirting board, then yelped in pain and began faking tears.

'Oh for goodness sake Wayne. Grow up.' Gina shouted. She pushed him out of her way and called to Carrie to get her shoes on. It was time they left.

'You always rush me. Like you're ashamed of me. We never get to speak these days.'

He was right. She was ashamed that she had scraped the bottom of the barrel and slept with him in the first place. He was the very last man on earth she would have looked at; but when her marriage had hit the rocks he had been a mirage in a sea of trouble – a long standing friend, a listening ear to her troubles, a shoulder to cry on.

But things had spun out of control. She had been under some sort of spell. Had been temporarily detached from reality. Their torrid affair had spelt the death knell of her marriage to Nick. Looking back now, she had no idea why she had entertained a relationship with a man who looked like Mr Bean, acted like Mr Bean and had the same ability to irritate as Mr Bean.

'Wayne we're over. We've been over a very long time. In fact there never really was an us. You were in the wrong place at the wrong time. I'm sorry.'

She remembered how she had discarded him like a broken hoover. Wayne had been the leapfrog relationship. That was all a year ago: high time she met someone she wanted to be with long term.

'There *is* nothing to say. I'm going out. I've got a train to catch.'

She glanced at her watch again. She needed time alone to check her make up, her hair before setting off to meet Clifford in Brighton.

'Where are you going?'

'What's it to you? Carrie...shoes. Now.' Gina barked, stepping into the lounge - Wayne at her heel like a puppy.

'Don't you want to be with one of the fathers of your children?'

'Oh for goodness sake Wayne.'

She locked her front door, feeling proud to own her own flat. The financial settlement of the divorce had been amicable. She'd wanted to get back on the property ladder even if all she could afford was a two bed flat on a council estate. It was a roof over their heads and money invested.

There were times when she wondered if she would have had the courage to get divorced if tax credits hadn't existed and Wayne hadn't been there – her rescue package. Her marriage had hit troubled waters around the time Gordon Brown had introduced them back in 1999; sold as a solution to poverty for hardworking families. All her other friends were discussing tax credits in the playground, the cafes and the toddler groups whose marriages were also up the creak. They were coming to the same conclusion. There was no financial benefit to remaining in a bad marriage. This tax credit made divorce possible. There was a positive excited feel to their chatter as they planned their freedom. Some might have left regardless of the costs but tax credits certainly helped them take the plunge.

Tax credits had given her a massive step up. After the marriage break up she trained to be a registered child minder and earned the same again in tax credits. She had more than enough to live on and within a couple of years had paid off her mortgage on the flat. But trying to buy a bigger place now was proving difficult. No mortgage company would lend to her.

She began the short walk to the station. She was meeting Clifford in Brighton at noon.

At first she'd loved the freedom of life without a man but there were times when she felt lonely. She didn't like being back on the shelf, gathering dust. The dream of finding love once more was out there.

One bored weekend Gina had loaded a picture, put up a profile. Internet dating felt like a giant candy store. But over time it was in fact like panning for gold – most of it turned out to be fool's gold.

The dating site was an art gallery of meaningless faces. Some reoccurred each day like the repetition of an advert for a pay day loan. There were toothless men with icy stares, balding men with facial scars, tattooed arms radiating danger. Sagging bellies and rippling man boobies in tight vests. There were builders and window cleaners, lorry drivers and carpet cleaners and football fanatics and bungee jumpers.

And then... just as she was about to give up, bored with the tedium of the searches, the meaningless emails back and forth that felt so like Groundhog Day, the virtual winks and smiles, the virtual champagne, chocolates and roses - Clifford arrived in her inbox one Saturday afternoon. In all the months of on line dating this was the first *long* email she had received.

He didn't list his food tastes as a tedious shopping list.

He wrote:' Ducks do not have souls. Please don't tell me you are an animal rights protestor swinging your anti gavage placards outside my favourite store Fortnum and Mason. You'll see a lot of cruelty in British farming. Foie Gras is no more the evil delicacy of despair than battery farming of hens. Every decent restaurant should have it on their menu.'

He didn't list the restaurants he liked he wrote about the ones he didn't.

'You won't get me in a carvery. They're full of dribbling pensioners in wheelchairs and bloated chavs queuing for their weekly blow out; as much as they can fill their gobs for a fiver. Carveries stink of old congealed gravy and brussel sprouts.'

She laughed. She couldn't have agreed more. From that first email they became drawn into all sorts of discussions.

He looked a little like the gorgeous George Clooney. He hadn't selected the clearest of pictures. He was sitting in the desert. It looked so breathtaking, so healing that she was reminded of a poem by WH Auden. 'In the desert of the heart let the healing start. In the prison of his days, teach the free man to praise.' He was squinting against the evening light, friendly creases radiating gently around his eyes. His face was beautifully tanned and stubbly, his sparse hair short, a salt and pepper mix of grey and dark. She liked the sexy way his red rimmed trendy glasses rested on his head and her eye was drawn to a light sprinkling of hair revealed in the opening of his navy shirt. His skin was fairly dark. She wondered if he had Indian blood. He was in India, after all.

They began to text and this became a daily pattern from the moment they woke:

'I'm Jewish. My grandparents were from Eastern Europe. I'm on business in India. Tomorrow I'm taking a train to Dhaka in Bangladesh.'

'That's sounds like an incredible experience.'

'I won't get to see much. The visit is mainly a tour of a recently opened tyre plant.'

'I guess you could link the article you're writing to their way of life.'

'In a sense. Bangladesh is a rapidly changing country. The people have no collateral, but they have ability. In the west we're screwed by the banks more than we know it. I can't convey in text the chaos, dirt, the sheer numbers of people here. The way business works here is like a building society model. It's not like western lending. The economy is growing at 6% but it's not a capitalist model. They aren't relying on debt to do things. Once you can start to tax people you can start to develop a society. These people have cultural and educational aspiration. They aren't ashamed of their abject poverty.'

'I feel as if I'm there with you.'

Texts pinged from the moment she woke to last thing at night. She felt as if she'd been in India and Bangladesh with him during the past week.

One rainy evening, as she sat with the kids watching Coronation Street on her chinzy sofa the phone bleeped.

'We're taking a rickshaw.'

'Where to?'

'To eat. Where do you fancy?'

'Pizza.'

'We're in India, silly.'

'Curry?'

'What about spinach curried kebab? Vegetarian is amazing over here.'

'What am I drinking?'

'Tequila.'

'Nice. Only one ice. It has to be 50 degrees plus to have more than one lump. Actually you're in India. Maybe no ice.'

'Dire Straits is playing in the corner.'

And the following evening there were more texts.

'What dress size are you?'

'12. Why?'

'I'm choosing a long floaty dress for you in a bazaar.'

'How will you know what suits me.'

'Darling I just will.'

And on that Saturday morning as she sat on the train heading to meet him for the first time she continued to text.

'I'm sitting opposite two nuns with huge metal swaying crosses. One of them is on her mobile!'

Gina joined the throng of people squeezing through the barriers at Brighton station, swarming down towards the town and the sea front.

She crossed the road at the clock tower, diving between taxis. She was less than a minute from the '3 for 2' stand in Waterstones where they had arranged to meet. Crumpled receipts danced around the entrance.

A bearded man with a dog and a blanket looked up at her as she went in.

'Big Issue?' he asked.

8
Clifford

March 2009

Clifford waited for Gina by the '3 for 2s.' He thumbed through a fat biography on the former prime minister he referred to as *that evil woman*. At some point in the future he would enjoy raising a glass at a 'ding dong the witch is dead party.' But what the hell was he doing about to date a Tory and single mother? Single mothers were firmly on his list of 'thanks but no thanks' – another group to look down upon along with the workshy, drug addicts, benefit scroungers and more.

And yet when he looked at the age group he was in who were likely to find him interesting a high percentage would be single mums. He wondered if he had the mental resolve to deal with the other angles of such a relationship if it developed.

With reservations mounting Clifford watched her come into the shop, pull her jacket zipper down to reveal a beautiful cleavage and trim figure. An inner voice chirruped '*three kids, two dads.*' He pretended he hadn't seen her. He picked up another book '101 Things To Do with a Dead Body' and waited for the Afgan roadside device that was this sexy single mother of three kids, two dads to recognise and join him at the stand.

Gina

They were laughing - engulfed in great gulping uncontrollable tidal waves sharing the silliness of the coffee table book he was browsing.

The book now returned to the table they were exposed and vulnerable, their buttress gone.

'I'm a dead ringer for Groucho Marx?' He sealed a smile. Her eyes locked onto his thick eyebrows level to her own. He was indeed like Groucho Marx; or Denis Healey or Alistair Darling, but politely she denied it. He was much shorter than she'd imagined. The vision of George Clooney melted away. *'Steve Irwin could go hunting for snakes in those eyebrows'* she wanted to admit. She laughed it off embarrassed for staring but as they walked out of the store down West Street towards the sea front a hot slap of disappointment burned across her face.

They chatted on buoyed by humour. The sparkling sea ahead and the chewing gummed pavement below and the pleasant tones of his voice were distractions from the reality beside her. By the time they'd reached the front she wondered how to reconcile her developing feelings for him in the virtual world with the crushing downer of him the man, in flesh.

They crossed the stream of traffic chatting over the thunder of motorbikes and the wail of police sirens diving to the safety of the green faded railings. Tatty posters advertising events long gone, fluttered in the breeze. She caught a glimpse of the top of his bald head and a Gorbachev strawberry birthmark. Why had she imagined he would look like George flipping Clooney?

The screech of a seagull overhead and its descending splat suddenly sent Clifford into theatrical mode.

'Arrh, the seagull's had a dodgy ruby.' Soon they were laughing again. Clifford wobbled his head like a weeble. The weight of disappointment had started to lift.

'Miss Gina India is full of stinky poo. One day I take you there.' He bowed. And as they continued walking he talked about his trip to India and the Indian worries about terrorism.

He carried on. 'Taxi driver charge me seven rupees for visit to Aga Khan Palace and market to buy fine lady a garment.'

'Oww.' Gina waited. Clifford stopped walking and presented her with a brown parcel.

'I'm impressed. I've never had a present on a first date.'

She blushed as she unwrapped the parcel. A black and white dress escaped from the packaging. It seemed to go on and on, like a magician's trick tumbling from a top hat.

'Do you like it? Will it fit?' Clifford looked concerned. She liked his concern.

'How big did you imagine I would be? Did you ask for tent size?'

She held it up to her body laughing.

'If we ever find ourselves without clothes or in need of a parachute we'll be ok.' She grinned.

'It would fit my ex. She's hideously large - an elephant!'

She stopped laughing, told him it wasn't fair that some women grew to be so big. She looked at him trying to work out who or what he reminded her of. Was it Bert from Sesame Street or a bloated pink jelly baby?

His body was a bendy metal coathanger performing a very poor job of supporting his weighty clothing: jeans that were too wide, too long, too baggy, too bunched up. He was drowning in a weathered brown leather jacket, which reminded her of an antique sideboard in a bric a brac. She felt sorry for him. Her heart tugged slightly. She couldn't work out what she felt: a mixture of repulsion and intrigue.

A police helicopter hummed and a plane embroidered the blue sky with garlands of vapour as they headed for the pier - Brighton's magnet. Clifford was telling her how he had spent two days of his Indian trip on the toilet. He described the heat and intensity of the place. Soon they were comparing notes on airport experiences across the world.

'I hate the fucking Disney experience of airports - endless queuing for security checks.'

She found his constant swearing amusing and disarming and she liked his open and honest opinions.

Her boots clattered along the planking out to sea, adding to the thud of fun fair music, different tunes and beats competing from every direction. They paused to lean over the railings, sticky with salt.

'It's more like a British Ibiza each time I come here.' She sensed his shadow over her face as he spoke studying her, her eyes closed against the sun, breathing in wafts of nauseating grease, candy floss and sugared doughnuts.

'One day I hope I'll come back to live here. Brighton has everything.' She sensed his sadness in the silence that followed.

'The city itself or further to Saltdean?' She opened her eyes to the wavy outline of the cliffs.

'I might find it too painful. I miss the house –lying in the field watching the sky. She forced me to leave over a year ago. Now she's refusing to sell. She rents every room to DHSS. She's too idle to get a proper job and the business she runs has never made a penny. The house has been on the market for months but who's going to buy it with dirty trash living there?'

Gina couldn't work out his political thoughts. They didn't seem to make much sense. He had called himself Left wing but there was nothing about him that she found at all Left wing.

'She forced you to leave? How? Nobody can do that.'

'They can. If the police get involved. I had 24 hours to go.'

'What did you do?'

'I pushed her. Against the fridge. She was nagging about something.'

'We all do things in the heat of the moment we later regret. By then it's too late.' Gina thought of her affair with Wayne.

She turned towards the helter skelter and for a time they looked towards Shoreham. Seagulls hovered overhead in battle formation.

'Bloated seagulls. They seem to get bigger and fatter. See that one looking at us with it's beady eyes. It's like a copper.' She observed.

'They're like MPs on the scrounge.' He eyed a gull pecking on a discarded wrapper.

The comparison made Gina smile. 'Pigs with snouts in the trough. That's what the papers said. I suppose you can't blame them. If there's a loop hole people will abuse it. MPs don't earn enough that's the problem.'

'None of us do anymore. The country's finished. It'll be irrelevant who wins the next election because there are no big visions any more or great visionaries. It's just about managed decline.'

'Lots of people still want to come to Britain so things can't be that bad. Look at London. It's booming. Gina kicked a chip through a gap in the planking and fixed her gaze on the pier – a pile of little black matchsticks in the sea.

'The West Pier. It's like the tangled wreck of our lives. Do you not think?'

'Maybe. Or it could symbolize the tangled wreck of the British economy. It's the remains of Northern Rock. No amount of cutbacks are going to raise our economy. The debt is the biggest issue facing this country.'

Their arms were touching, their eyes transfixed on the steely sea. Gina caught a glimpse of his stub nose and his tight mouth. She thought of a cat's arse. She didn't want to imagine kissing him. Wiry black hairs shot from his nose in every direction, from the ridge at the top to the bulb at the bottom. She wanted to attack him with a pair of tweezers.

'What about quantitative easing? It could lead to hyper inflation. What's your take on that?' Gina was enjoying his opinions. In her world she mingled with mothers who didn't talk much about current affairs.

'It's totally unique. A bold move on the part of Gordon Brown. That man will go down as one the country's greatest leaders.'

'Labour have ruined the economy with their massive spending projects. I should know. I'm one of the recipients of their great tax credit system.'

'Arr so that's why I pay so much in corporation tax.' Clifford nudged her teasingly. 'To support all you Karen Matthews out there. The woman who pretended her kid was missing to claim a reward?'

'Oh yeah. She was on loads of benefits. Six kids, six dads I think. I'm better off than when I was married. Tax credits make a huge difference. I don't think the government's aware just how much they've contributed to the rising divorce rates. I left the marriage when house prices had peaked and interest rates were so low that I was able to pay off the small mortgage on my flat. I'm basically a Tory but I've done well out of Labour.'

'Women gain and men lose. I lost thousands. My divorce was a shipwreck. And I'm still trying to salvage the remaining treasures.'

Clifford

They ambled past the crowds drinking in the seafront bars, the stalls selling hair braids and ethnic style dress, chatting about the mistakes of their past; sharing regrets, losses and dreams. Hope for a better future fizzed through every conversation and there were small suggestions of where they might go on future dates.

'I've always wanted to walk the South Downs.' Gina said.

'Let's do it then.' Clifford was enthused. He was liking this single mum.

'Are you interested in coming to the London Book Fair?' she asked.

A woman in black lycra and trainers ran past them and Clifford called out.

'Don't bother love. You'll only die one day.'

'You're mad Clifford Chancer,' Gina exclaimed. She moved closer and linked her arm into his. It seemed a natural move.

'Hey we should celebrate. A happy new beginning? Do you fancy cocktails at the Grand Hotel?'

He waited for her to confirm the idea of a 'them.' She had opened up to him about her life as a single mother and the struggle to juggle work, kids and a social life. Part of him felt a tinge of sadness for it all. But he admired her too: her thrift, hard work and determination to pay off the mortgage. He was shocked at the small sums the kids' dads paid in maintenance. That was unfair and selfish. The CSA levels were pitifully low. He was glad he had stuck the marriage out and seen Ben through to university.

He was beginning to think that maybe his ideas about single mothers were a little harsh. But whatever he thought of them as a group he knew he wanted to get to know this particular single mum. She was young and full of life; had an infectious energy about her.

Gina

He took her hand guiding her up the steps. It felt as if she were holding a child's hand because of his height. She'd get over it. He was an interesting person. She liked his travel stories and when she mentioned radio 4 programmes he knew what she was talking about and they shared thoughts. Their daily routines were similar - waking around 6.30, listening to John Humphreys or Evan Davies until 7.30 before making strong black filter coffee. She couldn't imagine life with a radio one listener.

The Grand Hotel a reminder of a former age loomed above. She thought back to the conference and night in 1984. Prickles of fear skittered up her arms and across her back. She'd never forget the vision of Maggie, resolute yet exhausted, keeping her nerve, carrying on.

She studied the white peeling facade as they crossed the busy road. It looked like Miss Haversham's wedding cake, Charles Dickens character.

'It's seen better days,' Gina said as they waited to cross the second line of traffic. 'You've no idea what a treat this is. Single mothers on tax credits don't go to the Grand Hotel.'

He was striding up the steps - a socialist making a presence among the British establishment. 'We're fighting a ridiculous war in Afganistan to keep the streets of Britain safe – so the politicians tell us.'

But she was remembering when the IRA threatened daily life. As she looked up she recalled the night of the bomb attack. She could see the debris, the falling chunks of concrete and plaster, the twisted balconies, the bits of veranda. She could taste the dust again, felt slightly giddy as they ascended the Axminster carpeted steps. It seemed surreal.

'It's a new kind of terrorism now. Back then...' She looked around at the chandeliers and pianist and people enjoying afternoon tea. Her voice trailed away, her mind wheeling back. And seeing the sedate atmosphere, calm, sophisticated she thought of the Titanic and how everything could be transformed in an instant.

'Ding dong the witch is dead,' he sang as he strode to the bar. 'It's a great shame they didn't get the old cow.'

He seemed to enjoy being the bull in the china shop, the little man causing a stir. Newspapers rustled in front of a few pompous faces. The memory of wailing sirens, screaming and Kate Adie reporting filled Gina's head.

'I would raise a glass to the IRA,' Clifford said to the Eastern European behind the bar. 'But they failed.'

He took a swig of his Kir Royale, handed Gina hers.

'The plot was a complete disaster. It was on a long delay timer planted under a bath. Christ. Bin Laden would have succeeded. Different cause. Different time. Or maybe not such a different cause if you think about it.'

The barman curtly smiled and offered a dish of peanuts.

They sat and he removed his laptop from a leather case to look up the London Book Fair.

'Cheers.' He clinked her glass.

'Can't quite believe I'm on a date with a Tory. A not so young, Young Conservative. The party that destroyed this country.' He leaned over to touch a flower in a vase on a coffee table. 'Christ. These flowers are artificial. The age of austerity has begun.'

'Labour have done a pretty good job of that.' Gina rose to the challenge.

'*She* destroyed all sense of community,' Clifford provoked.

'Oh that argument. The coal mines were uneconomical. I met Rhodes Boyson at a Conservative conference once. He explained the economics to me.'

'The policies of *your* government were pretty short sighted and despicable from 1981 onwards. She had no belief in science, supported the city elite. The types that come in here, pretty much.'

Clifford sniffed. Glanced round. 'Miners couldn't be turned into city bankers. These were big men, built like brick shithouses. The miners were on the scrap heap. Treated like old computers. And now we have whole communities with deep social problems created by *your* government.'

'You Luddite. What about evolution? Transformation? Economic change. Come on. You're a business man. You have to adapt all the time.' She was enjoying the challenge of conversational tennis.

'I've always got my eye on the next development but these people needed government to help them. They still do. There's a moral duty to help.'

'You're supposed to be a socialist?' It was more a statement than a question. 'I bet you try to cut your tax bill. Every businessman does. Would we really have wanted to carry on sending people to work in complete darkness for hours on end? It was dirty and hazardous. It was about progress, development and that came through blue chip enterprise. The country is far wealthier now and especially since the unions were smashed once and for all.' Another bat across the net. It felt good.

He leaned back in his armchair, huskily cleared his throat, resting his red framed glasses on his head to read an email. He had an air of authority and charisma which lured her in. She took a sip of her drink and thought to herself yes, maybe I'll stick with this, for a while, see where it might lead. I might grow to like his looks. But an inner voice screamed from deep within *don't settle for someone you don't physically desire.*

9
Clifford

March 2009

'Have you got time for a relationship?' Gina asked the next day over the phone.

'My life is like the M1 - fast and furious. I've no idea if we're a possible match but I'm willing to find out. What about you?'

'I can't just dismiss you after one date and a thousand texts.' She swooned.

'We've got a brain connection.'

'Feels like we've known each other for years. We've vomited our thoughts via text like shipping forecasts; every minutiae of our daily lives sent up into cyber space.

'If you don't hear from me assume I'm dead rather than not keen. I'll be flying on one of those 777's with the high probability of its' fuel systems seizing up with ice.'

He could see a relationship developing. Wondered where it might lead...

A few dates later he suggested the cinema.

The Audi snaked across the Downs towards the inky sea passing a failing school and the doom of Brighton's tower blocks – Lego sets by the sea containing fractured communities and social problems and all the many reasons why he had readily agreed to pack Ben off to boarding school.

They past the road where his mother used to live.

'My mum used to live along there.' He suddenly felt a stab of guilt and tried to stamp on it but as they descended the hill he was consumed with tangled emotions playing over in his head. Maybe he should visit her. But he didn't want to. He half wished he could have taken her to Dignitas to escape the creeping dementia. That seemed far kinder. She had no life. She was now in a middle zone; the zone between life and death.

'Why don't you visit her in the care home? I'm sure she'd like to see you.'

It was as if Gina was reading his mind.

' What's the point? My mum died in 2007. By now she might not recognise me and I can't forgive her for what she did. It's all too painful. I don't want to reopen that painful door into the past.'

There were times when the only thing he could think of in relation to his mum was the inheritance he'd get when she snuffed it and he hated thinking like that. He was always lecturing others about how you could never guarantee inheritance and mustn't rely on it but he couldn't help wondering how much he'd get and saw it as a solution to his housing problem. The money was slowly trickling away the longer she stayed alive.

They reached the car park. He momentarily scrunched his eyes, gripping the steering wheel as emotions ran in circles round his head.

'You feel guilty don't you?' Gina asked.

He sighed. Took the key from the ignition.

'Yeah. Yeah I do. I feel lots of things. Guilt. Sadness. Shame. I abandoned her but she abandoned me. I know she didn't really. She had dementia. She wasn't in control. But what she did was hurtful. Unforgiveable. I can't bring myself to go. I'm waiting for that call to say she's gone. It's awful. I know I shouldn't feel like that but I can't help it.'

Gina

After the film they had a curry at the Marina. He tore a naan, took a swig of lager.

'Knat's piss.' He pulled a face in the direction of the waiter.

Gina savoured each mouthful of Korma. It was much creamier and nuttier than the 99p cartons of Korma or Masala Wayne used to serve up on a Friday evening on his messy dining room table, surrounded by washing hanging on racks to dry and piles of ordnance survey maps littering his filthy, threadbare carpet. Even the poppadum had the edge on the slightly chewy ones they sold on the end aisles of a value store.

He swapped his Cobra for a Kingfisher.

'So. This weekend. Is it yours or the dads? I can't keep up. Glad I'm not a single mother. Think I'd want to shoot myself.'

She sniggered. She found his comment both amusing and slightly insulting.

'They're with me. Sorry.' She wondered why she was apologising.

'You won't be able to compartmentalize your life forever.'

'It's convenient. For now.'

'I couldn't have handled all that single parent shit. All the tooing and froing.'

'Your own family is broken. Remember?' Gina watched him cram shards of broken poppadum into his mouth.

'I stayed for as long as I could. I didn't want him damaged. Christ, I wouldn't have wanted what your exes have to put up with – maintenance bills and fortnightly visits. The ex wasn't up to bringing him up alone.'

'She would have managed. It's only one child. What about me with three?'

'She returned to full time work when he was tiny. She didn't care about him. It was only a crappy little job at the council.'

'Kids don't suffer. It means a second income.'

'I was earning more than enough. She didn't need to work. Kids need their mothers.'

'That's kind of old fashioned these days.'

Clifford

He reached over and placed his hand over hers.

'You're a lovely earth mother.' Clifford thought back to the previous week. An impromptu visit to Gina's flat with a gigantic chocolate egg wrapped in yellow ribbon to surprise her. Watching her spoon-feed a spinach mix from a pink plastic bowl into Carries's mouth, in her high chair that afternoon had stirred something in him. Was it a deep longing for another child? Or even love? Or maybe just lust? He hadn't made a big deal of the visit, hadn't wanted it to be puffed up into some big important and awkward 'meet the family for the first time' occasion.

Gina

Gina took a mouthful of korma. She remembered him visiting her flat bearing an early Easter egg: his faraway hooded eyes, hypnotic, rather like a dog communicating hunger to its owner following her round the kitchen. She couldn't work out what the look had meant.

'Ben still has a way to go to complete his veterinary training?'

'If it wasn't for me he'd be on his own. She's a waste of space and a liar.'

'What lies?'

'She said she could afford Ben's private schooling using an inheritance from her parents and her earnings. She was also meant to set aside some money for a new kitchen and bathroom. We'd agreed. Well that never happened.'

'Where did the money disappear to?' Gina had no concept of debt.

'She probably ate it.'

Gina looked at the lump of naan on her plate.

'That's what the judge said. God knows she was fat enough. Ate her way through every fucking buffet. Probably put mayonnaise on aspirins. Ben discovered she was up to her eyes in it. He was in the house one day and answered all the debt callers, saw the red reminders in the post. Clever lad. He showed me how to use Experian. It wasn't difficult. My heart wept when I saw it all there on the screen. Everything I'd worked for gone.'

'Blimey. So you had no idea?' Gina found it hard to grasp the idea of not being aware of what the other half was up to.

'Stupid cow had no idea what she was doing. When I confronted her all she did was cry for weeks. And me? What do you imagine I was doing? Shitting bricks. The scale of the debts was so enormous. We'll be lucky if we come out with a few thou' when the house is finally sold.'

'I hate lawyers. I think it was Robbie Williams who said that for men divorce is the removal of the testicles through the wallet.'

'He's not far wrong. A Polish woman told me once Clifford, you divorce, what you expect?' Gina laughed at his accent.

'An old school friend of hers removed my testicles. When they were kids she'd conned Roda out of her Barbie dolls - then went on to work for the law firm that is now fleecing the pair of us.'

After the curry and cinema Clifford glided the car out of the Asda car park over the ramps and up the flyover.

'I'll show you the house. It'll mean more if you see what I've lost. I left her with nothing. Not a single stick of furniture. I'd been working from my garden office and had to find new premises. She wasn't going to ruin the business and make it impossible for me to carry on. Silly ungrateful bitch treated my work with utter contempt after everything that business had given her – the lifestyle, the beautiful home.'

They drove up a steep hill next to an open scraggy landscape. Clifford parked the car in a pool of orange light.

'This hill used to keep my weight down and my bloods low. Now look at me.'

From his description she had expected grander housing but then she noticed a discreet driveway surrounded by tall foliage and straggly trees tucked in the corner a little way from the other houses.

They got out the car. He led her a short way along the graveled drive until they reached a corner in full view of a primrose painted Edwardian house.

'Jesus. I haven't stopped paying the mortgage. And we're creeping about like a pair of burglars.'

'It's beautiful. I can't quite see the detail but is it wisteria and climbing roses around the windows? It reminds me a little of a period drama.'

'We had a local gardener twice a week. It was too big to manage. I didn't have the time and she was basically too lazy. I found out she had given up paying him too. It was embarrassing. He was a nice guy, trying to earn a living like the rest of us. He became more than a gardener. He was a friend and doing that to a friend is a real shitty thing to do.'

'Looks like she's having a party. There are lots of cars.'

She was standing a little way off. He stepped onto the verge pushing a branch aside for a better view.

'Probably all the lodgers cars. They're bound to trash the place and make it impossible to sell. The place will go to rack and ruin.'

'Oh God.' He suddenly said.

'What's that little shit doing here? That's my son's brand new VW Polo on the driveway. The ten grand car I've just bought him.'

'It's his mother. He's allowed to visit.' Gina looked incredulous. 'He loves you both. Why would he take sides?' Gina started walking back to the car.

'He saw the debt. He's still not woken up to what she became.'

Gina said nothing. He carried on.

'She destroyed the wealth that one day he would have received. He won't be seeing a penny now and he feels no remorse, no bitterness about that. He shouldn't have anything more to do with that piece of scum. He should cut ties.' He made a scissor action with his hands.

'But what are you hoping to achieve?' Gina put her hand on his arm.

'She needs to be shamed by her own son into seeing the damage she's caused. I'll confront him later, ask him what he's playing at. 'You're a sweet girl but you haven't a clue really what I've been through.'

She prickled under the condescending comment, gulping, but gently pulled her arms around him kissing his neck. 'It's ok to be angry.'

Clifford

Clifford held her head with both hands slipping his fingers through her hair, feeling its soft bounce for the first time as they stood in the beam of light streaming from the lamp post. Then he raised his lips and planted a simple kiss on her forehead and another on her nose. And soon they had found each other's lips. Her taste was sweet, her mouth deliciously moist, almost succulent. Thoughts of Ben, the ex and the past momentarily melted away in a haze, the physical contact a relaxing aphrodisiac.

Gina

Gina hadn't planned to kiss him. Was it pity or desire? As their lips met he became a slobbering Labrador who had eaten the leftovers of his master's chicken vindaloo. His lips smacked clumsily against hers missing the target then edging round meeting once more. His tongue was a shy cave snake. He wasn't going to succumb to tongue hockey, even when her tongue courageously and boldly made encouraging gestures. Tiny ripples of confused pleasure travelled downwards. She slipped his leather jacket off and began kissing his thickened neck all the time thinking that it was possibly the ugliest neck she'd ever kissed. And then she noticed *them* – a whole mass of huge unsightly black and brown moles like splashes of mud. She pulled away straightening his shirt, physically and dramatically recoiling.

'We better go. I need to get back for the babysitter.'

Clifford

It was after midnight when Clifford dialed Ben's number. This was about principles and loyalty.

'I'm not going to stop seeing her Dad. She's in a bad way. She's not earning much at the moment. She's in real difficulty.'

'What's new? The fantasy she calls her business has never made a penny.'

'Her money is her concern. You need to get over it.'

'Get over it? I'm going to spend the rest of my life getting over it.'

'Leave me out of it. Sort it out between the two of you.'

'That's so incredibly self righteous of you. You think you're above it all, conveniently removed. What a little shit you've become. I used to think you were the one good takeaway from the marriage. But I'm discovering you're weak and pathetic. You can't stand up for principles and do what's right. Just you remember who is supporting you.'

Ben was quiet.

Then he said ' remember all those years ago when we used to sit on the bench at the bottom of the garden reading bear stories?' He paused, breathed out. 'Bye Dad.'

'Yeah.'

10

Gina

April 2009

'Nick used to grope me at the kitchen sink.'

'You're starting to turn me on. Naughty girl.'

'But when I stopped wanting him he bought a pink vibrator to use on himself.'

'Yuk. I don't feel so turned on now.' Clifford sounded as if he'd just trodden in dog dirt.

She wasn't sure how they had ended up in Clifford's bedroom naked. It was a tidy bedroom – for a bloke. No clothes strewn over a chair or socks dumped in the corner. No dirty coffee cups or screwed up balls of tissues. The carpet looked freshly hoovered, the surfaces dusted. After the pit that Wayne had lived in Gina was immediately impressed.

The bathroom door creaked in the breeze. Dodgy hinges. An instant turn on, warming her below -the Pavlov Dog effect. She tried to ignore the door and its enticing creaks. Tonight she'd be getting the real thing. She'd ditched the huge knickers she called Rover and had donned a silky black pair of Ann Summers, with red ribbon and matching bra. Just putting on this new set had made her feel alive again, a warm fizz shooting through her body.

There was something strangely horny and appealing about sleeping with a man who was much older, who looked older and was basically unattractive. She felt like a prostitute and suddenly her mind had escaped into a brothel. She looked at the colony of mud splashed moles, the sagging belly, the sprouting nasal hair; smelt the whiff of bad breath that never seemed to go away and cast her eye down to his very short legs – which looked like those of a pit pony.

Her head screamed. *What am I doing? How have I managed to press the 'disgust override' button to be standing here naked in front of him?* But her revulsion had become a curious turn on.

It had been a long time since she'd bedded a guy. Wayne had been the last. He had a seriously wide girth, a cock well hidden in a nasty baggy foreskin. Clumps of Gorgonzola clung in its folds. She shuddered at the memory and the pain of intercourse with such a well endowed man.

Gina twirled her naked flesh as Clifford lay on his bed looking up, that faraway look in his eyes. He was wearing a tatty hearing aid beige toweling robe that had seen better days but at least covered his lower region. His belly, much bigger than she had imagined it would be unclothed protruded from the robe with not an ounce of shame. Gina wondered how it had grown so huge, for everywhere else he was slim.

She knew every guy loved her pert nipples, her small compact breasts and her peachy bottom. It was her saggy middle that let her down – the folds women called 'the mother's apron.' She held her breath and pulled it in but she could see Clifford's eyes upon it. She suspected he longed for the smooth outline of a woman in her early thirties, whose body hadn't been wrecked by childbirth, stretched and pulled and twisted in all directions, leaving its marks and sags. Sometimes she felt like she'd fulfilled her purpose, as far as men were concerned. She was borderline too old for more kids, had 3 already and certainly wouldn't entertain any more.

A gentle breeze fluttered the curtains; distance ringing of church bells. She wanted the bells to stop - nausea was building. Sometimes the sound of church bells made her heart briefly pound; sometimes she came over faint. There was no escaping memories. She went over to the window, shut it tight.

'Get that va – Gina over here,' he thumped the bed.

'Oh my God how many times have I heard that.'

As she climbed onto the bed she began to dread what she'd find under his robe. In his texts he had referred to it as the anaconda. Her friends had warned her – little man, big dick. Penetration was going to be painful. Again her head screamed *what am I doing?*

He looked so old. But he was old. Twelve years older. In a strange and dirty way this was a turn on and she started to feel warm below, sordid thoughts creeping into her head. She was the young mistress, he the grandfather but not her equal or partner. This was a strange fantasy. His wispy wiry grey hair added several years to his appearance. Leaning closer she saw how scraggy and turkey like his neck was and saw mottled liver spots across his bald head. His brown eyes flickered over her nipples; that same dropping, far away hypnotic look - the same look she had noticed in his eyes at Easter when she was feeding Carrie. Soon their bodies were entwined, his belly wobbling and distended against hers and his wiry chest hair tickling her nipples as they embraced in slobbery kissing.

She wondered where he kept the condoms. The way he had referred to it as an anaconda made her imagine it might be too big for a standard sized condom. When he failed to produce one, embarrassed she asked if he had any.

'I don't think I've got any. Not used one in years.' The way he said it he was turning the condom into a quaint antiquity - an ancient relic found under glass at the British Museum. He made a cursory glance towards his bedside drawer making no effort pull out any drawers. 'You'll be ok. I'll explore you with my tongue,' he laughed.

'But there might be a stray strand of toilet paper.' She'd just been to the loo. Her face flushed.

'Well I'll soon find out.' Clifford smiled, unabashed.

'Or a bit of fluff.'

'Where's the fluff likely to have come from?' He laughed.

'I might taste of wee.' Gina had turned a shade of crimson.

'Are you usually like this? I'm used to ammonia. I'm a diabetic after all. Stop analyzing.'

Minutes later she was staring at the stained ceiling, charting rivers in the cracks, while his tongue made sloshing, unappealing noises down below, like a toddler slurping a bright red Slush Puppy in a swimming pool canteen. What was it with men? She'd not met a single man who could be creative with his tongue, who knew where to hit the jackpot. It wasn't about big gulping licks to an ice cream it was about curving and flicking and twisting the tongue into cigars. It was about an artist making careful actions with a paint brush.

The sooner it was over the better, she kept thinking, but she had no intention of doing a 'When Harry Met Sally' full scale fake. She'd have to just lie there and wait for him to come up for air or his tongue to go numb and drop off. At least she felt in control. If his technique had been good she'd have been tempted to forget the condoms and whizz down to the chemist first thing Monday, to buy a £22 morning after pill – an expensive shag.

It seemed to go on forever. Most men got bored if they bothered at all. Most were desperate just to plunge in. When it was finally over Gina knew she'd have to match the time otherwise it would look selfish. She hoped he wouldn't make her gag. She reluctantly began to pull his toweling robe off, which had clearly seen better days. His chest was the hairiest she'd ever seen. She had never made love to a man with a hairy chest, let alone one with grey hair. Her eyes stared at his belly. It was far bigger naked than clothed and totally out of proportion to the rest of his body which was really quite trim and petite. His belly looked almost comical when compared with his narrow hips and slim short legs and painfully thin arms. And then her eyes moved to the mass of brown hair around his groin. For a few seconds she thought about how different the hair was to the wiry, grey hair of his chest.

Then... suddenly she realized she couldn't see anything.

She tried not to show alarm. Where was his dick?

Usually a man's penis was a hard rod which reached up to the belly button.

She could see nothing - just a mass of hair. She felt like a wild pig foraging in the undergrowth for truffles. Where was it? For one awful moment Gina wondered if he wasn't actually a man at all or whether it had been surgically removed and he hadn't told her. She stroked his belly, amused at the way it wobbled from side to side. Her hand moved towards the mass of soft hair. It was like delving into a bird's nest, not knowing what you might find, scared of damaging the delicate eggs. Gina fumbled through his bush, almost *afraid* of what she might find.

This was one of those mega disappointing moments, when your whole new relationship's future flashes before you. And the turning point came when she noticed it, coiled beneath the hair – something so small, so shriveled if she had been a Martian just arriving from space she really wouldn't have had the foggiest idea what it was.

It.... felt and looked pretty much like a squelchy button mushroom – the type you find in tin cans drenched in brine. And his balls were really no bigger than tiny marbles wrapped in flesh. It wasn't moving; looked like it had been beaten to death.

She looked at the button mushroom. Wondered what it would be like in her mouth. A tiny droplet trickled from its' head. She imagined a slippery fish in her mouth.

And then she thought of the 'Cock Trump' cards played at Ann Summers parties. Her mind scanned through the encyclopedia of cock types. This wasn't the Joystick or the Darth Vada. It wasn't even the Twinkie or the Witchetty Grub or even the Baby Carrot. This was the Weener – the card that lost you the game. In stamina, girth size and cleanliness this was a big loser way off the Richter Scale of cocks. For the first time in her adult life she could suddenly see the appeal of a Rampant Rabbit; despite the £49 price tag.

What the hell was she supposed to do with it?

11
Clifford

April 2009

Clifford wanted to spend a bit of time getting to know Gina and so the invite to stay over for the weekend was a natural progression of their relationship.

But oh boy – he was drained. He'd returned from India the day before to a house of complete chaos. Gina had mentioned she liked a decent cup of coffee so he'd dashed over to Brighton to pick up the very best in De Longhi bean to cup professional style coffee machines. At £1200 it wasn't the most expensive kitchen gadget he'd ever bought, but it looked great on the work top and the smell wafting up the stairs first thing in the morning was bound to put her in the right mood for some hard thrusting. But that of course would very much depend upon his little friend down below.

Things had been so different a few years back when the hydraulics worked. If only he could return to those virulent days when his cock performed to order. The work trips away, free to behave as he wanted sauntering into a brothel, making his choice from a selection of women and twenty minutes later pulling his trousers back on, feeling slightly ashamed and dirty but returning to the bar of the hotel to chat up a stray lass over a drink or two, ending up in bed till the morning with her. Sex had been so easy. But now? He couldn't work out when things had changed and why they had changed. Maybe this was his punishment for his appalling marital behaviour. But he still had hope that 'normal service' would resume. Gina was young and pretty and the thought of shagging a single mother was a massive turn on. And if things weren't any better he'd call in the 'engineers' to see what they could offer.

Gina's eyes and body begged – leaning over the bed her pert erect nipples hovering over him, her swollen distended belly drooping towards her bushy mound. Her pubic mound was like a raised platform; a helicopter pad. He slipped his hand inside his robe pretending to massage the anaconda. He reached for her red angry nipples, flicking one and taking the other in his mouth.

'Have you got some condoms?'

His fingers were now inside her feeling the wetness, thick and clear, like fresh egg white from a broken shell; forming great peaks, baked as delicious meringues. He wanted, at that moment to push her down, climb inside her and come for England.

Condoms. What the fuck? Putting a condom on a limp dick was like trying to put up a tent in the pouring rain. It was on the tip of his tongue to say you didn't worry about condoms last time you did it, you dirty slut. Look what you produced that time? He held off, slightly irritated that she was happy to shag Mr. Neanderthal Man Wayne without a condom but not him.

'The anaconda would like to explore inside but that's ok there are other things we can do,' he licked his lips suggestively and flicked his tongue, his fingers rubbing her bloated vaginal lips. She'd soften. With a fanny that moist and a tongue that could weave magic how could she resist the anaconda? She was bound to succumb. If it mattered that much she'd be on the pill. She'd have whisked herself down to the doctors' days ago. Why were women so unprepared he wondered?

He spread her legs and began to explore with his tongue. She lay motionless; her body rigid, no sign of enjoyment came. It tasted good – sweet. There were none of the unpleasant odours he'd encountered with the ex. The smell of her fanny had been as rank as a walk through Billingsgate Market. It was no wonder that he'd strayed. He hadn't enjoyed dipping his wick in, let alone his tongue. But this was good, he thought, as he flicked his way around, hoping to excite her into receiving the anaconda.

And then she reached up and began to untie his robe. She looked desperate for it. Perhaps he'd been wrong. Maybe his tongue had fired her. She looked like she needed an orgasm. He looked down wishing beyond all hope that he could be as stiff as a piece of Brighton rock.

It was not to be. His cock lay curled and lifeless. He might as well be exposing himself in the centre of Oxford Street's Marks and Spencer on a Saturday afternoon for the embarrassment he felt.

At that moment it felt like he was sitting down to a plate of the most delicious food in the best restaurant in town with raging hunger like there was no tomorrow but then picking up the knife and fork, moving them towards his mouth but realizing at the last moment that he had no mouth.

This was unbearable. He couldn't tell her how he felt. He hoped she was going to stay quiet. He didn't need therapy. She was gently moving her hand around, down to the balls, fondling his shriveled penis - which refused to pay any attention whatsoever. At that point he wished he had a baseball bat because he would have wacked it, if it was detached from his body like a wounded animal in the road that you needed to put out of it's misery.

She stopped. She had full marks for trying. She said nothing; nothing that would make him feel any smaller than he already felt. But part of him felt slightly irritated that she had ignored the issue that lay between them, that prevented them from making love. He imagined her working on a corpse. Would she silently work away hoping it would stiffen?

And then from nowhere he started to laugh; a laughter which rose from his belly.

'Stand up, stand up for Jesus,' he sang, coughing and spluttering between verses.

'This cock is well and truly beyond its' sell by date Gina, Gina VaGina... and your fanny is within date. I think I'd like to take another taste. Call it the dessert, it's so sweet it's like sorbet. Fanny sorbet. Never mind the anaconda, next time will be better. Ride a cock's travelled to India and back. It's probably knackered.'

12
Clifford

April 2009

For Clifford the whole relationship hinged on his unreliable cock. He'd call in the engineers; fight the problem with chemical warfare. Then he'd take her away on a romantic relaxing weekend to the Scottish Highlands, ply her with chilled champagne from a bucket and they'd swallow lemon drenched oysters seductively. He'd book a castle with a four poster bed and a massive sunken bath. He'd feed her with good food, good company and quality spunk. It sounded like a Tory party initiative.

It felt as if they had so much to see and do to make up for lost time and all the wasted years spent in lousy marriages. He emailed his bucket list.

Subject: My Bucket List
Date: 04 May 2009 00:55:02

1. USA. I have to take you to all the places I know well. Each time I go there a little bit more of me wants to live there. Would that ever be possible do you think?
2. Vancouver. GORGEOUS BEARS.
3. Rwanda to see gorillas.
4. The Galapagos. Very doable and probably last chance in next 10 years.
5. India.
6. China. Cheap hotels; only £25 a night. And get your laundry done for £1.50!
7. Weekend in Marrakesh. You'll hate the toilets though. You end up shitting everywhere.

8. Japan. You'll love the toilets – the famous arse washing, blow drying Toto.
9. Manchester Science Museum – real sewers that smell.
10. Not on the list: South of England Show.

And she emailed him her bucket list.
Subject: My Bucket List
Date: 04 May 2009 02:45:06
1. New England in the Fall. (My mum went there)
2. Memphis to see Elvis' Gracelands. (Tacky I know)
3. A cruise to Alaska. (Did you like baked Alaska as a kid btw?)
4. India. (I studied Indian history at university).
5. Macchu Pichu. (My aunt went there).
6. Dubai. (My friend went there).
7. Belfast. (To see the graffiti on the side of houses in the Falls area).
8. A castle in the Scottish Highlands.
9. Anywhere on a cruise. (My mum raves about cruises).
10. Not Butlins or Pontins.

They'd work through those lists beginning with her number 8.

For a guy earning the best part of £150k a year a Harley Street £2k testosterone implant in the bottom was well worth the money. It would be like placing his cock in a Fison's Gro bag. It was a slow release hormone; a bit like Depo-Provera for dumb girls who couldn't remember to take the pill.

He hoped this magic cure would transform him from an old git into an Adonis. He was looking forward to the return of the early morning hard on. In a couple of weeks he'd be a new man swathed in silk sheets with Gina. He'd stock up on the little blue pills too –his back up measure.

He tripped up the steps to the clinic, his legs light and happy as if shot through with helium; his head full of visions of Gina's naked body, the curve of her belly. They'd hug and kiss - that total brain connection, sparking each other off with new thoughts, ideas.

His little problem hadn't put her off. He knew his problems were complicated and stemmed from the diabetes but also his head was filled with visions from the past; memories etched on his mind, returning again and again. There had been so many women - all used as toilets; money handed over, receptacles to wank into, then flies up and away; the scuttle of shame. Just at the point he thought he might cum with Gina, the memories would return.

Nursing his sore bottom he headed back to the tube. He knew there were no guarantees. And deep down he knew he couldn't reverse the body's decline. It had begun. This wasn't like exchanging a clapped out car for a sports car.

13
Gina

May 2009

The chauffeur driven Mercedes meandered its way down a palatial drive, took a final corner, sweeping past a cluster of tall emerald evergreens. A graceful mist swirled lightly between the trees like a veil hanging in anticipation and reminding her all at once of love; how it crept up slowly and ensnarled. And then she saw it. The castle - converted into a five star hotel. The internet had described it as one of the finest most imposing baronial mansions in the Scottish highlands - a mix of castle and mansion. Gina's eyes traced the outline of towers and turrets, porticos and crow stepped gables. It was framed by heath clad, snow capped mountains, grand and majestic like an oil painting in a gallery.

'You've transported me to the world of celebrities.' She rubbed his arm.

He reached over and kissed her ear.

' There'll be many more weekends like this. Champagne, fine food, stiff cock.'

'We always went on a Sun newspaper £10 deal to Pontins or Butlins when I was with Wayne. The kids sardined along the back seat of his swimming pool blue Nissan Micra. I can remember the wafer thin mattresses and plug in wall heaters and queues at the food court. Traipsing round carousels in pouring rain with overweight parents, dressed in tracksuits, garnished in tattoos screaming at their children who always seemed to be called Chelsea or Ryan.' Gina smiled.

' The man's fucking tight. I'd rather jump over Beachy Head than suffer Pontins or Butlins.'

'I can't stop thinking about something Nick said when I asked him to have the kids this weekend. It was quite upsetting.'

'What did the arse hole say?' Clifford looked in alarm.

'Off for a dirty weekend with your new lover?' When are you planning the next little bastard?'

'The man's a cunt.' Clifford spat. ' Relax and enjoy this weekend. We don't get weekends like this very often.'

They waited for the chauffeur to take their bags to the concierge. Clifford kissed her ear and ran his hand through her hair, sweeping her into an embrace.

'Love you.'

'Love you too.'

She studied his face. He wasn't good looking but had an alluring charisma and a sense of power and authority that appealed to her – the charisma of distinguished men like John Humphreys and Robert Redford.

A four poster bed with cream sheets in a sumptuous antique filled room awaited as they climbed the stairs which looked down upon a row of welly boots for the guests to wander around the vast estate.

'My feral mum.' Clifford leaned over her shoulder.

She gasped. 'The size of this bathroom. It's bigger than my lounge.

'I don't do down market. Are you interested in something else that's getting rather big?"

'Wow. Look at these soft white towels neatly folded like delicate sandwiches at a funeral.' She held one to her cheek feeling its softness.

He slipped his hands into her bra, cupping her breasts.

She ignored him. ' Molton Brown shampoo bottles. Wow! They're really expensive in department stores. Nice gold taps. And the bath. Crikey. ' His hands were still firmly clamped.

'We could sit in it together, accommodating all our middle aged wobbly bits.'

She looked at them both in the mirror. His hands were working round her nipples. His eyes were faraway, hypnotic. A fizz of excitement shot up and down her body. Within minutes she burned with desire for him. Something was different this time. And she was wet.

'Arrh my dear maiden this Irish priest needs you to perform your duty. Take off your apron my dear and your pantaloons.' He tugged at her top.

'Erm... how dirty. This fair maiden has been milking the cows all day. She needs to lie down in the hay.' He took her hand. Led her across the plush carpet to the four poster bed.

He pushed her hand to his groin as he continued the period drama. This time she was gripping a rigid slightly curved dick. She removed it from his trousers, struck by how it reminded her of one of those fun size bananas in supermarkets, marketed for kids' school lunch boxes. Whatever the doctor at Harley Street had given him - it was working. It was alive and waiting for her, no longer a shrivelled worm in the undergrowth. She didn't know much about Viagra but it was pretty obvious things had to happen fast; the moment would be lost – like charging the battery of a car or lighting a match. You couldn't just switch off the engine and hope the car would start later. You had to keep it running, foot firmly held on the accelerator.

Soon he was thrusting inside her. But all she could feel was his crushing weight on top of her pressing against her ribs; her swollen stomach and the taste of burning acid rising like fire in her throat, his clammy skin sticking to hers, wiry chest hair tickling. She couldn't feel the friction of a penis moving up and down, that tight sensation of pulling and the tip penetrating nerve endings. Waves of disappointment, not delight crashed around her. An orgasm wasn't about to happen and she was too old in the tooth to fake. When her orgasm was real it was raw and feral. She became a Pentecostal church goer speaking in tongues.

When sex was disappointing she always told herself it was just the icing on the cake. This was clearly hard work for him. She had to be patient, give it time. But she couldn't help looking over at the heavy door with longing. It felt as if Clifford was climbing to the top of a steep mountain, using every last drop of energy he had, determined to reach the summit.

And then it was over. Their eyes locked. She wished she hadn't made more effort to synchronise.

In frustration she considered reaching for a pair of tweezers to pluck the wiry hairs from his nose, but still felt a warm glow below that needed finishing off.

'I'm going to show you something I do when I can't. When I feel frustrated.'

'I'm sorry. I'm going to make you cum later. I'll be up for it again.' He had collapsed, panting.

'It's ok. Not your fault. I just kind of need to cum though. Watch.'

Gina slipped out of bed, padded across the plush carpet, grabbed a towel from the bathroom to mop the trickling sticky fluid from between her legs and went over to the inner door. She wedged the towel between her legs, grabbed each side of the door handles and began to swing on the door, clenching tight with her knees, pressed hard against each side as she rubbed herself up and down, growing hotter and hotter. This was exhausting. It had been easier when she was young, more nimble, lighter. Her hands burned. Her arms ached. She couldn't feel them. It felt like they would drop off.

They were in a sumptuous hotel with a four poster bed and this was what it had come to: her riding on a flipping door. But soon her stomach tightened. She was in trance. She gripped tighter, pressed harder against the wood. In a flash she could see her mother cooking and her sister playing in the garden and then her father telling her to stop. 'The door will come off its' hinges if that child doesn't stop'. She tried to blot them out focusing on imagining Clifford inside her. An orgasm came crashing from the pit of her stomach, radiating out, down her legs then shooting back up. She gripped tighter. Pressed her fanny harder against the door, clenching as tight as she could, moving lower, dragging her body closer to the ground, pressing and pressing, desperate to continue as wave after wave crashed. Her knees were sore, her hands were tingling.

When it was over she collapsed in a heap, then dragged herself up and limped back to the bed, hands red and burning, wheezing, heart pounding as if she'd sprinted round the hotel grounds 50 times.

'I've never seen anything like it. So a vibrator would be a waste of money? When did you learn that? You were like a wild animal. I'm going to start calling you Dorian. God I feel so inadequate. You reminded me of when my ex used a vibrator once. She had a massive orgasm, something I could never achieve for her. I threw it away. Couldn't bare it.'

'Never used one. What you saw, well it's been part of my whole life. Can't remember how and when it all started.'

'The return of the early morning hard on.' He pressed against her back the next morning. 'The testosterone shot is working.'

'More like the Viagra. You took a blue pill a while ago didn't you? I heard you doing something.'

She was beginning to wonder about all this medication. It put him in control. He was calling the shots. What if she didn't want it? The erection was there. It had to be dealt with, one way or the other. It was a bit like a couple who were having difficulties getting pregnant, having to perform the act to a tight window of opportunity in the cycle, robbed of the thrill of sex, reducing it to a mechanical act, spontaneity out the window. It was like cranking up an old machine and setting it immediately to work before it conked out again.

This time she needed to know if she could orgasm in intercourse. She suggested some cushions beneath the small of her back to raise her body higher. Logistically speaking she knew that was the answer to being able to feel his small cock. Maybe that would mould her into his body closer.

She gripped her legs around his waist and as he moved she moved too. With each thrust she pressed her hands on each of his buttocks pushing him deep, hearing him moan. It didn't hurt as it had with Wayne and Nick and soon she felt a tightening in her stomach, kept gripping, squeezing in, feeling the pleasure of their perfectly timed orgasms.

The sun streamed into the breakfast room. They ate a huge feast of thick creamy porridge with a knob of butter on top, fresh slithers of salmon and poached eggs with flecks of pepper and coffee...served by a wild looking Scotsman in a kilt and a lady who looked like she belonged to the Adams family.

After breakfast they had coffee in the the morning room, where newspapers were spread across a large oak coffee table and where she posed in a rather ornate gilt chair resembling the throne of a queen for a photograph. The photo would be the Scottish collection. And in the months to come there would be the Florence collection, the Paris collection, the Graz collection, the Istanbul collection.

They descended the tiered lawn, the tranquill grey waters of the River Awe before them. Clouds hung over the heather patched mountain – the slopes of

Ben Cruachen. Standing at the waters' edge she imagined they were part of some Celtic myth. He was the warrior, she the hero ready to slay the beast and carry her in long flowing garments to the small boat tied next to the rippling water.

'Hey look this way,' Clifford called from a short way off, breaking her day-dreams with the snap of his Nikon. He neatly framed her head with its tumbling curls, under the rain hat she was never without and her pastel green mac contrasting against the dark mountains.

'I feel like Princess Di and Prince Charles in the Highlands posing for their engagements photos. Where's ya kilt?' Gina chuckled.

He carried on clicking as she walked towards the wood skirting the hotel grounds. A squint in the sun; a backdrop of beautiful bright pink rhodedendrons; a view of her bottom bending to pick bluebells; a close up smile as she peered round a twisted knotted branch in the dim light.

'Take your hat off now. I want to see that beautiful springer spaniel hair that I fell in love with,' he called pursing his lips into a kiss from afar.

'That's perfect. Look at this one. Your hair looks luxuriant – the light has captured it so well. Can you see the tones? This camera is sharp.' He was scrolling back looking at the pictures.

They walked on, crunching leaves curled like tobacco under foot and into a darkened area, where the trees hid the light and moss and lichen lined the route. They began to kiss against the rugged bark of a tree, his fingers gently touching her face and reaching into her top to caress the hardened nipples.

'Remind me again why you love me,' she whispered as slivers of passion stirred.

'You're bright and sparky and I fell in love with your springer spaniel hair.'

'Looking after kids all day has given me a bit of a mushy brain.'

'I've found your re set button.'

It was beginning to drizzle as they came to the end of the wood, through a clearing into a secret walled garden. A blanket of bluebells spread before them.

'Bluebells grow in ancient woods.' He bent to pick one. They tiptoed to a broken greenhouse on the far side of the four walled garden.

'There has to be the perfect combination of sun and rain for so many bluebells to grow. They can quickly spread, as they have here but it's getting the right combination.' He bent down and took a tiny drooping head of the dainty violet flower in his fingers.

And then he became David Bellamy - 'The Botanic Man' strutting up and down for Thames TV stamping on the grass arms waving, mouth wide. He looked the part; dressed in a dark green gore-tex, a comforting thickened middle. His tufty grey hair stood wild in the wind and looked endearing for the first time.

'One hundred and fifty million years ago,' his voiced boomed, 'plants *w*uled the earth.... deep within the booooowels of the earth.... these bluebells depeeeeend upon the daaaaaarkest, daaaaampest conditions... and this is the first ever film prod....duced on bluebells, what a story this bluebell can tell you, these bluebells *w*hite-ful place is here.'

His voice grew in intensity, rising and falling. Gina realised that he could make her laugh in a unique way. But it was more than that. He knew so much. She wondered what he could teach her kids.

They wandered into the greenhouse tiptoeing around the broken glass and pots. 'Those silly voices you put on. I'll always remember the first date when you spoke with an Indian accent. Made me crack up. You've got something I've not seen before,' Gina gushed.

'If only I'd met you 30 years ago.' He looked sad. 'But then with our age gap I would have been labelled a child molester. You've come at the end of my life. What you see is a crumbly old 54 year old, battered, beaten, broken. I won't let you go now I've found you. Promise,' he pulled on her jacket, drawing her into a kiss.

'We connect at brain level totally. You're my equal. I know you care about me.'

The air was still and silent. She sensed he was about to say something more but then he frowned slightly, turned into the drizzle.

Gina wondered how their life would have been if they had met first time round. She often dreamt of the security of a long marriage. In her perfect little dream they would have stayed together. There wouldn't have been any rifts, just blissful contentment. The hum of radio four and the smell of toast each morning; a house with a view over a village, a river or the sea; mortgage paid off and no debts; a pension pot for retirement. By now they might even be looking to buy a second property and their son and daughter (because they would have been blessed with one of each, of course) would be at university while they tinkered round the house fixing things and improving the garden and travelling the world..... city breaks, cruises, relatives in far off places. The dream she had of what might have been made her suddenly feel sad.

She marvelled at couples who'd lasted the course.

'What is the secret glue that holds some couples together? What really is happy ever after? Do you know? I'm damned if I do. Maybe there are moments of happiness but I think you have to experience periods of unhappiness to understand happiness. At this moment in time, in Scotland, this afternoon, I would say I'm happy...blissfully happy in fact. I wish I could hold onto the moment. Capture it forever. How corny is that?'

'I don't know what I think. I know the couples you're on about though that stay together till the bitter end. You see them in the local papers, hugging, beaming up towards the camera from their built to last Parker Knoll settees. Those are the respectable marriages.'

'Love honour and obey and all that crap. An impossible mission, rather like flying to the moon must have seemed before Neil Armstrong proved otherwise.'

'My dad was only my age when he died. He'd had three heart attacks. Probably caused by a Jewish diet of fried fish. I think they had a happy marriage but he was away a lot, playing in an orchestra.... Vienna, Paris. She doted on him and when he died she went to pieces. She cried into his unwashed pyjamas for months and wouldn't leave the house. It was the end of her world. So sad to watch her go downhill. I'd ask how she was coping but always got the aggressive reply, how do you think I'm coping? She hardly encouraged sympathy. The longer you're with someone and the closer you are the worse the bereavement and loss is.'

He seemed far away. 'Fuck you've got me thinking of my poor mum again. I still can't face visiting her.'

She didn't know what to say. She'd tried to get him to visit. Even offered to go with him.

'Those couples are in bubble wrap world, blissfully unaware that one day the bubble will pop. Divorce makes you strong emotionally or maybe it makes you weaker.'

Clifford was listening, walking slightly ahead.

She carried on.

'I often see big groups of girls in Brighton at night, like a group of wild animals hunting in a pack, on hen weekends, drinking to oblivion, tarted up with matching pink fluffy bunny ears, fish nets and flashing sashes saying Chloe's hen night. You see them sucking huge willy lollies. Maybe I'm just a prude. It's as if marriage is one big joke - an excuse for a party. What are they thinking? See how it goes? A handbag is for life, but a husband...'

She wondered if those women knew that the L plate would be needed each day for the rest of their marriage... to steer their way around differences of opinion, reversing down ditches of despair at three in the morning or driving in the fast lane to blissfully wedded happiness via the junction of compromise, through the tunnel of communication and reconciliation.

'If only ACAS could arbitrate every time there was a dispute over which TV channel to watch. I suppose its called Marriage Guidance, or Relate. They didn't do much for me.'

Later on in the room they undressed each other at the window.

'A full moon. How corny. But so romantic,' she said.

He pushed her onto the four poster bed. She felt the soft sheets under her naked body. He pulled her legs wide apart while kneeling beside the bed and took his face towards her, as if she were a meal to consume. This time he didn't slosh or slurp. He flicked his tongue around her clitoris while tweaking both nipples which sent shock waves up and down her body and soon she was thrashing, a deep moan - her head moving from side to side like a wild creature. And then he was climbing on top of her, pushing his way inside while she quickly positioned two cushions under her back and for the second time she came, a different sensation, but equally pleasurable.

As they took their seats on the plane Gina wondered when the romantic bubble would burst. They fastened their belts and started to kiss. They didn't care that people might find it nauseating.

' I'd miss your wit, your lovely warm charm and the rapport we've built up. I'm a risk taker Gina. I hope you are.' Clifford leaned towards her, his shirt buttons popping open, curly greys escaping.

'Life is a risk.' Gina smiled.

Clifford unclipped his belt, put his jacket on the floor. 'I'm just nipping to the loo. I won't ask you to join the mile high but give this idea some thought.'

He looked down at her, a serious look spread across his face. He paused before saying 'Life's short. Marry me.'

'What?'

'You heard.'

She watched him walk along the aisle to the loo. Her heart pounded. Too stunned to focus on any meaningful thoughts she stared out of the window, her stomach knotting. She half registered the tiny houses and the meringue capped mountains - the fairyland that was Scotland.

He returned to an awkward silence and then she talked about the view from the plane as if the question had never been asked.

'Well? What do you think?' He asked.

'I know we've had a fantastic weekend but that was just two days. We've only known each other for eight weeks.'

'We could have a great future together. We don't have to rush into it but life's short. You know that.' He looked at her with those soppy eyes, brows pleading.

Gina sat up, taking control.

'I thought you said you didn't want to do the wifey bit again.'

She pulled the plane's magazine out of the slatted rack in front of her, started curling it into a large Havana.

'You said something along the lines that you'd always thought the wife thing was like one of those old style power tools which you could turn from drill into circular saw sander. But those tools were useless.'

Suddenly the tension was gone. They were laughing and kissing all over again.

He took her face in his hands, kissed her forehead.

'You're life partner material Gina. I've told you that before. I can see us carving some sort of future together. We can get a nanny and you can come on some of the trips with me... China in the Autumn, Japan in November... you'll love the arse washing, drying Toto toilets.'

'Not those bloody toilets again!'

'Think about it will you?'

The kids hardly know you.'

'I've bought one kid up. He's well adjusted. He never gave me any problems and he's a bright lad. I've not done too bad a job and I certainly wouldn't fail your kids.'

Gina heard his voice but her brain was a jigsaw of competing voices, stepping in to join the discussion. She didn't know the way forward. She liked being on her own but part of her wanted to be looked after. Maybe he was her lifeboat rescue. But he was more than that. As clichéd as it sounded he made her laugh. He kept her entertained. But was that enough? She had to think of the kids too. It wasn't just her life anymore. They didn't know him. They might not grow to like him. But they were growing up, they wouldn't be around forever and she had her life to think of. They would have to fit into her new life.

'I don't know those kids but I'm a big enough and generous enough human being to care about them. And they are the closest thing to the person I love.'

They climbed down the clanky metal steps onto the runway in drizzle and wind. An airport bus waited, filling fast. A queue had formed.

'Yes. Ok I will.' Gina grabbed his arm smiling before they reached the bus.

'Really? What? Just like that?' He put his bag down.

'Life's short!' She dropped her bag and flung her arms around him.

'We're off to Hatton Garden next weekend then, to buy you the biggest most expensive ring... well... there is a bit of a budget but it will be a four figure budget!'

For a few moments they forgot the bus and stood on the tarmac – gooey eyed and grinning. She was getting married. Again. And this time - she told herself it was going to be different. This was her second stab at happiness and she was going to make it work.

Clifford

In a haze they forgot Nick was meeting them at Gatwick with the kids.

They were relaxed walking through the airport terminal, laughing hand in hand. Suddenly Nick was in front of them, stoney faced clutching the kids hands ready to hand them over.

Clifford was taken aback. Catapulted back to reality he hadn't expected Nick to look so young, slim and trendy.

What was he supposed to say? He reached out his hand, tried to act casual while nerves danced in his stomach.

'Ok?'

But Nick looked far from ok. How could he be ok? His wife had kicked him in the bollocks, taken his kids, his money. He'd swapped reading bedtime stories each evening for a meal for one in a shitty rental.

Their faces met, eyebrows raised. In a brief moment Clifford saw the pain he carried.

What's she doing with that old git? He knew that was what Nick was thinking.

The encounter put a dampener on what had been a glorious weekend, a feeling made worse by the suffocating silence of the kids all the way home.

But then Clifford's heart sank as they pulled up at her flat.

Wayne was sitting in the window seat, waving to them, all comfy, drinking a mug of tea, reading to Carrie, as if he owned and lived in the place.

'What the fuck?' Clifford was fuming. His face pumped with blood.

'He still has a key. What can I do?'

'Ask for it back. What the hell are you doing Gina. It's time to move on.' He shouted.

14
Clifford

June 2009

Gina was watching the glint of her new diamond solitaire in the afternoon sun.

Ducks were bobbing on the fast current of the river Arun; toys in a draining bath. Gina loved to watch the ebb and flow of what was one of England's fastest flowing rivers. In places it was tidal. It was a relaxing way to spend a Sunday afternoon. They watched the cars stream across the bridge, mused about what it might be like to live in the imposing castle which dominated the landscape of their favourite historic town - Arundel and they thought about which tea room to pig out in – probably Belinda's on Tarrant Street.

'It's a wonderful feeling to be a couple again. There's a future to look forward to. Ever since divorce I couldn't see any future. Having this beautiful ring on my finger sort of makes things feel perfect. I've got a good feeling about this. We're older, wiser. It'ill work second time around. Don't you think?' She smiled confidence in his direction, squinting against the light. She pulled at a blade of grass. Took it between her teeth.

'You're my two legged Prozac Gina. We're two woodland creatures going into hybernation. It feels like the shit could be behind us.'

'We could burrow a den somewhere.'

'I'm still worried about the spousal maintenance. She's still there, in the background of our lives. I'd rather serve time than pay that evil bitch a penny.'

'You're like a dog with a bone. Just pay it. It's like paying council tax. Nobody wants to but we have no choice.'

' Gina.' Clifford sliced the romance in one hit. 'It's the principle. Why should I work my bollocks off to pay that lazy woman a grand a month? Answer me that?'

Gina shrugged. Stared at the water in silence.

'It's not a grand. It's more than that when you factor in the tax I've paid to earn it. Christ.' He spat the words.

Was she deliberately trying to stoke his embers? He watched her hold her hand towards the sun, still admiring the rock. She wove a blade of grass through the band of the ring.

'I've been mulling over an idea.' He braced himself.

'I'm going to call the solicitor in the morning.' He paused. ' Two guesses what I'm thinking?'

'I've no idea. We haven't developed telepathy yet. What are you thinking? Will I like it?'

'We could marry really soon.'

She jolted. Her face turned to hardened clay. 'Why rush into it? I haven't told the kids yet. Give me a chance.'

' They'll love the idea, you see. They'll get to live in a big house and have plenty of money spent on them.'

Gina said nothing. She looked away, watching a terrier scamp up the bank in the tall grass. Clifford nudged her.

'Just think we could go on a luxury honeymoon to the Far East. Sit on the beach for a week and have endless sex. What d'you reckon?'

From Gina's expression he knew she was processing this forbidden fruit, an idea hard to resist.

'Don't fight against something that feels so good.' He stroked her leg.

'Is that why you want to get on with it? You've seen a holiday.' She smiled.

'Sounds exciting. Maybe I could be persuaded.' She stretched out the last words, as if savouring a dessert.

'Not exactly. Having three dependents could work in my favour. Get me out of paying the maintenance. I'll get the solicitor to check it out in the morning. Imagine Roda's face. The final death knell in her claim.'

'So I'm just your life raft? Great. Hardly romantic.' She scoffed, leant down to pull a blade of grass with force this time.

'It's an idea. If it's a no go we'll take our time. Plans things slowly.'

'That sounds better. Take our time to choose a venue, enjoy the whole build up.'

'I'm thinking beyond the dress, the venue, the honeymoon. We need to discuss pre nuptials with the solicitor.'

'You certainly know how to demolish romance in one massive hit.'

'I'm not taking the risk of being fleeced twice over. Gina we're not 20. Doesn't experience tell you anything?' He wriggled on the grass.

He was Clifford Chancer and he wasn't prepared to play the Vegas style divorce game a second time around without an agreement. He knew the hard facts; women could be complete cows, hoovering up the pennies and the pounds.

'Are you thinking of a pre nuptial? They aren't legally binding. They're pretty pointless.'

'One day they might be legal then they'll carry weight. I've got my business to protect and a future inheritance from my mother.'

Clifford saw a change sweep her face – a child whose toy had been removed.

' You don't trust me? I'd run off with all your money. I didn't do that to Nick. We didn't need to use a solicitor. It's what amicable grown ups do.'

Clifford didn't miss her tone.

'I don't trust anyone. Not after being shafted.'

'Well I don't need a document to protect my money. If I didn't trust you I wouldn't be marrying you.'

'I'm not marrying without one. It's as simple as that. You're being niave. The courts could make decisions otherwise.'

'Everything has to be about the courts with you. What about what *we* decide?'

'What if I have another heart attack and need carers? They might award me more of the money. It's all about need. You don't know the first thing about how the courts work.'

'And I don't want to know. Two people should be able to work things out without the cost of a solicitor.'

'This is real life, not Lego Land, Gina. We both stand to lose.'

She looked down at the diamond again and in her mind it had transformed into a rock of salt on her finger for the sting on her face. Then her face melted and she began to twirl the diamond.

' We've just got engaged. Couples are supposed to start married life trusting each other.'

A fortnight later, having argued and discussed the details of a pre nuptial agreement they drove to North London and sat with his solicitor to discuss the formulation of a pre nuptial.

'I want you to pay my moving costs if we split up. I don't want costs eating up my equity. Otherwise I will end up in a smaller flat. That wouldn't be fair.'

'I'll be paying big payments on the mortgage. That's capital building up. I want that protected.'

'I'll be putting down the deposit. From my flat. You wouldn't be able to buy the big house in the first place without my help.'

'I feel exhausted now. That was totally draining. All this talk about splitting up and pre nuptials is destroying the romance,' she moaned on the journey back from the solicitors.

'Things are different second time around. The first time two people marry they don't have money to worry about. They can throw caution to the wind. We can't afford to.'

Clifford looked at her, could see sadness and disappointment in her face and hurt in the tart way she responded when the word pre nuptial was mentioned. But after a diet of deceit, deception, lies, debt and huge loss he had to be resolute. His head had the last say, not his heart. The future was founded on firm pillars of trust and honesty, enshrined in a formal document, not taken for granted in a haze of romantic platitudes.

The pre nuptial was a distraction from other issues playing on his mind. His solicitor had told him that marrying Gina would make no difference to

Roda's spousal maintenance claim. If Roda married again then he had a case. But not the other way around. 'Who's going to marry that fat ugly woman?' he told the solicitor.

One idea he had been contemplating was to get out of the country. He'd never belonged in Britain. As a child he'd been a Jew in a Christian school and as an adult an atheist in a Jewish family.

Moving abroad would make things difficult for Roda. Britain was broken- a country in decay socially, morally and economically and he, broken too. House prices were still rising. Everything he had worked for over these years was gone.

And there was another good reason to leave the country or even to move up to Scotland. He had a strong sense that Wayne and Nick would create problems for him. The path wasn't going to be smooth. It would be much easier to put thousands of miles between them. How was he ever going to win the kids over otherwise? They need consistency. It would be confusing for them otherwise growing up being told so many different things. Gina didn't need their maintenance. He earned enough to support them all. The kids would soon forget them. They were nobodies. They weren't fathers. They added nothing of any value to their lives.

He decided he would confront Wayne; he'd visit him one evening. He needed to put his stamp on the situation. He would keep it quiet from Gina. Gina was too weak to change any of the routines and ways of doing things. Wayne needed to face up to the fact that his relationship with Gina was never going to be restored. He didn't feel comfortable as things were.

And if he was going to take her away on more trips he needed Nick to be more obliging to have the kids. He needed to win him over, with a pint in the pub.

He wasn't looking forward though to meeting either.

15
Gina

Summer 2009

Sit down, turn the TV off. I need to talk to you about something important. The words stuck in her throat like scratchy toast.

She looked round the lounge as if searching for a manual that would explain how to break delicate news to kids. This was the most difficult speech of her life.

Her heart thudded. She felt like a naughty teenager. She strutted the room bracing herself.

'We're trying to watch Scooby Doo. What's up mother?' Saria looked up. Gina wondered why she called her mother, not mummy. She could see Nick referring to her as 'your mother.'

Gina began strutting again, her heart now in her throat. Big announcements were so cheesey, cringey, corny.

'I can't do this, I can't do this, I can't do this.'

'What are you muttering?' Saria huffed.

What happened next was crass. Immature. Farcical.

She took her hand from her pocket and flashed the ring at each in turn. Her face burned. She waited for the big response. Joss strained to see the TV. Saria gasped and gave several 'oh my Gods' in quick succession.

Carrie put her blanket down. 'Can I try it on?'

She looked at the other two.

'What do you think?' She waited for their approval. It didn't come. What an idiot I am, she thought. *Maybe I'm turning my life into a middle aged fairytale.*

Saria began to laugh; deep and mocking from the pit of her belly. On and on. The kid had morphed into the adult and Gina the blushing child. They were Eddie and Saffy in Ab' Fab.

'It won't last.' Saria mopped tears of laughter with her sleeve.

'Thanks for the vote of confidence. Am I that crap at relationships? Second thoughts don't answer that.'

'What do *you* think Joss? You like Clifford don't you? He brought you the computer. Remember? And Carrie? He's nice to you. He reads bedtime stories. He's been staying over for a while now.' Questions drummed across.

'He read me one story about a bear and then he stopped when his mobile rang.' Carrie momentarily unplugged her thumb from her mouth. But then it was back in and her gaze fixed once more to Scooby Doo.

'It was an old computer he didn't want any more.' Joss sniggered.

'We don't like him.' Saria made the big and bold announcement.

Gina's sky fell in. She didn't know what to say. She tried to push the words underwater holding them there but they were out and staining the room and the future.

She sucked in air.

'You know... one day you're all going to grow up and leave home and what about me? You want me to be all alone?' Gina's voice started to crack.

'He'll probably die before that. He's old mother.' Humiliation burned inside. Gina wanted to walk over and slap Saria across the face. Maybe she'd taken it for granted the kids would be ok with the news.

She had to win this. It was her future. She was the adult. They were the kids.

She'd also taken it for granted that Clifford would fit in around her kids, but she was about to find out how wrong she had been.

Gina was on her way to the Peak District. It was school half term.

'Look Gina don't bother taking them all the way to the Peak District if you're going to complain. They're your own flesh and blood. You're supposed to enjoy their company at half term.'

They weren't the reassuring words she had expected from Clifford. She wanted him to tell her she was a brilliant mum.

She was in the toilet crying at the service station having negotiated foreign lorries on the M1, trying to listen to news about the corrupt elections in Afganistan above three kids yelling at each other in the back of the car. A week in a cottage now seemed like a terrible mistake.

'I'm at my wit's end Clifford. Wish we'd not come up to the Peaks. Carrie's been kicking off in a retail outlet because I refused to buy a pair of Dora the explorer shoes and Saria has been moaning all day about an orthodontist appointment in several weeks time. And Joss has been asking when we're going home. Carrie's crying lasted a couple of hours. She cried herself to sleep.'

Gina's heart thudded. She wanted him to listen and become the reassuring step parent - backing her up, encouraging and offering support. His response wasn't the sweet honey she craved.

'Why the hell didn't you smack her?' He shot.

'The kid needs a big wallop and you're not prepared to do it. If you start smacking the kid she'll soon learn. Do it my way.'

Gina's heart sank. His words echoed around her head muddying her thoughts. Smacking was wrong. Every adult knew that.

His methods worked, he told her and hers didn't.

Then he revealed his real motive, catching her in her tracks.

'Unless you toughen up and get a grip they'll get the better of you and ultimately that's going to impact on me.'

The rug of independence and freedom that single motherhood had brought was suddenly yanked from under her feet. At the same time she clung to the dream that the castle of coupledom might bring.

By the time Clifford arrived in the Peaks for the weekend Gina felt utterly deflated. Despite his negative comments over the phone she imagined having his adult company for the weekend would help.

The kids had been saying they wanted a holiday abroad. Why couldn't they ever be grateful?

She was sick of reminding them she had no money and why couldn't they just enjoy it? They complained that National Trust properties were boring and for old people. And sealife centres were for school trips.

'Why did we have to come up here? What was the point?' Saria kept asking and Joss said he would rather just sit in the apartment and watch telly than trudge down a dark slippery cave to look at old rocks. And because Joss didn't want to do anything neither did Carrie.

Clifford arrived.

A quarrel broke out that evening about where to eat.

'We're starving. Can we go to the Red Lion over the road?' The kids were asking.

'It's a dive,' Clifford glanced across the road from the window. 'We'll find somewhere nice and cosy with ambience.'

They drove for miles in the dark. Found nothing. Ended up back at the Red Lion.

'I told you we should have gone here in the first place. You wouldn't listen.' Saria had a told you so look on her face.

'Oh you know everything.' Clifford sounded tired and wound up. Gina wished he would laugh at the situation.

They took a table at the back of the pub.

'Obviously you haven't learned any manners living on that council estate. Get down child.' Carrie was standing on the leather bench.

'For Christ sake learn how to use a hanky. We don't want to eat our meals watching you behave like an animal. Do you not teach these kids anything Gina?' Clifford shouted at Joss, catching him wiping slug trails with his sleeve.

'Well this is really awkward.' Saria piped up, rolling out the words as if it were a song.

Gina felt crushed from all directions. Whatever she said she wasn't going to be able to change the atmosphere that had settled around the table. All she could do was paint a white wash across the scene with polite gestures and a pleasant neutrality and hope that things would improve while at the same time quietly seethe.

Clifford

'The kids heard us having sex last week.'

'Fuck.' Clifford was speechless. He turned the engine off. It was getting late. They had just returned to Gina's flat after a mid week meal at an Indian.

'I'm sick of this pack a bag and go lifestyle, all these mid week treks to yours. I don't want those kids to see me as the man who just comes to shag their mum.' Clifford shuddered. The thought made him feel sick.

'We know it was you mummy. It was definitely your voice, Saria kept saying. Joss of course went bright red. I was so flipping embarrassed.'

' We can't carry on like this.' Clifford was in despair.

' We need to start looking for somewhere to live. We need a big house. Some space.'

'You still hardly know them and some of your attitudes are a bit Victorian. Did you read that step parenting book I recommended?'

'Fuck off Gina. I'm an old dog. Old dogs don't learn new tricks.'

'When we live together you're going to have to fit in with how things are. You can't wade in and try to change everything. Kids are sensitive. They like consistency.'

'I can only be me.'

'I wish you could be the fun person I know, not the serious you who visits on a Wednesday, delivering a weekly Reith Lecture. Quantitative easing, liquidity crisis and complicated theories about science and physics float right over their heads. Sometimes I wonder what you're trying to achieve by talking *at* them. It's pompous.'

'The weekend in the Peaks didn't go well did it? What did they say to you? Anything?'

'It's like I say you need to get to know them. Go easy on them. Be patient. Try and win Saria over first. She's the one who's not so keen on an us.'

'It's not complicated to work out the basic psychology of a child. They're all pretty selfish creatures. They'll be asking what's in this for me? Let's face it kids only care about themselves. They're only interested in what they want. And when they've worked out exactly what I can give them – a bigger better house, holidays, computers, fantastic Christmas presents, everything will slot into place. This isn't rocket science.'

'Kids need love more than they need money.'

'I need to sell them the package.'

'And how are you going to do that may I ask?'

' I have an idea. You'll like it. You told me the other day what Saria's big dream is.'

Gina

'It probably won't last. He's old and squitty, but I don't care mother. Keep him. I'm in New York and I'm living my dream,' Saria shrieked, spinning round the room on the 28th floor, like a ballerina, then crashing on to the emperor size bed.

'He's got hair sprouting out of his nose and oh my God really bad breath, but I really don't mind anymore. I don't want any more holidays in boring England' she yelped, sweeping her arms and legs, making snow angels on the white sheet. 'I can't believe it. I've been on a Virgin flight, in a yellow taxi and this massive room all to myself with amazing views over skyscrapers. It's cool. Clifford's cool,' she yelled.

Gina stood in the doorway to Saria's hotel room, instructing her not to open the mini bar and not to use her mobile. But she'd jumped from the bed, too busy looking out of the window; wasn't listening.

'It's like the whole universe is concentrated right here. I want to call everyone I know. But what would I tell them? That it is all so crazily amazing and so very different to anything I've ever seen before. I can't wait to tell Joss we're on 44th avenue. How cool is that? I feel like I'm inside a film set.'

She went into the bathroom flicked on the light, picked up the shampoo, the bath gel, read the gold writing on the side of the bottles then arranged the collection back on its tray.

'Funny size bath. Bit old and this shower curtain feels damp. I don't think I want a bath and the shower looks too scary and complicated. I may not bother washing... You can go now mother.'

Saria was fumbling for her phone, inspecting the massive TV. She began to take shots of the TV from every angle.

'It makes more sense to turn it on and take photos of each channel but God I bet there are so many channels I wouldn't know where to begin. You two can go out for the evening. I don't mind staying in. I'm not hungry. This room is way too cool to leave. I'll just plump up the pillows and watch TV all night. I don't care what I watch. I'll watch rubbish adverts because it's all so weird and amazing. God, mother why can't we move here? Just imagine what it would be like. No more charity shops or Primark or 99p stores. I could buy handbags and shoes in Macys and Bloomingdale and feel all glamorous.'

She grabbed Gina's arm.

'Pleeeeeeeeese can we move here? How difficult would that be?'

Gina tutted.

The following day Clifford took them to Macys to buy new dresses and a trip to the top of the Empire State, after a huge breakfast of pancakes and syrup in a cafe Saria thought was 'so cool' because it was called the Red Rock 99.

'The UK is finished. Soon it will look like an Eastern Bloc country. You have dreams. This is where you should be. Where we all should be. There's no future in Britain for you. University funding has suffered, scientific research has been starved of cash for years now. There's no investment in manufacturing. The country's shit. Every time I come here I realise that.' Clifford ranted on.

Gina looked at his plate of sausages, stack of pancakes, cream and syrup. It felt as if a syrup of despair was settling in her stomach, never mind his arteries. The cumulative effect on his blood sugars and the inevitable consequences not only for him but her as well seemed of no concern to him. She looked from the plate to his face, gave him a schoolmistress *you don't care* look but he didn't pick up on it.

It was scary Gina thought how easily a child could be won round with a bit of attention and money. The kid was overwhelmed. Clifford acted the perfect gentleman, complementing her on her beautiful figure as she tried on different outfits in Macys, telling her what a stunner she was. She felt proud that she had met someone who could fulfill the dreams her children had. Money was no object. A part of her felt guilt leading her down a pathway; fooling her own kid just as he was fooling her regarding his diabetes. Maybe Saria would see what they were both colluding in.

Gina's irritation mounted as the trolley got closer.

'Chocolate muffin and orange juice or Granoala bar and sparkling water?' The airhostess asked.

She'd spent the weekend watching him gorge pancakes, syrup and milkshakes. He didn't give a toss for his sugar levels or the implications of a high fat, high sugar diet.

Resentment curdled. 'How predictable. The unhealthy choice yet again.'

'What?' Clifford was still dazed from sleep. Switched on his overhead light.

'Why are you being so bloody dismissive of your health? A diabetic diet isn't hard.'

'Christ.' Clifford rubbed his eyes. 'Give me a break.'

'You're turning your diabetes into my problem. One day I shall be the one nursing you.' Bits of sunflower seed sprayed onto his tray. She thought of the trip up the Empire State and the Rockerfeller Centre. She thought of the museum at Ellis Island. She remembered the lovely meals and thought of the cost of it all. Pushing the guilt aside she ploughed on, ignoring his tired *here we go again* expression.

'What the hell are you going on about? You don't know anything about managing diabetes or about travelling.'

'It was a simple choice. Granola bar or chocolate muffin? What's so hard?'

'I shouldn't have taken you both to New York. Bad mistake again Clifford, along with all the other mistakes I've made.'

His tone was sarcastic. He folded his arms. Closed his eyes.

Gina stomped off the plane ahead. It was impossible to shake off her anger. She brushed away Saria's questions about what was wrong; gave them both the silent treatment.

As he dropped them back he called out 'don't bother calling me. We're over' but later on all was well when Clifford sent her a placatory text saying 'silly cow. Snap out of it. We're all going to die one day.'

16
Gina

Summer to Winter 2009

'I'm your escalator to foreign travel.' He yawned, bunched his jacket under his head.

He was sprawled on a park bench in Graz in Austria overlooking a river and cathedral.

'You certainly are. I'm a really lucky girl.'

Gina couldn't believe how much travelling they had done since Scotland. They'd been to India, America, Venice, Madrid, Austria, Florence and Paris.

'Being away is like living in a bubble. I can forget work and all our exes.'
'Everything is somehow placed on a shelf to deal with later.' Clifford yawned.

Cyclists, joggers and walkers were passing by along the path that skirted the river. The whole of humankind seemed to have past in a couple of hours.

Clifford fell asleep sprawled across the bench, head resting on his rolled up leather jacket. The sun was sinking in the late afternoon sun. Gina was enjoying the flecks of sunlight through the maple leaves, the skeleton of veins revealed in each leaf and the sound of the fast river tumbling over boulders below. Cyclists crunched over gravel. A man with huge boobs and a swaying cross panted by. A blind couple felt their way with white sticks. Gina couldn't remember when she had last sat for so long. Doing nothing. Just looking.

He gave a loud snuffle, woke.

'Urg.'

'Good post orgasmic sleep?' He pulled himself up, squinting.

'Yeah. This is the life Gina. Well at least the money comes out quicker from my pocket than the semen from my penis. You'll be alright with me.'

'You made a huge deposit earlier judging by the grunts in Graz.' Sex, that morning had been wonderful.

'Did any of my little swimmers reach the target?'

'What after five hours of swimming or spinning or dancing or however they travel – economy on easy jet or rocket to the moon? I should hope not. Pregnant at 44 wouldn't be much fun.'

'Hopefully they've flown by Concorde. I'd love to see your belly swell. I guess our lives are too fractured. When the kids go to Nick and Wayne I always think of it being like a train arriving at Bognor and separating into two. Cameron is right. Society is broken.'

'They're good dads on the whole. Some aren't. I could have a lot more baggage you know.'

'You might do. The future's an open book. Let's imagine Saria gets pregnant at sixteen and Joss gets killed in Afganistan.'

'Thank you. Nice of you to imagine the worst. While you were asleep I watched people walking along this path. It's a bit like watching the M1 on a particularly heavy day. Every man woman and kid is on some sort of mission. It's a microcosm of life.'

'I'm expecting Arnold Schwarzenegger to appear. Give me your boots. Your bicycle.'

'Too many Hollywood babes jogging by. I need to lose weight.'

'You're fine as you are.'

Clifford leant back, closing his eyes against the sun.

'The sun is setting in the sky Teletubbies say goodbye. And look. Now they've all shat themselves.'

'Two women in burkhas over there. Imagine putting them in a time machine, zooming back to 1940. Wasn't long ago.'

Gina thought about the Nazis.

'Arh, they're like grubby little beetles crawling the face of the earth. Black bugs staring at their Blackberries. What if they have Victoria Secret's undies underneath and menstrual blood flowing between their legs? God, Hitler would be turning in his grave, cursing and I'd be joining him.'

Gina looked down at him, still partially slumped.

'Never judge a book by its cover. You looked like a homeless guy curled up next to me on your park bench by the way. Look the begging bowl is empty.'

'Not a dime. Lousy day's work. Either that or the ex has stopped off at our M1 service station to pinch it all.'

'You going to delve into the bin then for fish and chips?' she laughed.

'Yeah, I'm a wreck I know.'

Clifford stretched, sat up.

'Was that a hornet buzzing round just then? It probably thought your high visibility panties were a giant sunflower; thought it could pollenate inside your knickers.'

'What's wrong with my knickers? I bought them especially for you. Carrie said I needed to be careful not to do a wet fart in them because it would spray through the meshing like liquid through a sieve. You should have seen the knickers I used to wear.'

'I need a shower. Water over my belly. Escape to the bathroom to fart after that huge lunch. If you feel like breaking wind Gina you have permission from the higher forces, the powers that be but I want to feel you do it on my hand.'

'God why would I do that?'

'Dunno. While I was asleep I dreamt of making love then I heard the cough of a child. It's the dirtiest thing to hear the cough of a kid when you're having an orgasm. Oh God my mind is one big sewer. A crazy generation game never stops in my head.' He sighed. 'That was a Saturn five of a shag this morning.'

'You've lost me.' Gina was confused.

'Enough force to escape gravity. I experienced the pull of six times the force of gravity. It was a magnificent orgasm. Best one in a long time. My bollocks felt like the firing shed of a steam train. My techy in the office is into trains. Stupid prick. But he's too busy re arranging and maintaining all the track set up in his garden to notice his wife's coal shed.'

'How sad for his wife.'

'After such good sex, it's like being stoned. A slight depression descends. My mind is a rolling film during sex; the court case, the judge telling me I was a bully and then the judgement.'

'Well I must say I've never had a triple orgasm before. Nobody has ever given me more than one orgasm in a row. It feels greedy but nice.' Gina was still in awe that a small cock could give that much pleasure.

'I'm an experimentalist and ready to publish a paper on this one. Better before sex, better after? I'm willing to do it a hundred times to give it statistical significance.'

'I will present you with an award.'

'Arh, I'll be claiming the Golden Tongue Award in the Hall of Fame for fanny licking. The first orgasm was the missed train out of St Pancras. The second was the slow train down to Brighton. The third was the fast from Euston to Manchester calling at Crewe on route.'

'Imagine a ring tone with the sound of your orgasm?' Gina suddenly suggested.

'And the phone starts ringing in the packed foyer of Victoria as you wait for the 5.33 to Southampton, train dividing at Haywards Heath.'

'I would go bright red.'

'Imagine toilet pan mats with faces of MPs on them. I would piss on all the ones guilty in the expenses scandal.'

'Or toilet bowls and seats with members of the Royal Family.' Gina was smiling, her eyes fixed on the tumbling river below as they bantered.

'We've reached a new level of intimacy. You and me.'

'Yep. Life's pretty good right now.'

She felt truly happy. A feeling she hadn't felt in a long time.

Clifford took Gina to visit a tyre factory in Dubai late in the year and she was given the task of filming the production process from start to finish. After entertaining the owners over a gourmet seafood evening they had a week in a hotel by the sea and plenty of sightseeing. She wasn't sure she'd like Dubai. She imagined it was Croydon in the sun, a bunch of towel heads with money. But recently Piers Morgan had done a travelogue on Dubai and it looked amazing.

Dubai was more glitzy, glamorous and space age than she'd imagined. An upmarket London Docklands: an Arab theme park, Disney for adults, a fantasy world created in the desert with oil money. At the airport security the booths looked like they were manned by Opec members.

'What's the price of oil today?' Clifford asked.

As they drove to the hotel the taxi driver, pointed out the landmarks. 'Meester Clifford where you from, England?' Questions came thudding from the front seat.

'Yes. And our Queen by the way is just a little old lady who reads the 'Mail on Sunday' but if she came here she would like your horses, your kings and your polo. And if I came to live here I wouldn't miss England. I'd save half a million in five years in tax. They should sell Dubai on the basis of no politics, no tax. If I moved here it could be Jewbai not Dubai.'

'If you moved here it would be goodbye. I can't move away.' Gina said, still mesmerized by the view from the window.

'Would you miss England's green and pleasant land? All the priests and the kiddy fiddlers? Cameron's cutbacks? I wouldn't miss the old ladies in Eastbourne and priests sticking willies up little boy's arses. Burn the cathedrals, torch the lot. Eliminate religion. Kill the Tory Bastards. Where did you say you are from?'

'Manilla, Meester Clifford. Phillipines Sir. I been five years now.'

Gina was in awe; wasn't listening to Clifford's rant. The skyline looked like a futuristic space scene, the tallest building sitting next to a crescent moon bright in a red, purple sky. She thought she'd arrived on Mars and imagined seeing people travelling in bubble cars in the sky.

'England's over mate. Well and truly over. The banks are screwed and I'm sick of paying more into the system and getting less out. I have diabetes. More and more people are being diagnosed. In the future more and more of the healthcare budget will go on fighting the illness.' He sighed.

'Oh come on Clifford you get a lot out of the system. All that diabetic medication and treatment. You can't keep saying Britain's over. We're still the 6th largest manufacturer in the world the third largest in Europe, I think. Our aerospace industry is the second largest national aerospace industry in the world and pharmaceuticals make an important contribution. Just because we don't see headline grabbing inventions constantly on our screens doesn't mean we aren't productive and inventive – hello, you have a Dyson, don't you? And what about satellite technology?'

'And this is why we're together, my feisty spirit. We love to argue and debate.'

'I can't do dull, bland pipe and slipper men that agree with me on everything and don't have opinions.'

'I hate all the PC shit out there.'

'Meester Clifford, look this way sir you see area to left? They build Universal Studios. And Meester Clifford and madam too we have new airport is being built. Going to be biggest in world.'

'You drive fast. I like speed.' Clifford smiled, clutching his red satchel. 'I'd love to drive out here'.

'Speed limit 160 kph. Police allow to go over by twenty, sir'.

'Un-bel-iev-able. I'm moving over here Gina. I've never liked the ridiculous restrictions in the UK.'

As they approached the hotel Gina spotted a row of Ferraris and up market motors parked up.

'So much wealth. In the UK you go shopping and think can I afford it? All these beautiful cars and nowhere to piss off to apart from the desert,' Clifford laughed.

'You go to desert while here? See camels?'

'That would be fantastic. Apparently you can go to a bedouin village and watch belly dancing and watch the stars twinkling in the sky. I love views. Can we have a cocktail 120 floors up in the Burj Khalif and look down on all the man made islands and waterfalls?' Gina asked.

'We're gunna do it all princess. Only the best for you my love,' Clifford leaned over and kissed her tenderly. The kiss lingered and as they withdrew their tongues she felt almost giddy with excitement and anticipation - a child in a candy store. His cotton checked shirt was undone and wisps of grey hair poked out. His red glasses were sitting on top of his head, i phone in one hand. Looking at him now he was her George Clooney.

'They say camel milk is natural Viagra Meester Clifford.'

'Oh we won't be needing that,' Clifford laughed.

'There is no fat in camel milk. You can't make cheese from it. It very salty you may like to try.'

Sitting on the hotel veranda eating breakfast, drinking lime and chilli smoothie overlooking the most perfect beach Gina felt that she had 'arrived.' Ravens sat on pillars squawking and screeching, waiting for crumbs. Stray kittens moved between table legs. She felt an important part of Clifford's life; felt valued.

The beach was the most perfect beach Gina had ever seen; soft white sand and a low winter sun. It felt like being on a beach right in the middle of London Docklands, an Armani creation, for tall metallic buildings with amazing curves and angles; some lit up in different colours which changed periodically. Some buildings dazzled and glittered in the sun, lined the shore, reaching to the sky. Helicopters flew overhead.

' It's an upmarket Benidorm Gina. Those helicopters are on an Arab suicide mission.'

'It's nothing like Benidorm. I've been there. Perfect white beach yeah but full of trash and the call of bingo and cheering of football matches everywhere you go. Ghastly place.'

'Out here there are no beggars, no impoverished elderly, no drunks, no rubbish, no drinking and singing in the streets. The sheiks just think what do these people need? Nice houses, jobs.'

A smiling, relaxed Indian topped up Clifford's coffee and they chatted about Sri Lanka and Tamil Tigers.

He took a sip of coffee. Looked at the man.

'I called you about my phone bill last week, why are you still here?'

' You're outrageous,' Gina smiled into the sun.

'What the hell are you doing Wayne? You snide creepy little man.' Gina spat into the mouthpiece of her landline.

'I'm only thinking of my daughter.' Wayne whined.

'Ringing my friends to ask them what they think of Clifford. How dare you!'

'I'm worried about you moving in with him.'

'When are you ever going to move on?' Gina was fuming. He had no right to ask her friends what they thought of Clifford. It was an invasion of privacy.

'I don't care about *you*. I'm thinking of *my* daughter. If you don't want to be with me, that's your loss. I don't want my daughter living with a man that's constantly swearing.'

'Oh piss off.' Gina slammed the phone back on its' cradle, slumped onto the settee.

It was useless. She would always be shackled to the past; to Nick and Wayne and nothing would ever change that. They would always be there in the background making life difficult. Wayne would always be jealous of any partner she had. Gina was the one and only woman he'd ever love; she knew he'd never look for another, was only interested in her.

Nick was equally difficult but in a different way.

'I can't believe we've missed the train.' Gina looked up and down the platform at the Gare Du Nord and up to the roofing. She was close to tears.

'I'm so sorry.' Clifford tried to console her by gripping her shoulders and kissing her.

'We'll just have to stay in Paris another night.' He had a glint in his eye and Gina knew what that meant.

'I can't.' She screamed. 'I've got kids.' It was only supposed to be a weekend away.

She had visions of Nick dumping Saria and Joss on the doorstep. It was the type of thing he would do.

'Nick will have to keep them longer. So will Wayne. Just call them. Explain. Mistakes happen. Stop worrying.'

With shaking hands she stabbed the mobile buttons.

'You evil bitch. You've done this deliberately. Make sure you're back at 6pm. I'm dropping the kids, the rest is your problem. And if you're not back I shall stop the maintenance.' Nick screamed down the line. Her heart thudded in her chest.

Gina was distraught. They queued at the ticket booths at the Gare Du Nord and paid several hundred to get back from their romantic weekend in Paris that evening. Nick knew how to scare her.

Gina was checking emails and noticed one from Wayne. She scanned through the contents. Fear coursed through her. When was Wayne ever going to move on and leave her in peace?

'Why should you have custody of Carrie? Why can't it be me? You're only interested in having a good time these days going on all your holidays.' His email asked.

She phoned Clifford and through tears told him what Wayne had asked. 'Stop worrying.'

'What if he fights for custody?'

'Calm down and listen to me. He'd never get custody. Check it out with any solicitor Gina. You're safe. It's ok. No court would agree to it. Trust me. That ignorant bastard needs a visit from me. They both do. I'll sort the shitheads out.'

But Gina wasn't so sure. Her family felt more vulnerable than ever.

Clifford

He finally decided to email both Wayne and Nick inviting them out separately for a friendly drink to break the ice and reassure them both that he wasn't a nonce and could be trusted to look after their kids. He'd put it off long enough.

Wayne ignored the email. This only left Clifford more determined that they would meet, even if it meant he had to confront the little shit on his doorstep.

Nick responded swiftly. Clifford drove the 50 mile journey to Nick's local and although the meeting was strained he felt he'd achieved something.

When they sat down to drink their beers in the busy 'Moon and Stars' Clifford realized in a instant why he'd wanted to meet with Nick and it had nothing at all to do with the way Nick behaved towards Gina over child access arrangements. He was shocked by the sudden realization that actually he empathized with the way Nick probably felt towards Gina. He felt the same intense anger towards Roda, the same dislike of Wayne; they had more in common than he'd first imagined. But much more than that: Clifford understood what it was like to be let down by your wife; the endless excuses regarding sex - the rejection, the anger, the frustration. The more he thought about it the more he felt he was on Nick's side, not Gina's. It was a strange thought to have. Roda and Gina had both denied their men; frigid, frumpy women who had changed with the years.

He took a sip from the froth and asked him directly 'There's something I don't understand. Why didn't you punch his lights out?'

Nick looked shocked. Picked up a beer mat and banged it on the side of the table.

'You don't think I wanted to? There were many times I considered it. But what would that have made me? And where would I be now? In prison unable to see my kids.'

'I hate the bastard. Don't understand what possessed her to go with him. She had everything she could want with you; nice house, two kids.'

'It's all gone. I'll never buy again. House prices are rising by the month.' Nick said gloomily as he began to thaw towards this man.

'She wiped out my entire future. But hey, she's a good mother.'

Nick took the large swig, wiped the froth from his mouth, gave a sigh of resignation in the same teenage way Joss would have done if he was told he couldn't have a new pair of trainers. He offered Clifford another beer and the conversation switched to computers and cars where it remained for the rest of the evening.

17
Clifford

August 2009

Clifford squeezed his car into a cramped space and looked around. The neighbourhood was pretty much as Gina had described it; a non- descript, bland 1930s London suburb, like any other around the London perimeter. George Orwell had called them horizontal slammers in 'Coming Up For Air.' Clifford imagined Wayne describing it proudly as leafy - on account of trees lining the pavement - probably believing he'd finally 'arrived.'

Number six had a broken fence, unkempt garden and soggy mattress sitting on the cracked pathway. Weeds were thriving through the cracks.

'Deluded cunt thinks one day Gina will come to her senses and get back with him. He has no idea about women.' Clifford seethed under his breath, gave the mattress a kick.

'Piece of shit, forcing me to drive all this way. No social grace to answer an email.'

As he reached for the door he wondered why Gina would have slept with a piece of garbage; procreated with a low life.

One hand was curled into a fist, the other pressed the doorbell. He noticed the peeling, yellow paintwork of the wooden front door – which looked like crusty clumps of lichen. He kept his finger firmly on the button waiting for the bastard to answer. What sort of a prat would paint their front door yellow he wondered.

He glanced at the rubbish in the front garden, scoffing at the irony that this grubby little house was probably worth much more than his beautiful Edwardian detached marital home.

Then he remembered why he'd driven all this way. He was only doing what weak willed Nick should have done ages back after he'd discovered his wife's sordid little affair. The door flung open. Wayne's hulk of a body filled the frame. Christ almighty. The man had gloopy egg trickling down his chin. Gina had swapped a high flying accountant for this piece of trash.

He took it all in. The rubbish in the hallway - yogurt lids, beer tops, coins, nails, clothing, piles of junk mail and free local newspapers were strewn across the threadbare hall carpet. It looked as if he had thrown the contents of a bin bag across the floor. It was a squat. Gina had shagged this Neanderthal, had a baby with him; conceived in a swimming pool blue Nissan Micra in a Little Chef car park. He resisted the urge to swipe him one; kept his cool.

All at once he felt pity for Nick losing his home because of the actions of this man. She must have taken leave of her senses, maybe had a nervous breakdown even. He could fully understand Nick's continued bitterness towards Gina – the angry emails, the lack of cooperation over weekend arrangements, the references to Carrie as the bastard piece of shit. He couldn't understand why Nick had meekly stood by and let it all happen.

The door slammed in Clifford's face, no words were spoken.

He flipped the letterbox and screamed. 'I'm not going anywhere Wayne. Open the door before I have to break it down.'

He waited. The door opened, more cautiously this time with the chain on. Then the chain came off. Wayne had shrunk in size. Clifford thought he was about to start crying. His lip quivered and his eyes were scrunched up as if in bright sunlight. He muttered something about calling a solicitor or the police. In that moment Clifford had an overwhelming desire to thump him not for any one particular reason. What the hell did he know about the law? He'd never been arrested. He hadn't spent a night in a cell. He'd never been divorced. He hadn't lost thousands. He was still sitting in his pile. Smug bastard deserved a thump.

'What do you want?' he asked, except that it didn't come out like that. The words rolled into one, in a south London, whiny toddler drawl.

'Whadayou wan' was how it sounded. His tone was flat, monotone; hardly someone with fight. He remembered the biggest reason why Gina had dumped him. 'I couldn't stand the way he spoke, among other things,' she'd said. She did a good impression of how he asked mothers the age of their babies.

Harrod is 'e?

What had possessed her? Why had she wrecked her marriage for this?

'We either go to the pub for a man to man chat or we stand out here in view of your neighbours and sort this out. I'm not going anywhere. You ignore my emails. You slam the phone down. I've been trying to get in touch with you for weeks. For starters we'll have the key back.'

'It's my flat as well,' he whined grabbing a tatty grey anorak from the bannister and slamming the door behind him.

'Sorry?' Clifford said loudly, looking up at the coward.

'Your flat? You own 10% of the flat. It's bugger all. The doormat if that. It doesn't give you a right to walk in, stick the kettle on and sit on Gina's furniture.'

'My daughter lives there. I've gotta have somewhere to wait.'

His voice began to grate on Clifford as they headed for the pub. He'd only met the man once before but once had been enough for him to get an impression. He scuttled along shoe laces undone, head tilted to one side constantly pulling his trousers back up to his waist because he obviously couldn't be bothered to wear a belt. All of these traits made Clifford bristle with contempt.

Wayne ran slightly behind Clifford, like a child trying to keep up. While he ran he took the key off a ring and handed it to Clifford, apologising in a servile manner.

Wayne continued to scuttle along behind talking randomly about anything that came into his head.

'That house over there, well they're having an extension. I don't see the point in extensions' and 'the old Woolworths is going to be a carpet shop. We've got loads of carpet shops. We could do with a Halfords' and 'Kennedy's Butchers is closing soon. It's been there for years. Such a lovely shop' and then when Clifford said nothing he asked 'Which way did you come?' except that it came out as 'which way d'ya come.'

Clifford stopped. He felt a sensation on his skin as if he were falling through feathers. He put his hands in his pockets and looked up at Wayne. Gina was right. The top of his head did look like the hair of a black pig.

' I thought I was having a déjà vu moment when you said that. You sound like my ex brother in law. I hated that bastard. Many times I just wanted to whack him one. I had years of visiting him. He always said which way d'ya come? in the same irritating way. Jesus, I can see why Gina left you. Do you really care which way I came? I came up the A23, which way do you think I came? You saw my car parked outside. Look, this is all trivia Wayne. I don't give a damn about Woolworths pick n mix or sausages or any other damn shop for the matter. I didn't drive all this way to discuss your shopping parade.'

'Where did he live?' Wayne asked, innocently.

'What?' Clifford snarled.

'Your ex brother in law?'

'Fuck off. Which way is this pub?'

They carried on walking at a faster pace this time.

'The pub is going to be refurbished soon.' Wayne commented as they pushed through the swing doors.

'Do you ever shut up talking such fucking drivel?' Clifford asked as he passed Wayne a pint then took a bar stall.

'If you carry on insulting me I'll just go back home.'

'We've got things to sort out.' Clifford placed his beer on a mat. The froth sloshed over the rim.

'How do you mean? You're not making threats I hope? All I want is for my daughter to be safe. I don't care about Gina. It's her loss she didn't stay with me.'

'And she is perfectly safe. What do you take me for? I'm not a nonce.' Clifford took a sip, wiped his sweaty brow with the back of his hand.

'I hope you don't swear in front of my daughter.'

'Look I've raised my own kid pretty successfully. He's 23 now and at Vet School. If you'd given me a chance rather than snidely asking about me behind my back to Gina's friends and worse than that telling your daughter she can come and live with you if she doesn't like me...you would see that I'm a decent human being.'

Wayne scrunched his eyes again. His smile was fake.

'I'm warning you Wayne, that's all. Just back off and let us live our lives. We're getting married next year. Get used to the idea. Gina's not getting back with you. Ever.'

'And what about my daughter? Does she have a say?'

His voice sounded feminine, high pitched. He raised his eyebrows, looked triumphant.

'Maybe she would prefer to live with me. Did she have a say when you thrashed her the other week?'

Clifford froze. The words hung in the air like a dirty cobweb.

'Oh listen to yourself. I tapped her on the hand. What would you do if she were about to run into the road? Let her? Do you think Gina would still be with me if I was a child beater? Are you that stupid? Do you think I go around hitting kids all day? And no, she doesn't have a say. She's 6 years old and Gina is her mother. So you can stop planting ideas in Carrie's head.'

Clifford noticed how hard Wayne found it to establish eye contact. Maybe he felt intimidated. Clifford liked the thought, was determined to meet his raven eyes.

'Will you look at me when I'm speaking?' Clifford demanded. Wayne briefly looked up then quickly glanced away, a child in front of a headmaster with the threat of the cane looming for some awful misdemeanor and muttered something about the number of colourful drinks on display behind the bar.

'I haven't done nothing.'

'Anything. Not nothing. Learn to speak properly.'

Clifford shook his head, swore under his breath. This guy was seriously thick.

'All I'm going to say to you is this. I'll say it once and I expect you never to forget it.' Clifford took a deep breath, tried to remain calm.

'If you cause any trouble and I mean telling Carrie that if she doesn't like me she can come and live up here in your shit hole or talking to Gina's friends behind her back about me I shall make sure we put a distance of 600 miles between you and us. Have I made that quite clear? My business can go anywhere. We can even move to America. I think Gina would be up for that.'

Clifford's voice rose, an air of triumph entering his tone. He sat up on his stall as if attempting to match Wayne's height.

'We certainly don't need your pathetic 300 a month in maintenance. I can make that sort of money in an hour.'

'I pay more than the CSA guidelines. I don't want my kid to go without.'

'Well she won't have a great lifestyle on that shit money if that's what you're thinking.'

'Are you rich or something?' Wayne asked in a childish way, his voice squeaky.

'Wayne, look, I was shredded by my ex. You have absolutely no idea about real life and the damage that divorce does financially not to mention in every other way too. You're living in Noddy Land. You didn't have the guts to commit to Gina. When you could have sold that shit hole you call home you chose not to, even when she was carrying your baby. You owed her big time after wrecking their marriage. I'm working my bollocks off to rebuild my life and let's not forget we're living through the worst recession in living memory.'

'Well you are entitled to half the house.' Wayne replied weakly. 'Gina got half their house.'

'Wayne. You don't get it do you?' Clifford leaned in towards him, paused. He had an overwhelming desire to punch his lights out. The ignorance of the man was astounding.

'Do you know anything about debts the size of mountains and legal fees that run into thousands? You've not been married and by all accounts you never will. You whinge about the pathetic amount you loaned Gina to help her buy that dreadful little flat to put a roof over *your* kids' head. You should have done the decent thing and given the money to her. It's only 10% of the value of the flat after all. She gave you a child. Christ almighty. It's peanuts.'

'It's not peanuts to me. Talking of peanuts would you like a pack?'

Clifford couldn't believe it. Why did this man never rise to the bait? He was like a cowardly boxer hunched in the corner of the fighting ring, nursing a nosebleed. Did he have no backbone? He had skin the thickness of a Rhino - was dismissive, evasive, weak, and non confrontational on every front.

Clifford felt better for having driven to Wayne's, in the same way he felt better after bollocking one of the staff in his office. Had he achieved what he'd set out to achieve? He wasn't sure but he had Gina's key and a good feeling he'd put him in his place and established a few ground rules. There was a semblance of control back in the relationship. This man wouldn't be messing with him.

Gina didn't have the guts to confront him over the key and the things he'd said to her friends. He didn't understand why she hadn't; why she was so timid.

Was the pathway now clear to move ahead with Gina? Or were there more problems ahead?

18
Gina

June 2010

Gina remembered vividly the first Summer in her flat – the moment it felt like home. She had just hung Carrie's paintings on the washing line. Paint dripped onto the rich emerald lawn, casting long shadows, the paper curling and flapping in the gentle breeze. She was child minding. The girls were making puddings and biscuits in the sand pit. The boys were dressed for battle, rushing at each other with swords. Cradling a cup of tea, she studied the exterior - the bricks, the double glazed windows, the Laura Ashley curtaining and thought to herself - this is all mine. No one can take it away. And it felt good. And despite being a lifelong Tory voter she had Tony Blair to thank.

From that moment on she looked forward to coming home to the flat she'd made their home. She even started to like the estate. The faces of the locals: drunks sitting on the wall outside the pub, the mentally ill who frequented the cafe, the overweight mothers lugging their Iceland shopping off the bus, the kids messing around on the waste land opposite. It was familiar and comforting.

But it was now the Summer of 2010. Politicians were talking about the fair society; David Cameron the new prime minister was working out how to fix 'Broken Britain' and its massive debt problem. As she turned the corner into her road she could see the blob of red that was the Sold board pinned to the fence in her front garden. The past weeks had been a whirlwind. The flat had been on the market a week before she'd received an offer of the full asking price.

They hadn't expected it to sell so quickly. She was a tad offended at Clifford's warning 'I'm not expecting a quick sale or relying on your money. It's a shabby flat on a shitty estate. It may not sell. Be great as a deposit for a new place but I'm not banking on it. I'll be able to raise the lot on my own without your input if I have to.' To his surprise and her secret swollen pride the full asking price was offered within days.

'Are you lot sure about all this? You've not said much about Clifford.'

Gina had asked the kids several times, checking, re checking how they felt. It disturbed her that they didn't seem to have strong opinions. She almost expected them to violently disapprove and fight to protect the status quo.

'Don't back out now mother. We want a big house. Somewhere that isn't on a council estate.' Saria dictated.

'But what about living with Clifford? You haven't said anything about moving in with him?'

Saria didn't seem bothered. It was as if Gina had asked if she wanted pizza for tea.

'He's alright, I suppose. As long as he takes me to New York again or gets me an i phone, I don't really care.'

'For God sake. That's not what it's all about. He's not an open wallet.'

'Can we go to Disney next time we go to America? That would be so cool. Pleeeeeese.' Saria begged, as if the word please could turn a demand into reality.

Joss just shrugged. Was it possible, Gina wondered for a kid not to have any opinion at all? But in her heart she knew he had opinions but somewhere over time they'd been lost. She noticed how withdrawn and insular he'd become, little by little since the divorce and she didn't know quite what to do about it. She didn't want to have to address problems that might or might not exist.

Clifford

They found a house and were now waiting for mortgage approval.

'That'll be a piece of piss.' Clifford was confident. He was a valued client; had been with the bank for years and had taken out several large business loans.

It would be a quick wave in front of an underwriter and hey presto they were well on their way to a new and better future.

He was sick of living like a travelling circus, shunting his stuff from rental to shitty rental. He was looking forward to coming home from work parking his car on the drive, looking up and saying I own this place.

But one thing concerned him. What if the relationship broke down? There were no guarantees and if it did he stood to lose money. Two grand a month would be knocked off the mortgage each month and the equity would start to accumulate. And in a few years time, if he sold his business, maybe in the region of £2million if he was lucky he needed to secure that – preferably with a water tight agreement that no judge was going to dispute. He needed to make sure she couldn't get her hands on it if they split. He wasn't going to be fleeced twice. If there was the slightest risk that this could happen again he wanted to back out. He was certain of that.

Gina

Gina wasn't hungry. She felt overwhelmed. She picked at the pizza like a small bird. Clifford hacked away at his pizza - a butcher with a cleaver; the intensity of conversation in his cramped solicitor's north London office had given him a raging appetite and thirst for a large gin and tonic. This was their next visit to the solicitors to discuss a pre nuptial.

'This whole pre nuptial stuff doesn't seem clear. So much legal jargon. They aren't part of the law yet so it's probably a waste of time. I don't know what to think Cliff. What will it say?'

'You're not good with detail. From your point of view any money you inherit is yours. I can't touch it if we divorce. Same with me. When I inherit it's mine. You can't try and claim any of it for yourself, or the assets from my business.' Clifford called the waitress over, asked for another gin. It niggled Gina that drinking and driving never worried him. He seemed to take driving for granted.

'But what about the equity in the house we're buying? The equity I'm putting in stays mine obviously, but the equity we will be building up each month, each year, together. Whose is that?'

' We'll both get a proportionate rise in the value of the property according to what we both put in.'

'If I have to go through the whole buying process again I'll lose some equity and end up worse off.'

'I'm happy to pay your costs but bottom line I'm not their father. I'm not supporting them if we divorce. They're not my responsibility.'

'Nobody asked you to.' There was a strained silence. Gina pushed the crusts around the plate. Clifford poured some fizzy water. Her hands were shaking and she thought she might start crying.

'You can see things from my point of you.' His voice was stern.

'Sounds like you're starting to see my kids as a burden – baggage we've picked up by accident at Terminal Three. This whole pre nuptial thing isn't very romantic. I never had all of this with Nick. It's like you don't trust me. History isn't going to repeat itself. You have to get the past out of your head.'

'You don't know what you'll be like. You've got three kids to support. People will do anything for their kids, fighting till they've won.'

'I'm losing a lot getting together with you. I hope you appreciate that. I'll be losing a lot in tax credits.'

'Yeah well I'm going to be picking up the tab, supporting your kids. University is the biggest expense. You've conveniently forgotten that.' Clifford dabbed his mouth with a napkin.

'We're a team aren't we? Helping each other. That's how Nick and I looked at it. I've never asked you to help through university. I wouldn't dream of it. They'll have to support themselves and take out loans. If I was on my own they wouldn't have help.'

Gina had been curling the napkin. Now she was tying it into a knot of fury.

Clifford stepped into his car, plumb into a headbutt of heat. He was expecting mortgage approval any day.

He gunned along the lanes to the office, switched on radio four.

'Yeah, yeah, yeah. We have a Tory Government.' He shouted obscenities about Cameron and Osbourne, screaming to the wind.

If he hadn't switched off the radio he might have missed the new ringtone on his i phone that he was still getting used to. He pulled over. A withheld call. It was a non entity from the bank, at the end of a phone line wearing polished shoes. He'd never met the jumped up little prick, in all probability fresh off some overrated Business Studies course, at a polytechnic reassembled, repackaged, like Lego pieces, to pass off as a university, to third rate students with Photography and Sociology A levels.

This was the call he'd been waiting for - their future held in the balance. Now that Gina had sold her flat they were - to coin that ghastly expression which estate agents were fond of *all systems go, hot to trot.* He hadn't expected her flat to go so quickly. It was an area where cars sat on bricks, mattresses rotted in gardens and supermarket trolleys, beer cans, petrol cans, old tyres languished on drivesways and alcoholics shouted obscenities outside the pub each night. How Gina could bare to put her children through it he didn't know.

They had frantically dashed round one Saturday, agreed on a nearby town, a compromise area; made an offer on a modern detached five -bed on a quiet estate. It wasn't quite how he had imagined living in his mid fifties but the house at 450k was a good price. On his yearly earnings of £100k and Gina's equity the mortgage was very manageable. He'd easily pay it back within a few years and with any luck his mother would snuff it and leave him a packet for he was, after all an only child. And with that extra wad they could move on.

THE BANK. Everything hinged on those little non entities. And it all went back to Bin Laden - that hairy man hiding in a cave somewhere. He had a lot to answer to. Alan Greenspan, fearing more attacks thought America would stop spending and investing; created the QE concept; a massive paper injection of money into the system; interest rates were driven down to encourage spending and restore faith which had led to a nesting instinct; Americans suddenly placing higher value on their homes. Low interest rates had served as the catalyst to accelerate the housing market. Banks were lending freely to anyone; the country had gone on a debt binge. And now he - Clifford needed a mortgage at just the wrong moment in time. He feared the worst.

He could remember very clearly the start of the financial crisis and the broken property dream. He was in Florida on business in 2007 the year he split from the ex. He knew things were going to be pretty bad. He was watching TV and thought it was a real cash machine stopping moment. The papers were full of the housing downturn. The whole lending system seemed so wrong, so unsustainable. Everything was falling apart. Things were really getting bad in 2006/2007. The reality of the housing market was that people who shouldn't have been lent to were defaulting. It was obvious it was going to happen in the UK. After all America sneezes Europe catches the cold, Clifford told colleagues. Duff mortgages had been sold in the UK too. His marriage break up hadn't come at a more worse time because on top of the mortgage debt his wife had caused it wasn't going to sell for anywhere near what it was worth. And it hadn't, as predicted.

'Dan. I hope you've got some news for me. Application's taking way too long.'

'It's not good I'm afraid. The underwriters have rejected your application.'

'What?'

'You didn't pass the credit score. There's an old debt from one credit card company for £3000 which is still outstanding. It goes back five years apparently.'

'You are joking, I hope. Well I'll fix it then. I'll pay it off today. It's not a problem.'

'That won't make any difference. They've rejected the application.'

'It's £3000. Peanuts. A week's earnings. I'm not putting up with this kind of shit from you lot. You know how long I've been banking with you for? Do you want me to take my business elsewhere? The million a year turnover which is set to increase over the next few years but no thanks to you lot.'

'I'm very sorry this is not what you wanted to hear but it's out of my hands.'

Clifford drove on, unaware he was taking the wrong turns in a daze. This wasn't on his radar. Year on year his earnings had risen steadily. This was a kick in the teeth of the highest order just when the injuries from the divorce were starting to heal. He felt about as useless and inadequate as the cock in his pants. He'd thought his nightmare was over. The dream he'd carved of once more owning a home was obliterated in one swift call from a non entity in the banking world - a boy in short trousers, a complete nobody.

'So what does everyone think to Pot Hole Cottage? Or would you prefer to rent Crumbling Clematis Cottage? Both are awful. Two wrecks to chose from. Two grand a month down the drain to line some bastard landlord's pocket. And if we don't chose either there aren't any more rentals to look at because they're being snapped up in this crazy rental market.'

'That's because it's so hard to get a mortgage these days.' Gina stated the obvious.

'Don't remind me about those wanker bankers.'

The morning's rental viewings had been disheartening. They all sat in the Subway eating sandwiches. He would give it six months but no longer, then he'd make a fresh mortgage application. What a waste of time and money the next 6 months was going to be. £12k down the drain that could have been used as a house deposit.

The kids were discussing crazy ideas as they ate. Hide and seek at Clematis Cottage and creating a spooky film set in the dilapidated barns of its' overgrown garden. Sleepovers at Pot Hole Cottage watching the planes rise and land and late night snacks at the food court in Gatwick. Their minds were running away into a fantasy existence.

'You lot aren't paying for it all. It's an adventure for you.'

'Let them have fun Cliff.' Gina snapped, tossing her sandwich aside.

Gina

'The best properties are snapped up so quickly. It's a heated market.' Gina liked this latest rental. She stood in the hallway and knew it was the one.

Christingle Cottage was perfect. It had the edge on everything they'd seen. It was a 5 minute walk from the school and close to the station. Gina had never wanted to switch the kid's schools even though the kids liked the idea. Clifford was quite capable of driving the 40 minutes to his office. It was no big deal. Ok he wanted to be closer but getting together had to involve compromise. She had kids. They came first. Any man entering her life had to recognise and acknowledge that.

He was impressed. The garden backed onto open fields reminding him of his marital home and the happy memories he carried of lying in long grass staring at the sky. He liked the little wood burner in the sitting room, the open fireplace in the kitchen and the oak flooring. He could see his furniture in each room. It was a spacious house and even had a study at the front that he could turn into an office from home.

'It will be lovely in the winter, warm and cosy with the open fire.' He said.

When the kids saw it they couldn't contain their excitement, playing hide and seek within minutes and planning who was going to sleep where and what new furniture they needed. Gina knew it was the right decision. Clifford was happy, she was happy and more importantly the kids were happy. She felt a sense of calm. Maybe it had all been worth it after all.

Life was now on the up. But would a bigger home be enough to make them happy?

19
Gina

August 2010

'You want to be an architect?'

Ben smiled at Saria over the table. Gina watched the two of them chatting, sizing each other up. Saria was twiddling with the chopsticks, obviously nervous. She wondered if Ben found her attractive. After all she was a beautiful girl; long mousey hair and big brown eyes that any man would fall for. She was glad they were chatting so well. It couldn't be easy for either of them meeting for the first time. Yet the atmosphere around the table was so tense that Gina was aware of every sniff, every cough, every clink of glasses in the Chinese restaurant - on edge in expectation that something would go wrong.

Clifford said very little to Joss and Carrie. He looked over tutted, shook his head in disapproval as they folded and unfolded a napkin between them trying out different shapes - uninterested in getting to know their future step brother.

'There's been a lot of programmes lately about the construction of famous buildings. And going to New York with my mum and your dad really inspired me. New York is amazing.'

' I'm going to make a wonderful step father aren't I Ben? The kid loved New York.' Clifford laughed.

The waitress took the order.

'We'll have Dim Sum and your finest chicken soup. Oh and seaweed and duck and pancakes. No expense spared this evening. This is the start of our future together. Are we really moving in together in two weeks Gina? It's all happened so quick.'

'Dad likes to flash his money Saria. You'll soon learn that.'

Saria giggled and Clifford was quick to reply.

'I needed plenty of it bringing you up and this course is dragging on a bit. Hopefully you'll pass the next set of vet exams.'

A swift change came over Ben. It was as if a key had been inserted into his back and wound up. He had been asking Saria questions, had listened to her career ideas. He had shown a brief interest in Joss and Carrie. But now his conversation became erratic. His voice speeded up, the volume cranked up. He became a runaway train that wasn't going to stop for any passengers.

'I had a phone call from my old headmaster and he wanted to have dinner with me...' Ben rambled on. Joss and Carrie showed no interest. They were talking and laughing to each other and pointing to a fat man puffing his way up the road against the strong sea gale.

Clifford and Saria didn't interrupt.

'Last week I went out for a drink in Central London and I got chatting with a guy who runs one of the most prestigious veterinary practices in the country and he offered me a job when I graduate. He was really impressed by everything I said.'

There was strain behind Clifford's smile Gina noticed; as if a hundred balls were being thrown at him at once. His face said *I'm not sure I believe all this codswallop*. Gina was surprised he didn't interrupt, allowing Ben to ramble on and dominate the stage, only interested in himself.

On the way home Gina asked Clifford what he was thinking and whether he found Ben's behaviour strange. Gina had only met him a couple of times before. At first she'd liked Ben but now she found him arrogant and self centred. He gave the impression he was better than everyone else. He had treated Joss and Carrie as if they were wallpaper covering. Had made little attempt to talk to them. Gina had found this hurtful but excused him because he was 23 and too young to be interested in younger kids, yet too old as well.

'He did seem a bit odd.'

'Odd? That's an understatement. He didn't stop talking all evening. I've never heard someone speak so fast. Is he always like that?'

'Maybe he hasn't been sleeping very well or he's working too hard.' He shrugged.

He sighed. 'I don't know Gina. I've got enough work issues of my own at the moment.'

'Well... that will never change.'

Clifford

'This place is a bit greasy.' Clifford put his fork down. Eating at the American diner was like being on a business trip in the States. He wiped his mouth.

'We could have stayed in that Vietnamese restaurant.'

'Nah. I didn't fancy eating Agent Orange soup.'

'Fuck off dad. That's a sick joke.'

'I think I'll be delivering a napalm bomb in the toilet here after this nasty burger.'

They were eating in an American restaurant along Brighton's seafront. Bill Haley was rocking around the clock. A waitress in a crisp white pinny tapped her feet as she leant against the counter waiting for a strawberry shake to be handed to her.

'You were a bit weird last week mate.' Clifford said.

'Is that what her kids said?'

' They never have opinions.'

'They were ok.' Ben smiled. 'Carrie was a cutie. I talked to Joss about computer games. And Saria's a sweet girl. Bright.'

'But then you took over. You were completely manic. What's all this bollocks about a top vet offering you a job?'

'I think he did. I can't remember.'

Ben seemed to have forgotten everything he had talked about in the Chinese restaurant. Clifford found that strange.

Ben carved into his burger. 'I'm going on a trip to Israel with mum.'

Clifford stopped cutting, dropped his knife. This was some confession.

'You didn't tell me that. I'm the last to know everything. And how is your bitch of a mother financing this trip? And you? The maintenance I provide is obviously way too much.'

'Dad. Stop referring to her as the bitch. She's my mother. How do you think that makes me feel? I don't think it's any of your business how mum is paying for the trip.'

Each word stabbed across the table. The beat of the music thudded in his ears.

'Now that's where you're completely wrong.'

Clifford felt a hot coal of anger burn in his chest. 'That bitch....'

'She's your ex wife and my mother.' Ben jabbed back.

'I repeat...*that* bitch, you call your mother stole thousands from me. Your memory is pretty crap these days Ben. She should pay her debts first. How do you think she's paying? Out of my hard earned money.' His voice was rising but he maintained a tone that gave him control.

'I don't care Dad. The divorce is over. It's time you moved on.'

'You may sneer, brush it all aside. It's your future she's ruined. Are you too stupid to see that? No son of mine goes on holiday with a woman who bled his father dry. You should disown her. It's the only way she will see sense and drop the spousal maintenance claim.'

'Your divorce settlement has nothing to do with me. If you've been told by the courts to pay up, that's what you should do. They will freeze your bank account if you don't.' Ben picked his burger up.

This kind of non committal attitude stirred something deep inside. Clifford's problems were his problems too.

'Now that's where you're acting like a complete selfish cunt.' Heads were turning. He could no longer hear the music. Fries tilted on forks, glasses poised to lips, everybody freeze framed like when a video in a machine gets stuck.

'Dad, stop being irrational. She's allowed a holiday.'

It was Clifford's turn to boot where it hurt.

'You have no regard for my feelings or what I went through' he spat. 'You expect to come down here, sit around watching sport on my Sky package, let me take you out for meals. You know what? It's no wonder you keep failing your exams if you can't even reach the correct conclusion about your mother.'

Ben scraped his chair back. A waitress glanced across ready to take the plate. Clifford saw Ben's wounded look but was unmoved.

'I'm not going to let you treat me like this. My friends keep telling me I deserve better. When you've got something civil to say call me.'

Ben was curt, but calm. He scraped the chair forward. A knife clattered to the floor.

'The way you're going Dad you'll have another heart attack.'

'You don't just get up and walk out of a restaurant.'

If this prick of a son couldn't be transparent about money it was high time to cut the chord. Why should he carry on supporting his son through veterinary college? Anger bubbled and boiled and rose to the surface. Clifford reached for his glass. Without giving time to think how ridiculous he was he flicked the dregs of the sickly chocolate shake at his son's face. It felt good.

Clifford was driving to Heathrow when he took the call a week after the meal in the American diner.

A pleasant summer breeze thrashed his shirt like a sail at sea, wind smacking from all directions. He loved his soft top. It was a good sturdy car, safe but could handle speed.

His phone was vibrating in his shirt pocket. He didn't want to stop, lose time. The check-in queues were always horrendous, particularly when flying to the States. He headed for the long stay car park circuiting round, finally edging into a space zapping the car into neutral.

It was Ben. He wasn't making much sense. Clifford couldn't decipher what he was really saying and the thunder of a plane taking off didn't help. The minute Clifford asked any questions or tried to clarify Ben would talk over him. Something wasn't right.

'Slow down Ben for God's sake. I can't understand what you're saying mate. Deep breathes. Start again. You've locked yourself out of my house? I thought you were clearing your stuff. You'll need to before I move in with Gina.'

'Yeah. The gardener next door tried to help me get back in.' Ben rambled on. Clifford was confused. The houses along Wrencrest Court didn't have gardens. They all had concreted driveways and bricked over courtyard gardens. Nobody needed a gardener.

'I'm heading back to London now - got to get back. I don't feel safe in your house.' Ben said.

'Safe? What? You have your car keys then?'

'Yes, obviously.'

'Not *obviously* Ben. I thought they'd be on the same key fob as my house keys, that's all.'

'I stopped at Mc Donalds in Crawley but I didn't feel safe in there so I continued driving and stopped at a massive Halfords on the Purley Way. Dad, do you know what I saw in there?'

'Cut to the chase Ben. I'm about to catch a plane. What's this all about? You're rambling on about nothing.'

'I saw the bike you and mum bought me for my fifth birthday. So I bought it. It's beautiful, all shiny and metallic. Do you remember teaching me to ride it? I wobbled down the hill and you and mum were frantic I was going to crash into the road. It's in the back of my Golf dad.' And then as swift as a storm cloud his tone changed. 'But what the hell? What would you understand?'

'xcuse me? Clifford felt the slap of sarcasm. Wondered what would come next.

'You're a cunt dad.'

'What?' Clifford snapped. There was a pause while he tried to digest this latest gristle and lift his case from the car. The conversation was slipping into a dark and dangerous place he didn't want to go.

'Well fuck you,' he spat and ended the call.

He dragged his bags to the terminal, thoughts racing. Was Ben losing the plot he wondered? He felt so detached from his son. He couldn't work him out any longer. His moods had become unpredictable - sometimes sulky and evasive, sometimes manic.

Clifford moved through the tedium of security and slumped into a chair at the gate to await the boarding announcement. He had twenty minutes to check emails and watch the slaggy cabin crew from dreadful northern towns tripping along the conveyor belt in heels so thin they might snap off at any moment ready to be rammed up their pert arses. His eyes shot away. He couldn't bear to watch the male cabin crew following on, their hands and arms flapping all over the place as they chatted and laughed in their shrill voices. They were pretty boys looking forward to a short stop over in Alicante or Malaga or some other God awful place with the prospect of picking up a tan and a Gary or a Robbie on the beach for a quick shafting before the return flight back to the UK.

His phone was vibrating again but it was Gina this time. He filled her in on the brief call with Ben but she was already up to speed on what was happening.

'Jesus. I'm on my way to San Remo and the little shit calls to tell me he's locked himself out of the house. What am I supposed to do Gina?'

'Can I do anything? Maybe I should drop over there, check your house is locked up. If he's acting all weird how do we know he hasn't just left the front door wide open. I don't think you can trust him. There's something not right.'

'The house will be fine. I'm not worried about that.'

'He was saying he dropped into McDonalds in Crawley and didn't feel safe. *Safe*. Strange word to use. Don't you think Cliff?'

'What else did he say?'

'He said he then drove to Brixton and parked up near the Mc Donalds and he felt safe there.'

'Safe in Brixton? I *don't* think so.'

'No. Just what I thought. Of all the places that could be called *safe*.'

'He said the staff in Mc Donalds gave him water and he knew he could trust the water. That it wouldn't be poisoned. And then he went to the toilets and knew they would be safe too and the burger he ate was safe. Everything was either safe or unsafe.'

'What happened after that?'

'I don't know. I guess he must be back at his flat in London.'

'What can I do? He's an adult. He's out of my control.'

On the plane he closed his eyes and dreamt of Ben, the young boy. He was running along the beach. Then they were digging an enormous and elaborate sandcastle. He saw images of toddler Ben sitting on bear's bench at the bottom of the garden. But each image was slowly erased by the dark shadow of his ex spilling over the picture, turning it to grey mush. She seemed to drown out the happiness, the laughter. He wished he could airbrush her out of their past, his existence. She was a poison seeping through everything that had gone wrong.

Clifford fought the waking. Each problem hit like missiles. The financial wreckage of his marriage, the failed mortgage application, his health and now Ben. Ben had been the only reason he'd kept going. He wanted to see his son finish veterinary training and qualify. He'd chosen a stressful career. Clifford blamed himself. He remembered all the games they used to play; bandaging up teddy bears, putting stethoscopes to a fluffy toy dog called Barker; whisking toy cats, dogs, birds to the vets – the shed in the corner of the garden. He used to tell Ben that one day he would be a vet if he worked hard enough.

If it hadn't been for Ben he would have left the marriage years ago. But he hadn't wanted to be the absent dad with Sunday access joining the other single dads in the park or searching for happiness in a Mc Donalds meal. He'd tried to make things work with his wife. But in truth he should never have married her. On their wedding day he'd woken with a feeling of dread. How ironic it now seemed. Losing a grand for an aborted wedding was nothing compared to the thousands she had swallowed over the years.

Ben was the marital sticking plaster, for a time. Clifford had adored the kid. They had built a model railway in the garden when he was five spending hours playing with it. And when he was seven they started doing Air Fix kits in the shed. Ben was bright, he soaked it up like a sponge. He was a great all rounder, interested in lots of different things.

His ex couldn't have coped alone as a single parent. When she'd suggested Ben go to private school he'd thought it was one of her better ideas. Most of the state schools in Brighton were mediocre, massive comprehensives that churned people out like toilet rolls on a factory conveyor. He wanted him to have the best chances. But the lad hadn't found veterinary training easy. It was a long course. Ben had failed the second year and had to repeat it. It was a big knock. Clifford had been understanding but it was looking likely that he'd fail the next year and be put back another year. Clifford was beginning to feel a level of despair. He'd forked out enough money. He was paying Ben £10k a year. His pocket was a bottomless pit. It was all getting a bit beyond the call of duty. The kid wasn't young anymore. He was 23 for heaven's sake. Time he stood on his own two feet and supported himself. I'm an old engine he'd told Ben the last time he flunked his exams. I can't support you for much longer.

Clifford was checking his bloods in the hotel room when Gina called.

'I know you didn't want me to check on your place but I'm glad I did.' She told him assertively.

'I appreciate your help but I told you not to. It was unnecessary.'

'I wouldn't say it was *unnecessary*. Not after what I found.'

'Oh?'

'He's built some kind of shrine to his childhood. It spooked me out Clifford. It was as if someone had died. As if *he* had died.'

'My worst fear.'

'What?'

'Him. Killing himself. I can see it happening. I don't know why. It's just a feeling I have.' Clifford sat back on the bed, put a pillow behind his head, unrolling his sleeve with his phone pressed between ear and shoulder.

'I'm glad I saw it. At least you'll be prepared when you get back.'

'And will I be prepared if he tops himself? What then?' Clifford was starting to shout.

'Don't shoot the messenger. He'd set up two tables on your landing. It was a big display of stuff, all neatly arranged, with a table cloth underneath. What 23 year old boy would use a table cloth? I don't know where it had all come from.'

'He's probably been rummaging through boxes. I hadn't unpacked everything.'

'There's a picture of him as a baby and you both on your wedding day. And a wooden ship. I can't remember everything. It's like that memory game kids play at parties and you get blindfolded.'

'That wooden ship has been packed away for years. We made it together in my old shed. We had such fun building that. I'm surprised he remembered.'

'His GCSE certificates are on display as well as his cycling proficiency and scout badges and a plastic soldier. There's so much stuff. It's a display of his past. Your pasts. All of you. He's even laid a table for her. All her exam certificates. Strange.'

'Did you say a plastic soldier? It was a freebie from a Rice Crispie or Cornflakes box. I remember the cute squeal he made when he dug into the packet and pulled it out. Roda and I looked at each other and melted. I took her paws and his little paw. We were three bears together, united against the world.

I told her I loved her. And in that fleeting moment maybe I did and maybe Ben saw the love between his parents. I think that was the last time we said those words.'

The air had that musty cloying smell all rentals had. Clifford began tearing open boxes resigned to his transient existence - his belongings a travelling circus. He was sicking of moving house.

With a sleeve he dusted a framed picture of Ben eating Spaghetti Bolognese splattered all over his smiling face, like bad acne. He tried to recapture the memory of Ben laughing and waving a plastic spoon, a cheeky glint in his eyes, but all he could see was the young man he'd metamorphosed into – moody and arrogant. Flecks of sunlight spilt onto his wispy blonde locks, filling the scene with radiance and earthy heaven. Was the past just an illusion?

There was a level of disassociation that made him wonder whether this faintly familiar stranger was really his own flesh and blood. In the first few weeks of Ben's life he had also felt like this - but those were feelings of joy and love; touching and looking at perfection, a tiny miracle, wondering 'is this little thing really mine?' He loved to feel the warmth of the small bundle lying on his chest. But now he looked at his son and felt an intense disliking. It was so hard to like someone that didn't see things the way you did or support your cause or understand the troubles you'd been through.

This wasn't the boy he used to laugh and joke with, or take to the beach to collect shells. Days of bliss now jagged shards of memory. He remembered with such clarity how he'd felt back in 1990 when Ben was just two, when he'd longed for the end of his working day so he could scoop the toddler into his arms and plant furious kisses around his neck. Then he'd chase him on all fours around the room, hiding behind the settee, jumping out, falling apart on the carpet laughing, teasing and tickling. They created the idea of the 'shamuzel' a fictitious animal who loved kissing and licking ears and would end up in a heap on the floor, both with soggy ears.

He remembered the times he'd cuddled Ben in the late Summer sun, stroking his mop of blonde curls. 'This will always be our special bench and our very own Bear Corner.' He'd smile down at Ben, whose bare legs dangled over the struts of the bench, pausing between pages of their favourite story about a bear who was scared of the dark. They loved reading that book. 'I can't sleep. This cave is so dark.' Clifford remembered looking up from the book and over towards the meadow undulating away to the cliffs and the sea in the distance. He never wanted his son to be scared of a single thing.

But now Ben was just the young man he took out for a meal now and again. He was part of a past Ben didn't understand or remember very well.

The relationship was sliding downhill - but just as he hadn't foreseen the development of dementia in his mother, he wasn't stopping to think about how strange Ben's behaviour was becoming.

Gina

Gina stood in the doorway with mugs of tea watching Clifford and Joss chatting to each other, reading the Ikea instructions for the new desk they had bought the day before and were now building, making mistakes with different pieces and laughing. It was late August. They had been living together in the cottage for a week.

In that moment she knew moving in with Clifford had been the right thing. Joss needed a male role model in his life. Fortnightly visits to his dad weren't enough. Something had been missing.

Clifford looked up. Took the mug.

'Ben and I used to build model planes and rail track. Young Joss and I are going to do all that too aren't we mate?' He nudged Joss and smiled. 'I'm glad we all went to Ikea yesterday. I don't like the shop but we had fun didn't we?'

'It was so funny when we saw those black women in long dresses carrying pots and pans on their head in the car park.' Joss laughed.

'Yeah. It was as if they were carrying water across the Sudan,' Clifford laughed.

'And Saria didn't stop going on about getting cushions for her bedroom. She didn't need any cushions.' Joss commented.

'That's sisters for you. They're a pain in the arse.' Clifford laughed.

Gina wondered if Joss went a little way to replacing his lost past. He seemed to have a soft spot for him.

She felt a tinge of sadness too - that it wasn't Nick doing these things with him, but felt optimistic that Clifford could make a difference to all of their lives.

October 2010
Clifford
'God damn it Gina.'

'It's what teenagers do. You've forgotten.'

'Well it doesn't have to be like this.'

'I shouldn't have left them with you. You said it would be ok. I only went away for a few days.' Gina dropped her bag on the kitchen floor.

'While you were up north with Carrie and your cousin I was having the week from hell. They stayed in their rooms all week. Hardly spoke. I feel invisible.

'You're winding me up?' Gina searched his face.

'They hardly spoke to me. Jesus. They live under MY roof. I pay the bills. I deserve some bloody respect. Not this.'

'It's just the way they are.'

'Bollocks. It's deliberate.'

'You take everything personally.'

'What sort of imbeciles are you bringing up?'

'Wooooo. Steady on. That's a bit harsh.'

If he'd had his way he would have confronted Saria and Joss. They remained in their cells, doors firmly closed, as usual, while she tried to placate him by flicking the kettle hoping his feelings would dissolve in a peace keeping cup of tea.

Clifford sat at his office desk, his mind drifting. An uneaten sandwich lay on a pile of papers, lettuce escaping. He felt sure women were programmed differently. Sometimes when he talked to Gina it was like watching something made of mud attempt to think.

Many arguments centred in the kitchen and were to do with food or cooking.

Women didn't understand the science behind cooking. They understood the pretty colours on top of cupcakes and the art of napkin folding. The kitchen was no different to a science laboratory. Cooking was experimental science. To be able to cook and get it right you had to understand the physical processes - how to control temperature to avoid a soufflé collapsing and how to tenderize the meat. But Gina didn't listen. She had a child like frustration with anything marginally scientific. She was like a Spanish dog – couldn't be changed. Getting worked up over heavy saucepans was like a scenario of a toddler throwing toys out of a playpen. He knew to step back, not to interfere at that point. She didn't see that practically anything technical was possible. It was hard to reason with her. Her voice took on a whine when she was frustrated and that became particularly apparent with technical equipment: hoovers, computers, telephones and dishwashers.

At the beginning of the relationship he'd admired her frugality more than anything else about her. She had an incredible ability to save money. She'd paid off her mortgage and managed to live on so little. This was refreshing after the way his ex had lived. He'd swapped a spender for a saver. But as time went by he wasn't sure he could live with either. It drove him mad to open an empty fridge.

Ever since Clifford was a young boy growing up in a Jewish home, living on fried fish and matza he was determined the fridge would always be full. Full of ham and bacon, prawns and mussels and as much non kosher food that could be crammed in. What a farce the Jewish food laws were with their restrictions and careful ways of preparations. He never wanted to go without. His childhood had been a bitter struggle. His grandparents hadn't been able to shake off the ridiculous war mentality of using up every scrape, cutting off the edges of mouldy cheese and squeezing tea bags out for the fifth cup.

'What am I paying you a grand a month for?' Clifford asked Gina. Ever since his lunch break in the office the day before he'd been thinking about money.

'When I set up that standing order you were expected to spend a minimum of 200 a week on food. What are you doing with it? I'm earning 100k a year for what? To live on olives and Petit Filous yogurts? We're going to have to start shopping together.'

He needed control back in his life. This was ridiculous.

He suspected she was scrimping, up to her old tricks and eccentricities as a poverty stricken single mother. At the flat they had all shared an inch of grimy bath water and clothes were only bought from charity shops and boot fairs. Her measures were so extreme she had even made toothpaste from baking soda, salt and peppermint oil, to save up to pay the mortgage off. Clifford couldn't understand this whole culture of extreme cost cutting. What was it all about? He hoped never ever to be in that situation himself. If things ever got that bad he'd buy a rope and tie it to a very tall sturdy oak tree and hope the end came swiftly.

Gina

Gina was proud of herself. Food needn't cost the earth or leave you broke she told Clifford. The words 'value' or 'basic' or 'economy' and 'budget' glowed on her radar, jumping into the trolley knocking a few pennies a few quid off the final bill. Swiftly moving up and down aisles she had the regimentation of a Korean army corporal and the organization of the Gestapo. Lists were essential, crossing out items, moving onwards, never lingering or lurking in the chocolate aisle. A bottle of budget whiskey - a once a year treat and the occasional stash of clotted cream rice pudding, hidden at the back of the fridge.

Gina loathed waste which was so hard when you had kids. 'Waste not want not' was her mantra. It was better to buy in small quantities than buy a fridge full of stuff and end up throwing half of it out. As a young child her grandma had made her recite a poem every time she felt the urge to waste:

I shall not throw on the floor
the stuff I cannot eat
cause many hungry little ones
would think it quite a treat.
Tis wistful waste make woeful want
and I will live to say
how I wish I had that little crumb
I once had thrown away

She was used to an empty fridge but unlike Clifford she hadn't rebelled against her childhood. She had been swept along with the values of thrift, frequently telling her kids 'I'm not asking you to like it I'm asking you to eat it.' Cooking for kids was a futile exercise. She dreaded the plates cast aside because the meal was 'gus gus' but when it was 'lish lish' there was never enough. The poor blighters were always fishing for a fill up of biscuits soon after dinner, much to the annoyance of Gina.

Clifford

He didn't like shopping but it was important to have a say in what ended up on his plate. He imagined a smart fridge that ordered food directly or a 3d printer that synthesized food, cooked it and recovered materials from human waste. 'This will come one day' he told himself. The Samsung Gastro 3. He could see it. At least this way you could by-pass the downtrodden cashier in her fifties, nursing a prolapsed womb; a robot that asked the same thing, over and over 'want a bag for life dear?' He looked at the old bag behind the till and gave the same answer each time. 'I had a bag for life, but thank God I've divorced her.'

Gina had a wallet full of loyalty cards but he hated the concept of loyalty cards; designed to cleverly or not so cleverly extract a customer's personal details and compile their shopping preferences. Saving up piddly amounts on loyalty cards was a complete waste of time and money off vouchers that spewed out of tills. Only the proles with their shortsighted mentality were conned by the farce of vouchers. Karl Marx could write a whole pamphlet on the subjugation of the proles by way of supermarket. 'I don't do loyalty' he enjoyed the shock on the assistant's face. 'I do infidelity, so if you have a card that clocks up infidelity points I would be more than happy to take one.'

But the biggest arguments – the ones that rocked the foundations of their relationship were toilet related. The first of those arguments came a few weeks after moving in.

Clifford heard a blood curdling scream from the cloakroom.

'What's wrong?' He scrapped the chair across the wooden floor, flipped the lid down on his Mac. 'What the fuck have you done? We've only been here three weeks. Jesus. I'm flying to Japan at four in the morning and I need to finish this article.' He screamed back.

Gina was watching water gush from the cistern like a liquid tornado. The toilet had come alive. It looked like a porcelain monster.

'Get the yellow pages. Quick.'

Her feet were fixed to the ground. She carried on screaming.

'The flush was too slow. I thought I'd just tweak the ball cock and this happened.' Her face was flushed. The toilet wasn't. She leaned over, peered into the cistern as if it were a mysterious cavern. The cistern, Clifford thought should be a no go area with a clearly displayed warning sign for women.

'You fiddle with this, you mess with that. Get the yellow pages NOW. You stupid fucking woman.' He screamed, inches from her face, feeling like a Nazi general. 'Move it.'

He went to look for the valve to stop the water. He slammed cupboard doors, cursing, frantically searching. Then he ran into the street looking for a manhole cover, came back to the cloakroom grabbing the yellow pages. Gina was still fixed to the spot, now hysterical.

'You're nothing but a cancer. A useless bitch.' He screamed.

He called a plumber and within half an hour was answering the door to a plumber and his tool kit; in all probability a toilet enthusiast for whom bogs were his bread and butter. By now the cloakroom looked like a documentary on the Niagara Falls.

'Get out of his way. Your life is like toilet paper – long and useless.' Clifford shouted. Already he could see the bill. This toilet geek would be raking it in, in call out fees to fix broken, blocked and buggered toilets, probably loving the fact that most people grabbed the phone not a plunger.

That night he dreamt about life without a toilet - shitting in the garden behind the shed, admiring a steaming pile, coiled like a snake in a pit. Good manure for the roses. And diabetic wee - death to ivy and mint creeping up fences, strangling plants - more economical than half the stuff sold in garden centres. Who was going to spot his miniscule cock at the bottom of the garden, except under a bright moon?

In the morning he felt just as angry about what she'd done.

'You fucking women are good at bleaching, scrubbing and wiping toilets. Fantastic at erasing the dribbles, the awkward, caked on skid marks but haven't the foggiest when it comes to the basic mechanics.'

Clifford told Ben what had happened, over lunch, three weeks later.

Ben laughed.

'I just want to weep.'

'See the funny side.'

'Fuck off. That mini Noah's Ark flood cost me £400.'

'You got to admit it is funny.' Ben belly laughed.

'I had a 4am flight to Japan the following morning. Her kids had been particularly obnoxious that evening.'

'Give them a break. Her kids are ok.'

'They were unsociable, doing their usual routine after dinner. I can still see the blank look of Carrie standing in the doorway. That kid is weird. I can sympathise with Ian Bradey.'

'That's a really vile thing to say Dad.'

' Might of known I wouldn't get your vote of support.'

Clifford looked in despair, fixed his eyes on the view over the Brighton Pavilion. 'Bloody women. She suddenly decides she's going to fiddle with the ball cock to improve the water flow.'

'It's not a big deal Dad.' He was stifling a grin, half watching a seagull strutting along a nearby wall.

'Why do women tamper with stuff they don't understand.'

'What happened next?' For a moment Ben looked as if he was starting to take the conversation seriously. He rubbed the stumble on his chin.

'Jesus I've never seen so much water. It was like a gigantic tidal wave crashing through the cloakroom, destroying everything in its wake.'

' Exaggeration? Or trying to sound amusing?'

'Hardly. She was hysterical. She wasn't going to call someone out. I took her upstairs to calm her down. She'd transformed into a wailing banshee by this stage. The only thing I could do was slap her, hard across the face. It was like yanking out the lead from a socket. She needed a new Sim card inserted. She was screaming in my face, inches away. I could feel the spital. The wild look in her eyes. I had to do something to stop her.'

'Bloody hell. What next?' Ben seemed only interested in the theatrics.

'She slapped me back. My glasses flew off, skidded across the floor. Christ. I don't know what would have happened next if I hadn't left the room.'

'And then something else happened a week later, you said?'

'Her sister had just arrived to look after the kids for a week while we went on a business trip to Istanbul. It was the kid's toilet this time. I'm forever telling them not to put so much loo paper down in. They never listen. And Gina defends them every time. Keeps saying it's a slow flush and not the kid's fault. I put a banana down the toilet, flushed it to show them it works perfectly well. But her snotty nosed kid uses far too much paper to wipe his nose. He hasn't learned to blow his nose properly yet. I've tried to teach him. Hopeless.'

'So it got blocked?'

'We couldn't leave it for her sister to sort out. I was cooking. Gina can't cook a decent meal. If I left the cooking to her on a Sunday it would be pizza. I flung her the Yellow Pages, told her just to call someone out. But she wouldn't. Started screaming again. In the end she made a phone call. Half way through the call she threw the phone at me. It hit me on the side of the head. Christ. My first thought...there's a screw lose somewhere.'

'Did it get sorted?'

'She used a plunger. Should have done that in the first place.'

'So you're not having much luck on the toilet front then?'

'All the toilets are useless. The en suite stinks of rotting cabbage or decomposing rats. I get the blame for the smell. She thinks it's my turds blocking the pipes.'

'You need to get the agency onto the problems.'

'And every time her ex, Wayne the wanker drops his kid back he lingers in the hall trying to amuse Gina with infantile jokes. His latest joke, by sheer coincidence is 'what's the worst thing you can buy in a charity shop? Toilet roll.'

Gina

Gina was enjoying Istanbul; winding her way through the bowels of the Grand Bazaar, a rabbit warren of stalls, looking at carpets and trinkets and colourful sparkly garments.

Sipping tea, enjoying the flirtations of the stall traders she thought back over the night the toilet had flooded. She couldn't shake off the image of Clifford shouting 'you useless fucking woman, haven't you got any common sense? Are you that dense?' The words played mental tennis in her head. They triggered childhood memories which should have disappeared with time but hadn't. As a child she'd lost count of how many times her dad had said she had no common sense. For years she'd thought common sense was a special and talented gift that only she didn't have.

Nick had always called her dense. Clifford was doing the same.

She accepted another apple tea and watched the throng of people moving around the bazaar. It was a shame he couldn't laugh about things that went wrong. They'd both end up having heart attacks at this rate.

'I just wanted to show you I could sort a problem.' She'd told him.

'Are you an expert suddenly on toilets? Why tackle something you don't understand? It's the most stupid thing you've ever done.'

He'd spat the words, anger filling his face every time the events were recalled. All she wanted was for him to hug her and tell her it was ok – it was only a God damn toilet.

When he was in a rage he became Nick and his words rang in her ears, feasting on reason, staining her, labeling her forever stupid, forever useless. Her hysteria had very nearly gushed over into something uncontrollable. She had never lashed out and hit another human being in her life. She felt ashamed to have lost control. But out of the fug she vaguely remembered him shouting that she was a mental case, a piece of useless shit. 'You're as much use as a cancer.' She was certain he'd said that and couldn't quite believe it. But she couldn't push away a nagging feeling that he was right but why would that thought have entered her head? Where had it come from? Trying to tell herself to have conviction and belief in herself was torture.

When they returned from Istanbul the drama was repeated when the kid's toilet blocked again.

'Your kids are animals. I'm going to make you lot pay the plumber's bill. You'll soon learn not to block it again,' he shouted.

'What did you do to it? Feed it a whole toilet roll, like an irresponsible visitor at the zoo? Jesus did you not read the DO NOT FEED sign clearly pinned to the wall? What animal precisely were you thinking of creating out of the brown papier mache mess?' Clifford peered into the bowl poking at the brown paper sludge with the plunger, holding his nose.

'A brown bog monster?' he looked over at a glum lifeless Joss standing at the door, who just shrugged.

' Something mythical that will come to life?' he added.

In the end Gina unblocked the damn toilet claiming the certificate The Queen of Bogs. Shit had splattered her face. She was hot, sweaty, annoyed.

The words *well done* didn't enter his head. She desperately wanted to hear those words. All he could talk about in the weeks that followed was the telephone she had thrown - allegedly at him after she had scoured the yellow pages, made some calls to plumbers. She had thrown it in a moment of pure animal anger and frustration. How dare he treat her like an idiot telesales girl. He could treat the people in his office how he liked. He could disrupt their phone calls but he wasn't going to do that to her.

'How much do you charge? How soon could you come?'

But he'd kept shouting in the background as he carried on cooking. 'Cut. Cut the call. Move on. Next call. End the call'. She was livid. She couldn't hear their answers. All she could hear was Clifford's screams 'end the call. They're time wasters. When are you going to realise? Dozy bitch. In a flash Gina had ended the call, spun round and in one stupendous, glorious moment of fury hurled the phone across the room, watching it bounce, then crack across the hard floor.

Her first thought was that he'd apologise. But he hadn't. 'You should be locked up and the key thrown away,' he'd shouted. She felt a bit like a helpless prisoner facing a firing squad. This was a powerless place. She'd been reduced to a childlike state.

20
Clifford

October 2010

'How are you Joss? How was school?' Clifford asked Joss over dinner. It wasn't a difficult question so why did he always get a shrug and a dumb whispered answer?

'About average.' Joss gave a cowering shrug.

'Does nobody have anything to say? Clifford looked round the table at everyone. Nobody spoke. It felt like he'd moved in with a cardboard cut out family.

He watched Joss put his glass down, an inch from the mat.

'Put your glass on the mat Joss.' Carrie screeched.

'Oh for goodness sake the pair of you. Every mealtime it's the same.' Gina sounded tired.

Carrie picked the glass up. Put it back on the mat. Joss picked the glass up. Took a sip. Subtly placed it on the table, an inch from the mat.

'Put it on the mat Joss.' Carrie shrieked louder then yelped as Joss gave her a hard kick under the table.'

Where was he supposed to begin? This was kindergarten territory.

'Pack it in both of you.' He barked. They looked at each other in surprise.

'Can I go upstairs now?' Joss asked.

'I need my blanket.' Carrie whispered. Clifford looked at her. He could see her future stretched ahead and it didn't look great; an adult tossed onto the pile of society's wasters.

'No. You can both sit there and finish your dinner and engage in some conversation for a change. I'm not putting up with silence.' Clifford barked. It was time for change.

Clifford looked at Saria. It wouldn't be long before she was applying for university but the kid was basically ignorant about life. There was so much he could help her with: science and maths, history and current affairs. The world was an open door waiting to be entered. But she wasn't switched on. He saw a daily obsession with mindless You Tube crap such as 'Charlie Bit My Finger Off.' And dumb teen speak such as 'is pizza a vegetable because apparently the American Government say it is?' or the suggestion that the breakfast cereal Cheerios 'is so up itself.'

Joss shrugged again, looked terrified and in a timid whisper, like the dying breath of an engine asked 'Did you know we are all related to tuna fish?'

'Well at least that's a start. Where did that idea come from?'

'I think its Darwinian.'

'Ah now we're getting somewhere. And do you know what is behind the theory?'

Joss shrugged. 'We've all evolved.'

Gina

Twenty minutes later Clifford finally finished explaining the Darwinian theory. Everybody looked like they were dropping off. He'd pitched his 'speech' at a much older audience. Gina watched as the kids looked at the door longing to escape scraping their chairs back - planning their surreptitious exit.

The following evening he asked Saria if she had anything interesting to say.

'Did you know that if you took all the space around an atom away the world could fit into an apple?' Saria was eying the apple she was eating.

Clifford seized on this crumb. 'That's an interesting theory.'

He began a long rambling lecture related to physics which went on for another twenty minutes.

In bed later on he told Gina how the conversations were leaving him totally drained.

' I'm not surprised. You do all the talking. Your voice becomes a monotone a bit like Melvyn Bragg on Radio four 'In Our Time.' You're heavy going.'

'They've nothing to say. One cowers and has been drained of all life form. One screeches or stays silent and the other starts a conversation then has nothing to add.'

'You barely give them a chance. They come out with interesting thoughts about apples or tuna fish or black holes and then *you* do all the talking.'

'I have to make a linguistic adjustment listening to them.'

'Is it so hard to be normal?' Gina was starting to rant.

She carried on. ' It's as if you're trying to fill three cups with ever more complicated concepts using words and ideas that go straight over their heads. It's no wonder they inch slowly to the door to escape.'

'Well fuck you. I'm tired of watching them step towards the kitchen door, fiddle with the knob as they nod and smile sweetly and politely, pretending to be interested in what I'm saying.'

'Jeez Clifford. They don't have PHDs. Are you doing it deliberately to put them off you?'

'They'll never accept me. You're happy with their baby talk. I'm not prepared to sit through a meal listening to a bunch of imbeciles.'

'Can't you be more entertaining, light hearted. They're easy going kids. They aren't into drugs or staying out late. They'll never swear at you or be rude. Any bloke would be delighted to have step kids like mine.'

Gina got into bed, started to take her make up off with cotton wool and baby cream.

'I sometimes wish they would swear. At least it would be a reaction.'

'When we're alone you're fun. Why be different with them?'

'Really?' Clifford felt lost. He squeezed his face, kneeding his chin as if it were a piece of dough. He let out a great sigh then looked straight at her. He loved this woman but for the first time in his adult life he didn't have a plan or a solution. Where was this going?

After a short silence, as they both took stock he said, 'Come here bitch. You gunna give this old bear a kiss.'

Clifford

Clifford loathed the way his work colleagues tried to give him tips on how to fit in. He didn't do fitting in. If people couldn't fit in with him then it was fuck off time.

'Why don't you have a Saturday night in with a takeaway curry and watch the X Factor together. Teenagers love it,' his office techy suggested.

He hated the X Factor. He called it mass produced, poor quality, manufactured entertainment for the scum. One evening he suggested a DVD but nobody could agree on the genre. In the end they sloped off to their rooms as soon as dinner was finished.

'You need to have a word with them – tell them how I feel. I can't go on like this.' Clifford poured himself a cup of tea, sat down at the kitchen pine table.

Gina looked incredulous.

'Have a word with them?' Tell them what exactly?' Her face looked pained. 'That they've got to transform into different kids. Sorry. They are as they are. Maybe I'm to blame for making them like that, or maybe that's what the big D word divorce does. Don't take it so personally. They're just very very shy. They feel awkward around you. Is that so surprising?' Gina ranted on.

It was a 'him and them' set up. He didn't belong anywhere. His own family had fractured, gone their separate ways and this new family were a collection of dysfunctional individuals who had lost the art of communication and couldn't connect with one another in any meaningful way.

'They shut down a bit more with each passing day, like union members working to rule. I can't stand it. I've tried to engage. When I come home at night surprise surprise they're always in their rooms, diligently coming down only when you call them for dinner. Then we have Joss cowering too afraid to speak, mumbling when spoken to, sniffing and wiping his nose on his sleeve. And Saria's face is always stiff. And a blanket permanently attached to Carrie's face as if it were an umbilical cord. I keep asking myself what am I doing here?'

Breakfast time was the worst time of the day. They sauntered into the kitchen in silence. He was invisible. What sort of parent dragged their kid up to be so unsociable? Each morning he made a point of trying to get them to engage. Christ, these kids would learn some manners if it was going to kill him.

Clifford poured coffee. The kids had gone back upstairs to get their school bags ready.

'How can this be right?' He stood tall now arms in the air doing the strut of despair. Then he turned to face her hoping for a direct answer.

'I shouldn't be here if that's the way they feel.'

He waited, wondering how she might turn things around.

'You're here for me.' She began to plead. 'ME.'

'It's not that simple. You come as one package. God knows everyone keeps reminding me.'

'If you love me you should want to work with me, not against me. Accept they're teenagers. Maybe you've forgotten what Ben was like. I'm sure he wasn't so God damn perfect.'

'He would have made some effort. They make no effort. They're all scowling mutes.'

'That's not true and you know it. They try their best. You have to gently encourage kids to talk. Tell them they have interesting opinions. It's about boosting their confidence then they'll want to talk more.'

'Oh Christ. I'm too old and long in the tooth for all this.'

Clifford could feel that heavy leaden weight falling to the pit of his stomach again and the prickling of a creeping headache like an insect across his forehead.

'This is way too complicated. I can't do it.' He raised his hands in the air, as if disarming himself.

'I bought one kid up. Now look at him. He's a mess, a wreck in fact. I'm in way over my head Gina.'

His arm fell to his sides, his head now hung low as if in shame.

She hissed. Pointed a finger at him.

'You're not listening to me. This is no different to encouraging your workforce to do better.'

'Well... I think we've hit upon a nail there.' Anger stabbed. He knew very well what she was referring to.

'I'm a dirty greedy Jew. Go on. Say it. It's all I know. Making money.'

He rubbed his thumb and forefinger together, hunching his back like Fagin in Oliver Twist.

'Oh shut up! My point is people need encouragement. They need their egos boosting in order to do better or gain in esteem.'

'Christ. You do talk bollocks sometime.'

Clifford hurled the 'b' word from his mouth as if spitting out a piece of nasty gristle. Gina shot him her animal wounded look. Her upper lip had started to quiver and she was standing away from him fiddling with the Welsh dresser drawers. He couldn't work out whether she would turn on the water works or fly into a rage. He searched for a compromise, a tempered olive branch. He had an idea. It might not work but he was willing to try.

But just as he was about to put his suggestion to her Saria burst through the door her voice shrill and jittery.

'We can hear what you're saying about us you know.' Her tone was laced with sarcasm, her face a deep beetroot.

Clifford's eyes widened. 'This is good. A kid that can speak.' It was like beckoning a spider from a crack.

Saria gripped the brass door knob, turning it round as she spoke. Nerves, Clifford thought. The knob rattled in her hand.

'Oh my God.' Saria shouted.

Then she burped and laughed.

'You're a prick. We don't WANT a serious conversation with you Clifford.'

Saria's pitch was rising, her voice wobbly. Her eyes were filling with tears. He didn't know what to think. Maybe the barriers were coming down. Maybe this was progress. His head started to thump.

'Stop rattling that door knob.'

' You're a prick. We don't care about your intellectual crap.' Saria continued to rattle the knob. Her skin looked mottled.

'We don't want to have heavy conversations every time we come through the door. We just want to go to our rooms and chill.' She drummed her point.

The door squeaked and Joss pushed through. His face was beetroot too. His hands were glued into his pockets.

'And what do you think Joss. Got anything to add to your sister's outburst?'

'Erm, no.' He shrugged.

'Well I just had an idea before your sister burst in. Why don't we try having family breakfasts at the weekends instead of everyone wandering down when they feel like it.'

'Cooked?' Joss's face lit up.

'Now where you go wrong Gina...'

'More put downs? Wondered when that was coming'. Gina swiveled round, the wounded look returned to her face.

'You let them wander into the kitchen to help themselves, do what the hell they like. You're their mother. Start acting like their mother. Serve them breakfast. A decent breakfast. Not wood shavings you find in a pencil sharpener.'

Gina bristled. He dreaded her voice rising to a hyena.

'They're not babies any more. I do enough for them. Cooking, washing, cleaning, ferrying them around all over the place. Life is rushed.'

'Well you shouldn't. Make them walk more. Make them help out. They could take turns in cooking a meal.'

'*We are here you know. We are listening.* Stop being horrible to mummy. She did very well before she met you.' Saria's voice was wobbly again.

'It would be a massive operation if I stood there serving toast on top of making packed lunches and getting Carrie to do her spelling tests. We could try family cooked breakfast at the weekends though. See how that goes. What does everyone think?' Gina looked from Clifford to Saria to Joss.

For Clifford happiness had always been dispensed through food. It was the key to any rift. There was something very basic and carnal about the power of food.

Gina

Gina was walking along the footpath from the cottage. She could hear Joss's voice. Maybe he was in the field next to the footpath. Then she heard his friends' voices. The hedge was high like a battlement. She couldn't see. She stopped. Strained to listen, waited for a woman and dog to pass.

'Now *my* impression of him. Listen everyone.' Joss was calling.

'Now then lad sit down will you and listen.' It was stern. Made to sound like an impression of a Nazi.

It didn't take her long to work out what was happening. Each one was doing a different impression of Clifford.

She carried on walking, smiled to herself. Joss was quiet but had a wonderful way of turning situations into humour.

Clifford

To begin with the cooked breakfasts were fun. He liked a busy kitchen. The atmosphere seemed to change with everybody thrown into the kitchen, doing something together - cracking eggs, sizzling bacon, turning sausages in the pan.

'Pass over a piece of that horrible white bread that tastes like Kleenex' he laughed, feeling relaxed for the first time.

The family breakfasts offered a small glimmer of hope but there was still a long way to go.

In the meantime bigger issues were surfacing on his horizon.

21

Clifford

Early November 2010

A milky sky promised the first snow of the season. Forecasters warned of a bitter winter. A few flakes swirled giddily in the darkness. Clifford was crouched by the hearth having arranged a stack of dry logs. The kindling caught fire immediately and he watched the flames leap and dance, blue edged and hypnotic. The curtain less room with its' stark magnolia walls and oak paneling beneath his shoeless feet was instantly transformed by the vibrancy of colour. The magnolia softened into peach, the richness of the oak deepened and Clifford's mood mellowed with it. Even the frozen smiling faces in the motley collection of family photographs on the shelf seemed warmer, more welcoming.

It was early evening, a Sunday in November. Saria and Joss had just returned from Nick's. They never spoke about their weekends away, compartmentalising their lives. Nick returned them at bang on six. It was as if he set his watch to Greenwich meantime. Even if the car pulled up five minutes early the engine would run till six, the kids emerging onto the doorstep just as the hall clock chimed.

'Constipated arsehole,' Clifford muttered to himself on hearing the doorbell. He gave a hard and pointless stab at the grate with the iron poker sending ash spinning, then another stab when he heard their feet pounding up the creaking stairs, as they retreated to their rooms without a hello.

At around seven the doorbell ran again. It was like a stream of postal deliveries. A sudden gust of chill air blasted through the open door creeping into the lounge.

'Shut the door will you,' Clifford called out.

He gave a hard, determined jab at the fire, the vision of Wayne in the flames. He still lingered; clearly hadn't given up hope of Gina getting back with him. Sparks splattered up, fell again, like small fireworks.

'She's 'ad a bath. She's all clean. She 'ad a bath this morning because the 'ot water goes off at ten. I've got a bit of a problem with the heating at the moment. The thing's gone wrong.' His monotone, South London drawl was like a cheap broken tin saucepan tapping against Clifford's head. He was a Mr. Bean version of Trigger in 'Only Fools.'

'Tell him you don't sodding care.' Clifford muttered. His whole body started to tense. He jabbed and twisted the poker into the oak flooring.

'I've washed 'er uniform. The tights are nearly dry. Feel 'em. Do they feel dry to you? They've been drying in the bathroom. I don't like to dry things indoors but they don't dry outside in the winter. Carrie Larrie, take those clothes off. They live at Daddy's house.'

'Do we always have to have this dreadful ritual of stripping her off on my doorstep? It's humiliating for the poor kid and cold.' Clifford willed her to be more assertive.

'It doesn't matter where they live Wayne. They're my clothes.'

Carrie's small voice was the voice of reason. Clifford smiled. He liked the way the kid called the sperm donor by his first name.

Gina sounded too calm, patient. He'd tell her that later. What was making her so God damn subservient to him? Why couldn't she ever tell him to fuck off? He was just a useless lump that walked the earth.

'He's taking the piss. He obviously still has strong feelings for you but you're not blunt enough. You let him linger. Be tough. Tell him to fuck off he'd told her several times.

He hated the way Wayne ignored Gina's wishes - insisting on stripping the little girl off in the hallway and taking the clothes he had bought at Primark for her to wear at his house.

'We've been doing the Tables. She knows the sevens now. Go on Carrie Larrie tell mummy the sevens.'

There was a brief silence. Clifford jabbed at the bricks surrounding the hearth. Sparks flew.

'Don't call her Carrie Larrie. I don't like it. She doesn't like it. I don't like your family calling her that either.'

Wayne made a dramatic sigh. Most people sighed quietly. But Wayne didn't do quiet. A sneeze, a whisper, a cough were the noises of a beast in the wilderness. Clifford put down the poker. Covered his ear with his small hands, pleading silently for the torture to end.

'Oh go on Carrie. Go on.' Wayne was almost whimpering. 'Do it for Daddy. Daddy's waiting. Ohhhhhh'. There was strain in his voice.

Clifford thought that he sounded like a toddler in a play park whining for the return of his trike. It took all the restraint he could muster not to burst through to the hall and throttle him.

'She can do it. Honest. We've been learning all weekend. And she done a rhyme. Go on tell mummy.'

Clifford picked the poker up again, grinding his teeth as he drowned out the poor grammar.

'Yeah yeah, I believe you.'

'Oh.' Wayne's voice descended with a thud. 'Stop knocking her. She can do the rhyme really well. After me Larrie.'

'First William, the Norman, then Willie, his son,
Henry, Stephen, Henry, Richard and John,
Henry and Edward, one, two and three,
And again after Richard, three Henrys we see.
Two Edwards and Richard, if rightly I guess -
Two Henrys, sixth Edward, Queen Mary, Queen Bess.
Then Jaimie the Scotsman, then Charles, whom they slew,
But receive after Cromwell another Charles (Two).
James Second the Stuart ascended the throne.
Then William and Mary, together, came on.
Queen Anne, Georges four, fourth William all passed.
Then came Victoria and long did she last.'

Clifford contemplated sending his massive turd of Soviet typhoon class, by text picture to Wayne's phone. But Wayne had a crappy little Nokia. The picture would be a brown blur. It wouldn't show the wonderful banana shape and its' amazing tones of brown gliding down the porcelain.

'Oh for God's sake. Why do you keep teaching her everything by rote? She needs to gain an understanding of things. It's an autistic way of learning,' Gina was telling him.

'Oh Gina.' Wayne droned each word, as if they were painful sores. 'You always knock me, put me down'.

' I'm telling you. Accept it.'

'Oh and you're so wonderful I suppose, you and Mouse.'

'His name's Clifford. Don't call him Mouse.'

Clifford couldn't bear it any longer. He wasn't going to put up with the nickname of Mouse. He'd show him. He swept towards the door, flinging it open, a gust a cold air rushing through.

'Out. Get out of my house now. And don't ask to use the toilet either. You can piss ya pants for all I care.'

And with that Clifford swept him away, a broom to filthy debris, with Gina stammering and cowering behind the door telling him not to be so cruel and Carrie shivering in her knickers and vest.

Gina

Clifford was rubbing his forehead, huffing as he sat at the table waiting for dinner to be served. Gina handed out plates of lasagne to everyone.

'I fucking hate the tedious paraphernalia of handovers. There's no reason he has to stand talking in the hallway for so long.'

Saria waved her knife in his direction. She was gaining in confidence, learning to confront him.

'You shouldn't swear in front of little kids. Anyway it's like well you knew mummy had kids when you met her.'

'Why do teenagers always litter sentences with the word like? You won't get through a job interview speaking like that.'

'Yeah yeah yeah' Joss sang in a jovial way masking a defiance he hadn't the courage to express. Joss knew his tone was sarcastic but it was also funny the way he said it. He was never offensive, a meek sort of boy.

'We could move to Scotland. House prices are cheaper there. A small mortgage wouldn't be a problem.' Clifford suggested.

'It's cold up there. We don't know anyone.' Gina sat down picked up her fork.

'We could even emigrate to New Zealand. The New Zealand government are encouraging business owners to relocate. My business can move anywhere. It's a much nicer way of life over there.'

'Yes pleeeeeeeeese. Oh yes please. Yes please.' Saria clasped her hands together pleading. She rested her head on Gina's shoulders pouting her lips with a soppy dog look in her eyes.

'That would be sooooooo amazing. Yes pleeeeeeeese.'

'My daddy could come too.' Carrie yelped.

'What do you think Joss?' Clifford asked.

Joss flushed. He was gripping his knife and fork in his hands as if in battle but his face was expressionless as if someone had asked him which ice cream he would prefer – strawberry or chocolate.

'I don't mind.' He shrugged. Looked embarrassed.

'Christ. Do you ever have an opinion? You've seen the Hobbit. The scenery is spectacular.'

'Oh yeah,' was all Joss could think of saying.

'Jesus. What you talk to your dad about? Do you say nothing to him either?'

Joss shrugged his shoulders again and looked increasingly awkward. Gina wondered what he was thinking and felt a rush of love and desperate need to protect her son. She sensed his vulnerability. She got up, put an arm around him. He flinched away.

'They just play on the X Box. They don't talk.' Saria said.

'I could never take them away from their dads. You know that.' Gina was firm.

'Those imbeciles aren't fathers. They're nothing.'

He spat the words across the table.

'You're always saying how fed up you are with Haywards Heath and its' attachment to your marriage and the pain of the past but when it comes to it you're intransigent to the idea of change. You can't see any further than getting the kids through school. The schools are run of the mill, churning uninspired kids off a production line.'

Shock filled Gina's face. What was she doing allowing him to speak about her children's fathers in that way?

'Why would the kids miss them?' he carried on his tireless catechism.

'I'm not going to listen to this. Not in front of the kids. They're good dads. They love their kids.' Gina was shouting.

'Go back to them then.' Clifford scraped his chair back across the wooden floor, huffing as he retreated to the lounge.

Suddenly Gina had a moment of clarity. Felt her heart harden. Her head was beginning to take control. She didn't know what she felt: anger or calm resignation. But she could see her plan B: they'd return to the flat in April when the tenants contract was up for renewal. Thank goodness the sale hadn't gone through.

But part of her hankered for Clifford to change. She didn't want to give in. The relationship had been good at the start. Surely it was possible to return to the good times?

She got up, followed him to the lounge, standing in the doorway.

'If we move away they might stop paying maintenance.' She told him.

He laughed. 'They pay a pittance. That's not support. I can earn that in a few hours.'

'They pay what the CSA guidelines tell them to pay. They don't earn vast amounts like you do.'

'Fucking CSA. Decent fathers pay more than the guidelines.'

She couldn't and wouldn't separate father and child. It was a precious bond not a flimsy spider's web. She had always done everything in her power to ensure they saw as much of their children as they could. Her life was on hold, rooted to Sussex. At times she desperately wanted to move away, to start afresh, put the past behind her. But change was the one thing she was resolute about. Stability meant everything.

Carrie was standing on a chair hanging red baubles on the Welsh dresser. She had just finished her breakfast. Anything to avoid learning spellings. In the corner of the kitchen John Humphrey's voice crackled on the radio as he reported the arrest of Julian Assange, founder of Wiki Leaks. An icy breeze buffeted the doors to the conservatory, a chill creeping to every corner of the room.

Gina shivered. 'Sit down Carrie. We need to learn these spellings.'

The child was still mixing up Ds with Bs and 'was' and 'saw.' She hadn't shared her concerns with Clifford. What was the point?

'Have you got any flash cards?' Clifford had been listening to the Assange interview, eating his muesli standing up at the counter.

'Why?'

'You had some Dorling and Kindersley cards. Bring them here.'

She opened a drawer, handed him the cards. He began to hold up each card patiently, calmly asking Carrie to read the simple words on the cards.

He tapped the cards on the counters, put them back in their box.

'Dyslexia. I'd lay a bet on it.'

'You reckon?' She looked at him incredulous and for the first time in a while felt warmth and hope.

'Get a psychologist's report. I'll pay. The school won't do anything. Budgets have been cut.'

'But what difference will it make? The school won't do anything.'

'Oh it will. Trust me. I love you. They'll offer support, maybe one to one help with phonics.' He took her hands, smiling sympathy and understanding. And in that moment she could see why she was with him. Wayne hadn't picked up that there was a problem. He lived in a bubble of Victorian rote learning; methods he believed in. He couldn't comprehend concepts and ideas that hadn't been generated from his own mind or own narrow world and experience. She dreaded attending parent meetings with Wayne. He was always focused on waiting for the teacher to finish talking so that he could proudly announce all the Times Tables he had taught Carrie. It was as if he wanted Brownie points himself.

'You were right. Dyslexia. We were there all morning. And the school want a copy of the report. I think they will take it seriously.' Gina beamed at Clifford.

'I'm so pleased. There's so much you can do to help her. I know a shop in Brighton with learning games to support children with special needs.' The caring Clifford was back. She felt a tug of love.

'Wow. Thank you.' She put her arms round him. They were together on this. Small stirrings of hope flitted in her stomach. Change was in the air.

It was a Saturday morning in the middle of December. Clifford and Gina were in bed nakedly entwined bathed in the smells and stickiness of sex. Clifford had been singing the Eton rowing song 'pull, pull, shag, shag' to gain momentum and keep going as he pushed and shafted, plundering the murky river waters. 'Come on boys keep going. Push push, shag, shag. Who's wearing the semen stained jersey? Team Clifford, keep going boys, my perfectly healthy spermatozoa.' Gina loved it. She responded with tiny shudders of pleasure. His humour reaffirmed to her why they were together.

'Christ.' Clifford nuzzled her neck, the bristles of his chin an emory board making her giggle.

'If I'd met you when I was a lot younger I would have used you like a urinal.'

Gina still found his filth amusing.

'Well that was a jolly good timed shag my little dick.' Clifford pulled at his dick, as if it were a loose bell cord.

'Maybe we'll have more later.' She suggested.

'We'll have to see. My dick is like a Morris Minor gearbox – the one exclusive.'

Gina started rubbing her fanny with two fingers, needing a little more satisfaction, pushing her sticky bottom into his groin, gently rubbing.

'When I lived in Fulham pussies used to walk along the wall outside my bedroom window. I used to lie there and watch them trotting up and down.'

'Is this a Mrs Slowcombe moment? We are talking cats not vaginas?'

'No. Not Va- Ginas.'

'Hey. Don't refer to my name in that way.'

Clifford laughed huskily in her ear.

'I named the pussies after all the women I knew. Once I leant out of the window and poured water on one. It went crazy, behaving like a cartoon cat.'

'Shushh. What was that noise?' They fell silent.

Gina grabbed her glasses, looked at the clock beside the bed. 7am and the peace was already disturbed by Carrie pounding on Joss' door, her frustration notching up with each ignored bang.

'You should have put a cooking bag over the retards head when you put her to bed last night. Sometimes I wonder whether the kid has dementia.'

Gina prised herself from his body, the stickiness of sex coated across their bodies like wallpaper paste.

'What? How bloody vile. I don't understand you. One minute you're helping - paying for an educational assessment, showing concern. Now this? What the hell's wrong with you?' She sat up. His words were like a hard cold slap of marble back to reality. It was like stepping out of a warm cabin into a biting storm. She stared at her reflection in the wardrobe mirror. Who was she? What was she doing here? One step forward, two steps back.

'You had a kid with a retard what do you expect?'

His words hovered then froze in the air between them, but still they didn't pierce her. She wanted to feel anger - the correct and natural reaction, like burning fingers on a kettle. All she felt was a slithering revulsion.

'Poor little girl. It's hard not having anyone to play with.'

It was strange hearing herself speak. What she really wanted to say didn't come out. It was like watching the scene from the ceiling having flown out of her body. She was disconnected from her tangible self.

She still hankered for the old Clifford. The one she'd fallen in love with in Scotland. The man who promised to be a good stepfather to her children. Why were his thoughts so inconsistent? If only she could read his mind. See who the real person was.

The pounding continued. 'He's probably reading Harry Potter.'

'The kid's always reading Harry Pothead.'

'I sometimes wish I could wheel back in time but with a different father. Be nice to have a father now. To help out.'

Gina started to create an image in her head of the perfect hands - on father.

'You should go back to Wanker Wayne.'

Gina turned to face him. She was sick of him suggesting that. Needles of frustration coursed through her body. He knew the buttons to press.

'What a ridiculous suggestion. I finished with him. It wasn't right. I didn't walk up the aisle with him.'

'You did everything else with him'. Gina felt dirty, punished for the sordid act of sex with Wayne.

'I would have thought her screaming every morning is a reminder of your sordid mistake. You're a moron Gina. And don't ever leave me on my own with her by the way. I'm likely to kill her.'

Gina couldn't process his words quick enough. Was he being serious? She wrestled with the duvet, pulling it away. Why didn't his nasty words make her react? Maybe she didn't want to react because to react might have pushed away the Clifford she hankered for, even further.

'He was the mistake. Not Carrie. It's not the same. At least I had another kid. You were too pathetic to bring another child into the world. You wouldn't have another kid because of something that happened deep in your past. Your baby brother. Get over it.'

'Fuck off.' His words were spat across the bed.

She felt his now cold semen escaping down her legs. She waited for the next missive, wondering what had really happened in his family long ago.

'You can't deal with her. You should get up. See to her. Stop imagining a fictitious father out there. We're all failed fathers. Failed offspring. Failed siblings. That's life. Get up before I have to strangle her myself.'

Gina unraveled the sheet, put her feet on the bare, cold floorboards.

'Call yourself intelligent. I don't think so.'

'*You* didn't have much intelligence to go with the moron in the first place.'

She looked in the mirror. Glanced at his reflection. She caught his eyes. Her heart flitted. His eyes were misty pools of sadness. His face had turned a shade of grey. This had nothing to do with Carrie. And everything to do with him. In a flash she could see it. A deep longing in those eyes. And she knew what that longing was. The desire for a baby.

22
Clifford

November 2010

There was a biting chill to the winter breeze on Rottingdean sea front. It had been beautiful when they arrived but the spectacular burnt orange sun was rapidly disappearing into the slate sea. Clifford was worried about the fading light, checking his watch. Soon it would be a struggle to drive with the oncoming headlights. What an old man he'd become. It was the same in airports. The bright lights had become dazzling.

He wrapped his angora scarf tight around his frozen ears as they watched the waves, come in, go out, reminding him of the problems in his life.

It was quiet on the beach except for the occasional barking dog. In the distance the glow of seafront entertainment went on, day after day. He longed for the merry go round of life to stop.

'Is it just me or does it look slightly foggy to you?' He asked Gina.

'The light's disappearing fast. I'm not sure it looks foggy though. I'll drive back if you like. I've noticed you're quite slow in the dark.' Her criticism was masked by an upbeat tone.

They walked towards a cluster of boulders. Clifford stopped, looked around squinting.

'Nothing wrong with my driving. I've been driving for 35 years now. I could find my way back with my eyes closed. I've probably driven round the globe several times.' He looked at his watch again.

'The people in front of those boulders don't look clear.' Clifford scrunched his eyes several times and took his glasses off, gave them a clean. 'I think it's these glasses. They need replacing.'

'You haven't had them long. Don't put them face down when you take them off. They get scratched easily. No wonder you can't see properly.'

He ignored her, stopped again scrunched his eyes.

'There's one dog in front of that boulder isn't there? I can see two dogs, not one.'

'Yes, only one dog. Maybe you should go to the optician. I noticed the other day the plates were still dirty after you washed up. It could be the glasses, or it could be your sight. Aren't you supposed to take eye drops for glaucoma?'

'The lighting's crap in that kitchen. There should be a spotlight above the sink. Now if I owned my own home...' His voice trailed off into a sigh. He thought of the latest mortgage application that had been declined.

He rubbed his eyes again.

'It's as if there's a film on my eye surface. There are tiny objects moving around in front of my eyes.'

'Eye drops?' He thought the silence had eased him out of the conversation but she had a motherly persistence when she wanted.

'Never taken them. I'll be dead by the time I go blind.'

'Glaucoma is the silent thief of sight. You should start taking drops.'

'I've got enough to think about. You try taking eye drops every day, on top of all the other medication I have to remember. They were unbearable. Made my eyes sting.'

She tutted. Said nothing. He was glad; too tired to argue.

But what he didn't know, as he struggled in the fading light was that further health problems were on their way.

Gina

'You're going to be very shocked when you see me.' Clifford's text bleeped.

Gina was ready to drive to Heathrow to pick him up from another business trip. 'What's the hells wrong? I'll be there as soon as I can.

'I'll wait at the arrivals, near M&S. My face is all crooked.'

A vision of the photograph on the back of ambulances of a woman's face following a stroke filled her mind in horror.

At Heathrow she parked the car, panic mounting, her heart racing as she rushed to meet him.

She spotted him a long way off. Stopped in her track, her hand clapped to her mouth.

He looked like a bulldog. His face sagged. He looked so different. He was massaging his face and pulled out a hanky to mop up saliva from his mouth. Taking a deep breath, adjusting her bag on her shoulders she hurried towards him.

'My God.' She gasped.

'You've had a stroke.' His face was a pillow with no stuffing. One eye was red and sagging. His mouth half drooped.

'That was my first thought. It's not a stroke. I woke up like it. It felt numb. I looked in the mirror. I've been googling and I'm pretty sure it's a condition called Bell's Palsy. It strikes the 7th cranial nerve causing facial paralysis. And guess what? Possibly another complication of diabetes. What a surprise that is. '

'I can't imagine what it's like. Poor you.'

He pulled the side of his mouth up with a hand to form a smile. 'I really am an old bear now. Where's the car?' He linked his arm into hers. As they walked she wondered if he would be permanently disfigured.

Clifford

'You ok? You've been tossing and turning all night.' Gina asked.

'You fucking would if you had face ache and couldn't shut your eye.'

' You've got to go to the doctor today. Take the day off work if you have to.'

'I can't do that. But I'll call into the doc.' Clifford knew that in most cases facial paralysis was due to Bell's Palsy; a condition possibly caused by the re-activation of the herpes virus, lying dormant in the body since a bout of chickenpox. He was also worried because he had been reading about Bells and anti-virals needed to be taken within 72 hours of the Bell's starting. The hours were creeping on.

He closed the doctor's door clutching a prescription for an anti-viral - Acyclovir and some eye drops, to prevent severe drying out of the eye because he couldn't close his eye and also an eye patch to wear at night.

He waited in the chemist for the drugs, conscious always of the time wasted that should have been spent in the office generating income. He thought of all the medication he was now on and felt like an inadequate bomber limping home. He jabbed his ear while he waited in an attempt to stop the stabbing pains. The doctor hadn't been able to tell him how long the condition would take to go away and so in the meantime he was going to have to meet clients with a drooping face and a runny eye. And worse – slobber at dinner meetings, massaging his mouth with his hand in order to chew the food like a baby.

The chemist handed him a large bag of the packaged drugs due, checked his address and asked if he would like to order a repeat while he was there.

' It's all down hill now. Life's a bastard. And I'm disaster man. I've spent my whole life managing disasters you know. I'm sick of it. I feel like George Bush when the second plane hit the second tower.'

The chemist just smiled. 'They've changed your medication I see?'

'Yep. My body is one giant cocktail of drugs. Shame I can't just put a flame to it, whoosh and I'm gone. I'd like to end up as brandy on a Christmas pudding,' he laughed.

Then he was serious. ' I've just had a long chat with the doctor. No I can't control my diabetes. Bloods are too high. Pancreas is probably fucked.'

He was off on one. The chemist held the prescription in mid air. Momentarily he didn't care who was listening. He thought back to the precarious way in which he took his medication. It wasn't possible to stick to a strict regime, especially when flying or at conferences when meetings frequently overran and different time zones messed up the body's clock. It was no wonder he frequently had diarrhea or felt sick. The regime the doctor wanted just wasn't happening.

He looked at the green prescription. The doctor had told him he was an ideal candidate for Victoza because he had an HbAIC of more than 9% but it was now critical that he started to take some exercise and to watch his diet more closely. But these doctors - what did they really know? Every person was different and diabetes was more complicated than most people imagined. The average country GP only had a quick five minutes to consider the finely balanced chemistry system of each body.

Was this really his messed up body? How had it come to this? It was like looking down from an aeroplane and seeing his body as a dried up ox bow lake system.

He yanked the chemist door open and thought of how Gina kept nagging him to lose weight. But he had no time for exercise. According to her he was carrying around a huge baby elephant.

'You look very slim from behind but massive at the front.'

In bed she would wobble his stomach from side to side, asking him how it had grown so big.

He got into his car, looked in the mirror and wondered how long this would go on for. His left eye was sore and kept streaming. He dribbled when he ate. He had to push the left side of his mouth up when chewing food because he couldn't feel the muscles. This could go on for months. The doctors had no time frame.

The doctor had suggested an idea. It gave him a tinge of hope. That evening he'd go on line and make a booking.

'Welcome to Champney's sir. May I take your name?'

Clifford looked around the foyer. There were polished green apples in bowls on every coffee table. People were floating past in toweling robes sipping bottled water. A smell of animal feed wafted through from the nearby restaurant. His stomach flipped. He didn't particularly fancy a plate of pumpkin seeds and a green pond weed smoothie. But he was desperate to recover from Bells.

'I've come here for the facials and saunas not a bloody detox.' He snapped at the receptionist.

'A general detox is part of the Champney's experience sir.'

'I don't think I'll cope. I can't survive on mountains of muesli and rocket salad. Life is too short. Oh well. Hopefully death will soon intervene.' He smirked.

'We have a good programme of facials and other treatments on offer.'

'Let's make the most of it. Hopefully it will help your face to recover.' Gina reassured.

The more a healthy regime was thrown at him the more he rebelled. He loved the clink of ice and the vibrant slice of lime in a double gin and tonic. He liked to spend time choosing the most sinful dessert in a restaurant. And in the quaint little tearoom, Belinda's in Arundel he boldly told the shy waitress that he'd like the full cream tea with extra clotted cream and jam because it was 'a wonderful gastronomic wank.' The crimson blush of the waitress' face toned well with the strawberry jam set in bowls on the dark oak tables. On other occasions he might ask for 'a heart attack tea with as much cholesterol as you can fit on the plate, with no statins please.' It was hardly the reaction you would expect from a man who had in fact suffered a heart attack.

Clifford's face felt no better after the spa facials. This was going to be a long illness.

But Bells was the least of his problems. A new problem was now on the horizon. With the constant moving of houses Clifford had lost track of which authorities he had updated. It had been a struggle finding rentals, organizing the move, packing, unpacking, sorting things out. Each time he moved it had become inevitable that something would be forgotten, overlooked or get lost in the moving process.

When he left the marital home it had been in a hurry. Emotions were running high and it was hard under those circumstances to get organized. He had overlooked informing the DVLA of his new address and several rentals on had completely forgotten to do so.

And so it was a complete surprise to receive a letter from the DVLA asking him to update his information. He had recently changed his car and this had alerted the DVLA to the change of address.

He was reading the letter over breakfast massaging his face. The slightest stress seemed to cause stabbing pains in his cheeks.

'The ex didn't have the decency to forward my mail on to me. Probably just binned all the car tax reminders.'

'Well it's hardly her job to be your secretary - beyond the call of duty.'

'She had an injunction to stop me returning there. I couldn't go and pick the post up. I don't think I've ever had this much contempt for another human being.'

He filled out the paperwork and returned it to the DVLA. He thought that was the end of the matter. A simple change of address, an updated driving licence. But several weeks later the DVLA wrote to him again, in response to their questions asking him to declare any medical conditions. He had informed them of his glaucoma. He hadn't thought anything of it. It had never affected his ability to drive before now. The DVLA it seemed, were unaware that he had glaucoma. Now they were asking him to have a fields test and notify them of the result before they could produce an updated driving licence.

'More hassle. Not had a fields test in a while. Never had an issue with fields or acuity. I should pass it.'

'You've been complaining a lot about your eyes lately. You sure about that?'

'I'm just getting old and it's a gloomy time of year to see properly.'

'What about what happened at that hotel last week when you were on business.'

He laughed as he remembered pouring coffee in the atrium restaurant with an upside down cup.

'I probably had a hangover.'

He failed the fields test. He'd had an ominous feeling about it all. Nothing seemed to go right for him anymore. The DVLA were notified of the results. But he wasn't too worried. He certainly didn't expect the next letter which arrived a couple of weeks later.

When the brown enveloped arrived he was picking up the car keys to his Audi A4 about to drive to Heathrow. He fingered the letter, turned it over in his hand a couple of times. He wondered whether to put it on the windowsill and open it on his return from China.

Fingering the envelope his mind reeled back to the landmark day he'd passed his test in North London years ago. Next to the birth of Ben - passing his driving test had been the most amazing day of his life. It had been his mechanical bar mitzvah - the passport to freedom and pleasure. He could control his destiny at last. He had truly entered adulthood and all that embraced.

That first evening following passing his driving test he'd showered, changed into smarter clothes as if he were dating the car rather than a girl. He couldn't explain the symbiosis, only that each time he'd opened the car door, stepping inside he felt liberated, sexually charged, ready for action in a way he had never felt until that day. The evening had been memorable in more ways than one. With mobility came sexual freedom and a new status that getting a number ten bus into town simply hadn't achieved. In those days he could line up all the beautiful labia for tasting.

Cruising round North London he'd driven through an area of Finsbury Park not realizing it was a red light district. Those were the days of kerb crawling. Through the driving rain he saw a woman waving at him to stop and in his naivety he thought she needed help so he wound down the window and she asked if he wanted to do business. Suddenly the penny dropped. The car made him feel like a real man. In a flash he had one of those 'fuck it' moments and thought 'hell why not?' They went to a cheap hotel and afterwards he felt as if he had emptied his bollocks into a toilet and couldn't wait to escape the shame. But as he stepped back into his metal monster he was in a different world again. This was his safety, his security, his friend.

He looked again at the envelope. Everything's up for sale he silently told himself. Women, cars... even false driving licences.

Life was cheap, he thought to himself. He only had to read the statistics of men dying in Afganistan to know that.

If he wanted a Greek to wipe his bum, a Romanian to lick his arse, a pair of smelly panties, adult nappies... it was all out there for sale. There was no end to the depravity. And everything made possible by the internet. But life was also not to be taken for granted. Various morals played a game inside his head. In a flash he saw driving as a privilege. And his licence a precious document he had earned. Had he taken it all for granted? Assumed he would be driving for the rest of his life?

He opened the envelope. Read the inevitable. In a daze he walked back to the peg in the kitchen where he hung his keys. He hovered at the peg for some time. Took the keys down again. Clasped them tight in his hand making a fist. Unclasped his hand. Twirled the keys round several times. Looked through the window at the stationery car. Just one more spin? He asked himself. He could claim ignorance and say he left the house before the post arrived. Just one last spin. He agonised; clasped the keys tight a rabbit caught in the headlights frozen to the spot. He closed his eyes imagining the breeze and the blue sky and his hands on the wheel. One last time, an inner voice spoke. But sense won the day. He placed them back. Never again would he be turning that key in the ignition. Never again would he feel the tyres scrape upon the gravel, his foot on the accelerator.

He took his licence from the drawer, the piece of paper that had given him his freedom for so many years and placed it in the brown envelope marked DVLA, Swansea, SA99 1AR and sealed the end of his driving days before he had a chance to consider doing something stupid he'd later regret. He couldn't believe he was returning it without a fight. This wasn't how he normally reacted to bad news. But he didn't see, at that moment what else he could do. This was a Government agency. There was no alternative but to send it back.

He went back to the window. Looked out at the car, almost too sick to look. She glinted and gleamed in all her innocence and then he wept - huge, uncontrollable sobs.

It had taken Clifford a week to master the strength, the courage to tell Gina. Admitting he could no longer drive was rather like admitting to impotence, or unemployment. It was a weakness, a tumour that had been allowed to grow and become inoperable.

'I was dumb. I ignored the disease for the best part of fifteen years. I didn't take the eye drops because they made my eyes sore. How pathetic is that? I can't turn back the clock. It's all too late.'

He huddled over the pine kitchen table, crumbled and broken kneading his face.

'With my background how stupid is that? Now I'll pay the price. I'll probably lose all my sight in less than a decade. Maybe faster. Nobody knows. You won't want to be with a blind beggar.' He looked up still slumped, his eyes questioning.

'You need a second opinion.' Gina started tidying the bits and pieces on the table.

'I know enough about glaucoma by now to know that the end game is blindness. It's just that no one can work out the speed it's going to happen.'

He didn't say anymore. He hoped she would take in the enormity of it all because he certainly hadn't. He felt paralysed. He didn't want to have to think about the reality of never driving again and all that entailed, let alone the nightmare prospect of ultimately going blind.

But it wasn't going to come to that. He was certain of that much. In the past few days he had been googling various 'end it' sites. It would be Beachy Head long before the lights went out.

'Surely they can work at preserving what sight you do have left. You'll have to start taking the drops. I don't know why you didn't ask the doctor for a different one years ago that wouldn't make your eyes sore.'

'Glaucoma doesn't obey any laws. 20% loss of fields this year doesn't mean 40% next year. It could mean more. It could mean less. Right now I've got other problems – work related. There's not much more the universe can take from me.'

'I'm here, you know.' Gina walked around the table that had divided them, leant down, buried her head in his neck.

'Do you still want this bear? Even if this bear is broken? You can walk away. You're young. Still fit. It wouldn't take you long to find someone new. You don't want to be saddled for the rest of your life with nursing me.'

'Don't say that.' Gina's eyes were starting to well. She gently pressed her thumb to his eye, blotting a tear away.

'I love your brown eyes. You won't go blind. You've got to stay positive. What else can you do?'

'We've got to be realistic. I don't want to be here broken and possibly broke because that's no good for you. I was supposed to look after you... at least that was my plan. Its like not being able to get a hard on I suppose - a general feeling of impotence. All I need now is a lower member of the tribe to start challenging me - like in the nature films when the old head of the pride of lions has to leave and die in the wilderness.'

Clifford sat at his laptop massaging his face.

'You've been pouring over that laptop every evening lately. It's not good for your sore eye. I hope you're taking the eye drops for the Bells. It won't help the recovery staring at a screen for hours.'

'You sound like my fucking mother. Oh God I wonder how she is. These days I hardly think of her.'

'Ben visits her doesn't he?'

'Yes. Only because the care home is near his college. Don't think he'd bother otherwise. I don't think she knows who he is.'

'So what are you looking at?'

'The more I read about glaucoma I don't think I should accept the decision of the DVLA. There are a lot of different opinions out there. It's not straight-forward. There's was more to it all than I'd originally thought.'

His feelings were changing.

'I'm going to challenge the decision.'

Gina stood behind him and rubbed his neck. Then she gently stroked the sore side of his face.

'I shall book an appointment to see the doc' and get referred to a private ophthalmologist.'

'What's the point?' Gina asked. 'At some point you'll have to accept the results. I know the truth is hard. I can drive you around.' She wrapped her arms around him.

' I'd make an awful passenger. I'm not going to have my life restricted in that way. I've been doing a lot of reading. There's a very sound case to appeal against their decision. The optician in Haywards Heath used a device called a perimeter which is a pretty crude assessment. It worked on old 3.5 inch disks which means its years old. At least twenty. There's another paper from one of the diabetic support groups which picks up its weaknesses. And that's why I'll use a lawyer to tear down the arguments. Obviously I'll only appeal if the medical evidence stands up to knock what the DVLA have said and right now I'm convinced it will. A grand or two in legal costs isn't much as far as I'm concerned.'

' I guess you're used to throwing money at problems.'

'What's the point in earning it if it can't make a difference?'

'Lawyers aren't always the answer.'

'Yeah well we differ on that. But if the fields are going in the 20° central field of view I'd have black spots in my vision when I read. But I don't. If there was central vision loss it would be end stage glaucoma which means blindness soon. The treatment for that is simple enough... Beachy Head.

I've read up quite a bit. The Glaucoma Association had a leaflet on driving and glaucoma. I'll send you the link. The DVLA test is a pretty crude test; testing both eyes at once. That's why I need to be referred to a private practitioner. The test that opticians use is basically a very easy, effective way of removing perhaps 40,000 drivers off the road every couple of years. And how many will bother contesting it I wonder?'

Clifford was standing now. Air filled his lungs as he gained in passion at each point he was making. She was witnessing the butterfly emerge from its' chrysalis.

'Then take into account others with medical issues and you can cull a lot of drivers in a country which has too many cars on the roads anyway. A good freedom of information request I think? How many revocations are there per annum and for what reasons?'

He was near to shouting his point spitting each word like venom from a snake. He moved round the pine table gripping each chair.

'I don't know Cliff.'

'I'm going to consult a solicitor. It will be a justifiable legal expense and I will appeal if the medical evidence is sound. There may even be a case for getting damages from the DVLA. Pain and distress?'

'So what did the leaflet from the Glaucoma Association say?'

'I'll pull it up. Wait a minute.' Clifford soon had the leaflet on the screen. 'Listen carefully.' He read slowly.

'Glaucoma damages the off centre parts of the field of vision first and does not affect the central detailed vision until the late stages of the condition.' He paused. 'See? Later stages. No way I'm in the later stages. I'd be practically blind if I was.'

He scrolled on. 'Arh, listen to this bit. The danger comes, especially in driving, when the damaged areas in each eye overlap: instead of an accurate combined visual picture the brain will insert the missing parts from memory and the driver will have no idea that this is happening. This may give a dangerously inaccurate picture. See? It's bollocks. There's nothing wrong with my driving. I've been driving for years.'

'Well I've noticed...'

'Noticed what? Spit it out.'

'Well. You don't drive as you used to.'

'There's nothing wrong with my driving. I drove 800 miles down the east coast of the States only a few months back. I could drive to Heathrow blind folded. These idiots think I'm a fool.'

'They don't. They just have a duty to protect people on the roads. They're only doing their job.' Gina went to make a cup of tea.

' They're just trying to drive people off the road. Oh and another thing the law has altered quite a bit on disability rules and driving. The European Commission changed the standards some years ago. Before that change I would have been fine to drive because the UK government didn't see that it was a problem.'

'So? What's that got to do with anything? The law changes over time because its about progress and improvement.'

'But small visual impairments don't necessarily result in accidents. What about all the drunks out there? What about you for starters? How many times have you nearly fallen asleep at the wheel?'

'I get tired. But it's my responsibility to pull over and have a break.' Gina poured boiling water into two mugs.

'There are plenty of irresponsible drivers out there and possibly thousands that have undiagnosed glaucoma. It's an insidious illness that goes unnoticed until its advanced.'

Clifford felt sure his driving days weren't over. Was he right?

23
Clifford

December 2010

'Fuck.'

'What?'

'It's a letter from the private ophthalmologist confirming the same results. Advises me not to appeal.'

In the coming weeks he had further appointments at the hospital to establish the extent of optic nerve damage and the optician prescribed him with eye drops, which weren't going to improve his sight but hopefully preserve the sight he had, halting further damage. He dreaded the thought of eventual surgery if the drops couldn't stabilise the pressures, but for now he didn't want to think about that.

He began to notice that things weren't right. He couldn't possibly have continued driving at night or in dim light, or in the bright glare of a sunny day. He frequently held his finger up to his eye, moving it from side to side and up and down, to the centre of his eye, then down while looking ahead. He couldn't see his finger when it was below his eye level. In bright sunshine he started to notice funny patterns, probably where the optic nerve didn't work properly.

'I can still see to wipe my own arse and check the toilet paper for evidence of effective wiping,' he told Gina. All was not lost.

'I've got an idea.' It was a crazy idea but would give him some semblance of independence.

He lifted the lid of his laptop took a swig of coffee, smiled a lob sided smile at Gina who had just returned from dropping Carrie to school.

'My useless mother never taught me to ride a bike.' Riding a bike to the station was therefore not an option. It felt like a double whammy. He couldn't drive and couldn't cycle.

He looked at Gina and rubbed his sore eye. He felt as broken and finished as Hastings Pier.

'I've been thinking about buying a trike with a battery pack. Now I'm on basal insulin my blood levels could hit seven pretty rapidly and if I used a trike every day I think that I can avoid the weight gain associated with insulin use.'

He felt optimistic he could even cut out the insulin altogether if he did some exercise.

Gina drew up a chair, put her arm around him, seemed to be excited for him. She leaned in, cradling her coffee.

'Exercise? Blimey you're beginning to realise then?'

They began to look at pictures of different trikes, studying the specs and designs finding out where he could obtain one and how long it would take.

'I'm not sure any more. Maybe it's not such a great idea. What if it rains? Or I have to wear a suit? And it would take too long to get around. Oh fuck Gina. My life's over.'

'I thought your optimism wouldn't last. You always worry about stuff in the middle of the night. Go back to sleep.'

'How can I? My face keeps me awake. Stabbing pains. I can't shut my eye. You have no idea what it's like.'

Clifford had returned to his usual downcast self. If he could convince Gina to move to the coast near his work that might be one answer. House prices were cheaper down there in any case. But Gina wasn't keen. She was constantly saying she didn't want to change the kids' schools. Schools everywhere were shit and run of the mill. It wasn't going to make a scrap of difference where they went. But she refused to contemplate the idea, despite him bringing home lots of specs of beautiful big houses.

Clifford sat on the windy station platform. Getting a train each day to work had become a daily grind. He stared at chewing gum on the platform, watching feet as they passed by.

The only way out of his struggle seemed to be to sell the business. It was his only option. He could see the future - blind in need of 24 hour care. Was that going to be Gina? He didn't want to burden her for the rest of her life. She was young. She had her own responsibilities. He felt more alone than he had ever felt. She was too new in his life to fully accept these challenges ahead. They didn't have the special bonding glue, the lifetime of shared history to make it work under trying circumstances. But he loved her. He cared for her more deeply than he had ever cared for another woman. He had known that for a long time. But life with Gina was no bed of roses; more a bed of Leylandii. How on earth were they going to make it work? He hadn't the foggiest; neither did she. And both of them had long stopped talking about marriage.

Clifford shook his head, stared at the posters opposite. Marriage. What on earth had he been thinking? The subject had dropped off the radar but he couldn't remember when that had happened. It all seemed irrelevant now, a fairytale dream that wasn't going to happen.

Gina booked tickets for the kids to go ice skating at the Dome in Brighton, then the American Diner for dinner. It seemed obvious to Clifford that they would drive down.

'I never drive to Brighton. That's ridiculous. Who wants to sit in endless traffic from the end of the A23 right to the seafront, drive round and round looking for a parking space? It's horrendously busy at this time of year.'

'A bus? You are joking?' Never before had he felt so powerless.

'Yes. We can take the bus. It makes sense. The bus stop is outside the house. If you don't use public transport it will disappear. All we have to do is glide on, sit back and enjoy the view and not have to worry about parking or getting stressed in a traffic queue. And it will be a treat for the kids.'

'A treat? Fucking listen to yourself.'

She put her hat and gloves on and they trudged out of the door. He expected her to change her mind once she reached the bus stop and worked out how ludicrous the idea was. But the bus had arrived and they all clambered up the steps. He stood on the pavement protesting and pleading with her. He wanted to go with them.

'You bitch. You're doing this to wind me up. How dare you humiliate me.' He called up. Put one foot on the bus, one hand on the rail.

'This is strictly a one off. I'm not fucking doing it again.'

He felt like a muzzled dog on a chain as he slumped into a worn grey seat at the very back. It was as if the key had been thrown away, great iron bars descending all around him as he fought bitterly to retain his freedom. He was slowly being choked by climbing ivy. He could still visualize his gleaming car on the driveway. And now when he came home each evening on the train there was an empty parking space. It felt like the car had been abducted by aliens; a surreal feeling. He kept thinking he would wake up and realise it had been a nasty dream. Being without a car didn't feel permanent. It was like losing a leg. How was he going to survive long term?

Saria and Joss sat in the opposite corner, no coats despite the winter. Saria even had a mini skirt on.

'Why the hell haven't you lot brought a coat with you? It's December. That means long sleeves, long trousers and definitely coats. You're both badly cared for. You're nothing but a pair of tramps. Very fitting that we should be on a bus.'

He looked at Saria's bare legs and skirt.

'Oh well if we get short of money we know the next business.' He watched her squirm at the comment, folding her legs throughout the journey attempting to pull her skirt lower.

'I quite like going on the bus. It's nice to be free of the constraints of the car. No parking nightmares. No extortionate charges in the NCP. And you can chat to strangers it's so sociable. I love to watch the world go by. It's great.'

'You're doing this deliberately aren't you? It's all about rubbing my nose in my misfortune. Well I didn't have you down as such a cow.'

'Of course I'm not. Why would I do that?'

He didn't like her cheery attitude. Was she an idiot or did she just love mixing with the plebs?

'Right now I can see that it would be rather nice to be a suicide bomber on a bus, or a train. If I could only pull the cord of my rucksack and that would be the end of all of us - great way to end my miserable little existence.

A whole manner of scum get on buses. Look at them all. Buses are full of smelly people, fat people, ignorant people using a seat for their shopping, buggies and mobiles ringing and teenagers texting or sexting. People who think they are cool not holding on then they collapse into your lap stinking of B.O. And twats holding a conversation with the driver. What was that all about? You don't go into the kitchen of a restaurant and start casually chatting to the chef so why talk to a bus driver?'

'Only men stink of B.O. Women glow. Think about the bus as a micro society. It's nice to chat to strangers. It's sociable. I like it.' Gina retorted.

'Well you would. I despise the way so many people rely on the state for transport. They're uncomfortable, they rattle along, stink and in the summer sweat drips off you because the driver can't turn the heating off. They're slow. Trundling all over the countryside. We're going to take a taxi home. That's the end of it.'

'A taxi? So basically the money saved is going to be wasted on a taxi back?'

Clifford enjoyed the shock descending on her face.

'Buses are the biggest gas guzzlers on the road. They burn diesel at a rate of a gallon every 3 miles. Cars are more efficient. If we stay together you better get used to driving me around.'

'Well all I can say is you're lucky we aren't on a bus in India with poultry and cockroaches and near death experiences at every corner. You're going to have to accept this big life change and make adjustments. There's not much else you can do.' Gina sniffed and turned to look out of the window.

Clifford had spent his whole life fighting: women, business partners, the authorities, as he found his way round loop holes, sidestepping road blocks, throwing money at issues and difficulties.

But this time there was no fight. His driving days were over. And over the next few months while he never came to terms with his fate he did begin to think about how he could make his life easier.

His greatest difficulty was work: getting to the coast each day and trips to the States and other countries involved driving between factories, between conferences. Not being able to drive was inconvenient and would affect the business in a huge way. Customers expected him to visit them. Skype calls weren't a substitute. Again, Gina seemed to have the smart answer. 'Employ someone just to drive then.' But it wasn't a clever answer. He didn't want to shell out more in salaries. He didn't want to be driven. And he'd have to pay for air flights for the driver, hotel costs. No. It was a shit idea.

And so in the meantime, until he could work out some solutions he was stuck with a ghastly routine of taking the train to work, listening to the same announcements on the platform, sitting on a windy platform at 7 in the frigging morning.

When he stood on the platform and alighted the train all he could see around him were society's failures, rejects, misfits and odd balls gathered together. He was part of their club now. They were the kids he'd loathed at school. People who could no longer drive, people who had no confidence to drive, too old to drive, too mental to drive. People on crutches, fat women in tight pink leggings chewing gum, bent over old ladies, paraplegics in wheelchairs. White trash of all shapes and sizes. The toothless, hooped earrings, tattoos, peroxide hair, screechy kids. Kids in flimsy buggies, Primark clothing. He wanted to line them all up, shoot them one by one, then turn the gun on himself. In a sea of faces they jumped out at him, poking and prodding and filling his head space. They became etched in his mind, a herd of elephants stamping and crashing in his brain. He was one of them; sinking into a quagmire a melting pit of despair. He couldn't climb out. He hadn't the strength. He couldn't see. It was all too late. And in truth he didn't want to be rescued. Rescued by whom? A bleeding heart liberal, pedigree dog face, overbred, very nice but dim counselor or clergyman. But old age, illness wasn't for sissys. He was staring up from the bottom of the well of self pity and despair.

As the first Crapital Connect made its' way down to the coast each morning he imagined he was on a journey to hell. He was in Cormac McCarthy's 'The Road.' This was his own personal catastrophe: Burger King coke cartons at his feet, sweet wrappers littering the seats, chewing gum stuck to the floor -sickly sweet smells of bodies and perfume in mortal combat. His world was burned to cinders. The trees were bare, the landscape bleak, dark and foreboding. Rain whipped and lashed at the windows.

The train clattered, rattled, glided and jolted. The passengers were zombies staring ahead and out. Moron faces going nowhere. Outside a dark mass of fields stretched to eternity. Corrugated roofing of warehouses, rows and rows of drab little houses, crammed in, boxes of glass tacked on the back. Divorcees mortgaged until death swallowed them, stuck in an apocalyptic nightmare. Everybody in post industrial, post Northern Rock meltdown. There was no wealth in these little boxes lined up by the track. They were piles of debt just getting bigger and bigger while people carried on spending what they weren't earning. Clifford looked at the houses and thought how like a tin of sardines life was. Everybody struggling to escape, searching for that sardine tin key.

The train journey was his test of endurance. Resting back, closing his eyes he wished that he could just switch himself off like an electrical device. Inside his head he was writing a suicide note. He imagined himself lying on the tracks below.

He wondered if this daily day dream would ever be any more than a day dream.

24
Clifford

December 2010

He woke to a racing heart. Was he having another heart attack? He felt clammy. Wondered where he was. And then he recognized the room: the cracked artex ceiling, the mirrors, the sheep in the field outside, the white floor boarding. Reality hit. It felt as if his recent life had been one long swim through sewerage with no exit pipe. For a time he lay on his back, his great belly escaping either side of his torso.

He turned to watch Gina sleeping; then felt her warm buttocks and the slippery crack. She reminded him of a toilet on display on a raised platform in John Lewis: clean and safe.

'The RAF are coming to bomb the target to smithereens. I want to leave you with a dollop of something to remember me by,' he whispered in her ear. She turned, nestled into the thick mass of grey hair, complaining that it tickled.

'I'm the spunk meister. My father's the fishmonger and I'm the whore monger. Do you have a smelly fanny this morning or can I go for a dipping?'

'You stink of BO. I'd rather be in bed with a Glastonbury toilet.'

Clifford rested one arm on his head. 'You've got the nose of a bloodhound. I should have bought you some Everglade from Poundstretcher for Christmas. You can go round spraying everything you don't like the smell of.'

Clifford huffed. 'I just want to die. Is that so difficult? I feel totally disconnected from you lot. I'm a walking disaster. Even human comfort and physical contact these days does nothing.'

He took his hand away from her pubic mound.

She put her hand to his limp dick, a sleepy animal in a grey nest, hibernating in a perpetual winter.

'We're a train wreckage Gina.'

She carried on touching around his saggy genitalia until he pushed her hand away and took her firm nipples in his hands.

'Are your tits going to give me the comfort I need? Your body's a playground. I wish life was a playground. Which part of your playground do I explore first? Your body's a clean toilet for me to trash.'

He moved down, teasing a nipple with his tongue, flicking then gently, pulling with his teeth.

'I'm waiting to find the braille on your skin to guide me. Is that what it will be like when I'm blind?' He huffed again. 'I wonder what fanny juice tastes like after death.'

'There are only two rides in my playground. Tits and fanny.'

Clifford loved to watch her thrashing her head from side to side like a wild animal in Africa, as he licked and sucked. She looked possessed when she came: a look which calmed to a faraway, drugged mist in her eyes; stillness and exhaustion transforming her face to airbrushed porcelain.

He loved to lick. These days it was only thing he was good at. She was whispering '*put it up me now, up me.*' She was like a Punjabi script. But he couldn't. He wanted to. He loved it when her fanny vacuumed him. He wanted to feel his body rising and being torn open and that pleasurable exhaustion that followed. But it was no good. There would be another hydraulic failure. When it worked he knew it was like Mr. Kipling sex... exceedingly good. But times like that were rare.

'It's asleep. I'm happy just for your fanny juice to decompose on my face. It's still lovely. I remember the first time I ever went down on you. Then I filled the car at the Shell Garage. I walked in to pay smelling of you all over my face. Some people jump up and shower off the dirty deed. I don't. But these days I'm just old British fuel.'

Christmas, during much of his adulthood was a very important occasion for Clifford because as the child of Jewish parents his family had never celebrated it. It was a confused upbringing. At school there had been too much Jesus: hymns and carols and dressing up in ridiculous costumes to perform on a stage as a shepherd or a lamb. He hadn't really understood what it was all about, just the feeling of being the odd one out.

At home Christmas had been just a day off. They exchanged a few presents but there was no turkey or Christmas tree. As a small child he wondered what the room would look like with a tree in the corner. It seemed such an odd thing to do. The Christmas of his youth had been a kit with missing and broken pieces. He remembered watching war films and cowboy films on Christmas day and a coal fire would burn in the front room and he would cry when the horse fell.

Yom Kippur was the most miserable day of the year, as he sat with all the other three times a year Synagogue attenders, not knowing whether to sit stand and where to leap to next, in the prayer book. He hated the confusion of the faith he was born into and the simplicity of the faith of his school as much as he would later hate Margaret Thatcher.

But as he emerged into adulthood Christmas seemed to beckon him –a magical allure of something forbidden, frivolous and exciting but at the same time silly. Being part of Christmas meant he wasn't a minority group, on the fringes of society, excluded from what everybody else was involved in and enjoying.

After Ben was born he aimed for a bigger and fuller tree than the previous year with more and brighter decorations that sparkled and glittered. It was liberating and modern. He felt naughty, slightly guilty. He loved the feeling of defiance that Christmas gave him. He hated the way his in laws had held onto the gastronomic, restrictive culture of the Jewish faith, with an almost racial superiority of the flock. He couldn't understand why they wanted to exclude themselves from the rest of society, turning up to dinner parties not being able to eat the food or properly join in. It was madness to Clifford. Each year he'd tried to change them but they resolutely brought along their own food. They were incredulous of the tree. He'd loved to see their shocked faces. And he'd ask them 'why not?' Having a tree was like having a dog. Another thing he hadn't be allowed to have as a child.

But this year was slightly different. Clifford wasn't in the festive cheer. He couldn't tour the farms in his car, looking for the greenest, fullest spruce. He was dreading the usual routine of her kids escaping to their rooms, not being a part of the occasion and his son making a short perfunctory appearance.

It was Christmas Eve. They were languishing in bed. It was getting late. Clifford had enjoyed his post coital orange. The sweet fragrance filled the air. The curled peel had been tossed onto the floor and the pips poked their bare bottoms in bed. The dregs of a Baileys lay sticky at the bottom of wine glasses.

'Well tomorrow night we won't be having sex because turkey farts put me right off sex.' And then he started to sing, his face a weasel.

'The smell of turkey up ya bum is really quite a shocker. The smell of faeces in the drain is really quite a bane.' And then the song fell flat. Clifford flunked his head back onto the pillow.

A few minutes later he sprung to life with another attempt and a different tune. 'Let it snow let it snow, let it snow... oh my outer lips are pulsating.'

He turned towards Gina, slipping a finger between her vaginal lips.

'My outer lips are pulsating and I should be masturbating... since there's nothing else to do let us screw, let us screw, let us screw.' He struggled up into a sitting position, his belly wobbly with the laughter and unwrapped his 5th or 6th liquor. Gina had tried to get him to eat diabetic chocolates, but to hell with the bloods.

'God, look at all the liquor wrappers.' Gina pulled the duvet off gasping at the mess.

He was examining the tray of liquors, wondering which one to eat next. 'This tray is a bit like the bar on the Titanic. I wouldn't have dressed in a penquin suit to play music on the decks. I would have asked the sea to take me. I feel like the Captain; drowning in style.'

'And I bet the ladies wouldn't have waved the cake trolley away if they had known.'

'Christ. This bed is full of semen stains, grey curly pubes, crumbs, wrappers, old farts, tissues, debris, rubbish. It's like Tower Hamlets. And what a stuck up place this village is. I was telling the taxi driver the other day that it's full of Tory voters. He said it's a nice place. Well I'm soon out of here.'

'Where are you going then? You didn't tell me. Your moods are constantly up and down like a yo yo. I can't keep up.'

'You won't come with me. I know that much. You won't put 600 miles between the kids and those semen donors. And why would you want to look after a blind man? There's no reason why you should saddle yourself with a defective product. Your kids don't want me here either. I can't put up with any more stifling and unbearable silences around the table. Christ, I'm not looking forward to tomorrow.'

And with that he pulled the duvet over his head sending liquor wrappers spinning, the tray tossing to the floor.

The kitchen was filled with the smell of cooking, the windows were misty with condensation and Clifford and Ben were busy singing songs. For a short time they were friends again as they prepared the lunch together. Saria and Joss were in their rooms on computers and Gina's mother who had to be persuaded to come was reading stories to Carrie in the lounge.

Clifford poured himself a third glass of red wine then began to waltz across the kitchen with Ben singing to Bing Crosby, 'Oh my partner's just got a stiffy and my fanny's all a whiffy and since there's no place to go this Christmas let it snow let it snow let it snow. My cock is all a throbbing, the fire looks delightful, the baubles of pleasure to be.' Soon the pair fell apart laughing.

Clifford sat down to Christmas lunch. He glanced round the table at the motley collection of people celebrating the day with him. What a pantomime it was. When he'd put his profile on a dating site, all that time back he never imagined sitting down to turkey and sprouts in such an incongruous setting with a dysfunctional bunch of people. His son was inches away but at times felt a million miles away. The singing and the dancing in the kitchen were fleeting acts of father, son bonding. The people gathered around the table were a cut and paste family, constructed from a cheap Christmas cracker.

Clifford raised a glass.

'Well.' He waited for everyone to pick up their glasses.

'Here's to our motley family. Here we are. Three years on from hurricane divorce and the United Nations is still bringing us Christmas dinner in a soup kitchen. I had hoped to move from the tent to a house in those three years, but I've landed in with this travelling circus. Three white rabbits who disappear when placed in a glove.'

He looked over at the kids whose faces were in limbo land, balanced between uncertainty and confusion. Gina's mother was the only one laughing. She was such a sweet innocent old lady. She probably didn't understand what he was saying.

'And that big bloated robin in the middle of the table is living on the fat of past credit. It should be a thin scrawny robin, a Cameron Clegg austerity robin.'

They began to eat. They were strangers around a table with fractured lives and broken pasts. He chatted with Ben about the people who used to be in their lives. And Gina chatted to her mother. The kids quietly bickered or ate.

'Well I'm sorry I forgot the stuffing. We're having an Alzheimer's Christmas this year. The Brussels and parsnips are a bit hard, the turkey's a bit too dry because the oven here is crap. Still, later on we'll have turkey and cranberry sandwiches and they'll look like I've murdered your three kids between two slices of bread... which of course, I'm sure I will if we're all still together next Christmas.' He laughed loudly, raising his glass again and gulping a mouthful wondered why Santa hadn't thrown a few hand grenades down the chimney over night. But then he realized that the only bomb delivered in his life was a useless pair of eyes and diabetes.

Gina's mother was laughing too, tears forming in her eyes.

'He is funny Gina. Where did you find him dear? At your local Tory club?'

'Were you warm enough last night by the way? We kept the heating on all night for you' Clifford asked Gina's mother. 'I hope you didn't sleep in the gammon sandwich you bought with you?'

'Oh plenty warm enough thank you dear. I've had to give up on hot water bottles. They just keep leaking.'

'You're probably incontinent and don't yet realise it.'

He enjoyed the shocked look from Saria and Gina. He watched the spray of fine brown gloop hit the clean red tablecloth and the big bloated robin through the spluttered laughter of his son and the blank expression of the woman who would have been his future mother in law.

'All the folk where I live seem to be using pads these days. I hope I won't be next. They all seem to be dying.'

' Put enough old folk in one place they do tend to die.' Clifford was quick to retort.

'Watch the gravy Ben. Use a napkin,' he ordered. 'Gravy is culinary hell. They serve it at all the nasty carvery chains. It's basically hot vicous engine oil draining from a sump. Anyone thought of it like that?' Clifford looked round the table.

'It's a very tasty dinner Clifford. I'm enjoying it dear. The gravy's not too thick. Not too thin.'

Clifford dismissed the compliment.

'It's fresh sludge piped through to your table from the local sewer farm. It's an amazing process you know to process raw sewer. You're basically taking out all the solid matter.'

Gina's mother had her next mouthful poised in mid air; fork hovering at her lips, uncertain whether to continue it's journey.

He was enjoying her hesitation. 'There's a glutinous warm sweet Christmas pudding to follow with delectable nuts and stickiness. I love the feeling of being pissed and the best defecation ever at the end of Christmas day. It's really quite something.'

Her mother put down the fork. Her laughter had turned to a blank look. She clearly didn't quite know how to respond. Saria and Gina were exchanging looks of embarrassed disgust.

'What a lovely meal dear.' Jesus, Clifford thought. Doesn't she have anything other than pleasantries to say?

'I don't think I can eat any more dear. It was so tasty and so very...... different. The turkey was tender, not too dry. That was plenty for me dear. Don't throw the rest away. I can wrap it up in tin foil and take it home with me'.

'Can I have more skin. I like the crispy skin' Carrie asked pointing with a greasy finger.

Clifford placed some skin on her plate. 'There you are, enjoy that bit of crispy foreskin.'

'What is the other meat on my plate?' Carrie asked innocently.

'You've got the turkey's thigh. The rest of the turkey's in a wheelchair. It had it's legs blown off in Afganistan.'

'Dad. Shut up will you. Just shut up' Ben had turned angry. 'There are men out there my age fighting. So just shut it. They're coming back in body bags or they're screwed up mentally and end up on the streets.'

A while later Gina asked Saria 'you're very quiet.'

'Your lot are always silent' Clifford responded. 'We have to insert a sim card for conversation, but the USB is fucked.'

Saria shrugged. ' I was quiet because of that comment about the turkey skin. And the weirdo comment about the gravy.'

'Well.' Clifford gave a big sigh. ' That was a successful lunch. And you won't have to put up with me much longer, Saria.' Sarcasm dripped like gravy.

Anyone for a Waitrose cracker? That would liven you all up.'

'I'll have a cracker.' It was the first thing Joss had said all meal.

'Be nice if you were crackers, boy.' Clifford reached out a hand and ruffled Joss' hair.

Ben left soon after lunch probably going on to see his mother. The thought of him seeing his mother filled Clifford yet again with anger.

Clifford stoked the fire in the sitting room as they all started to watch 'The Sound of Music.' This was the very first evening they had all sat in the room together, squeezed in on his leather settees and he had a very strong feeling it was going to be the last. He didn't have a plan for 2011 but he felt sure it didn't involve Gina and her dysfunctional kids. He loved her and wished they had met years ago, when they had no health challenges or baggage or painful history and a real chance of making a go of it.

Quite where his bags and boxes would land next he didn't know.

He took solace in the box of Quality Streets sitting on the coffee table. 'Anyone for an inequality street? Delve deep into the tin who'ill find the Poundstretcher, the homeless, MPs on the fiddle, Fred Goodwin drawing his massive pension.'

'Have you kids never watched 'The Sound Of Music' then?' He asked.

'I don't think they have,' Gina put the tin down.

Clifford sloshed back a swig of tea, took a large bite of mince pie. He'd always considered Quality Street to be an essential element of Christmas.

'There's some great music in this film and innuendo in every song. It feels like she's singing about my life.' And then Clifford broke into song changing the words of 'A Few of My Favourite Things,' as he went.

'Chocolate muffins and fannies, a gin and a whiskey, a brussel sprout bottom and a small turkey twizzler will be a dazzler in the toilet, with the help of Victoza. These are a few of my favourite things.

My driving is over, I'm striving for closure, I'll find my way of surviving. I'm considering my options when the eyes grow dimmer when the options look thinner, then I'll simply remember my favourite things.

A mother in a care home, I bid her shalom and a son who detests me. A business sale might fail, but I don't want a wanker for a banker or a half life with a new wife. These are a few of my favourite things.

When the kidney and the heart are fucked, I know I'm lucked out, I can't feel my feet and my muscles are dead meat. Then I'll remember the shit kit life I've had and the few of my favourite things.'

At the end of the song he noticed that the kids had quietly left the room but Gina was still perched on a wooden chair next to him stubbornly refusing to sit in his settee because she found it too cold.

'See. What a surprise. Your brats have sloped off again. You need to tell them how I feel.'

Boxing Day for Clifford was possibly the worst he had ever experienced. They took Gina's mother back to Maidstone.

'Can we have a good look round the DFS before you drop me home dear?' her mother asked, clutching leftover turkey wrapped in foil and a carrier containing her gifts – soap, talc and a pair of fluffy bed socks.

'I haven't been here in a long time.' Her mother said. 'Would be nice to look for a coffee table. I've been trying to find one for a long time. A nest of small tables in a dark oak. Is this the one that has fresh warm cookies and coffee? What a lovely treat. I hope they've got a cosy settee we can all sit on. Not being able to drive anymore has made me really appreciate these little trips out.'

They placed their polystyrene cups on a coffee table called Nathan.

'This has to be the worst place to take someone on Boxing Day -someone that doesn't have a house to buy furniture for. You just enjoy taking the piss out of me Gina. Like when you insisted on taking the bus to Brighton. It's all one big humiliation exercise. Next it's going to be a car showroom. Christ. That would be the end.'

'Oh stop it. My mother likes coming here. She doesn't get out much. It's a treat.'

'I may never own a home again. I have no home but I pay two grand in rent a month on a house with a leaking conservatory and broken patio.'

Clifford was fuming. He made his way to the exit, pacing up and down until they had finished their coffees and fill of chocolate chip cookies. What a Christmas it had been.

Would the New Year be any better he wondered.

25
Gina

January 2011

'You're back early. What's up?' Gina asked as Clifford slumped into his leather settee. His face looked ashen.

'I don't like my son any more. He's a c u next Tuesday.'

Gina knew he didn't mean it. It was painted all over his body language. He looked sad, deflated.

'I'll put the kettle on.'

Gina took a couple of mugs from the cupboard. She heard him huffing. Then he flicked the TV on.

He was a bastard – but one she couldn't help loving and feeling sorry for. He was a capable man but there was something needy about him. Throughout the Bells and the loss of his driving she felt desperately sorry for him. But he never seemed to help himself. His moods seemed to oscillate between increasing high and lows and he refused to climb out of the pit of despair. Each passing day he sunk lower into that pit. She wanted to drag him out but didn't know how. He didn't seem to understand his own emotions so how could she?

During the past months her emotions had lurched from anger to love, from shock to tears in a misty no man's land which felt surreal at times. Sometimes when he was nasty she didn't feel anger; could only see his failings as a human being. He was just a weak and vulnerable man, bitter with life and everyone but inside despite his bravado basic psychology told her he was angry with himself, not really with anyone else.

She handed him a mug.

'We had another row.'

'Not again. What about?'

'Fuck knows.'

'You must have said something.'

'Were you there?' He snapped.

'Well there must have been a reason.'

'He's not himself. He's a crap communicator. One minute he's manic and then the next he's sullen. I can't work him out. I think I called him scum.'

'Well that wouldn't help.'

She sat down. She still loved him but over the past weeks had pulled away little by little watching his moods slide, unable to help, telling herself to put her own future first and above all the kids first.

'Do you think he's depressed?'

'I didn't tell you but last week one of his friends called an ambulance.'

'Shit. For him? Why on earth didn't you tell me? What happened? Was that why you went up to London?'

'Yeah. He was talking rubbish in the middle of the night. He was ranting on. Got abusive. His friends were worried. They didn't know what was going on. He's been sectioned under the Mental Health Act. Is in a special ward at a London hospital with a whole manner of people who couldn't communicate, were freaking out. I'm getting a solicitor to lift it otherwise I'll collect him. It's not the right place for him. He was ranting about me apparently, among other things. Said I'm a useless piece of shit. He's got an appointment to see a psychiatrist. Fuck knows what's going to happen. Maybe he's suffering from schizophrenia. I hope to God's sake he's not. It doesn't bear thinking about.'

Clifford sighed. 'I can't take much more. I'll end up having another heart attack. It feels like a weight is descending. I'm completely overwhelmed.'

Gina perched on the arm of the settee. Schizophrenia was a big and loaded word. Maybe he was just depressed, over worked or stressed. But the more Gina thoughts about it the more she wondered if Clifford was schizophrenic too. He was going through a bad time but his mood swings weren't normal.

Clifford

'I think I've got the solution.'

'Really?' Clifford was talking to the owner of a northern factory in the bar at a conference in the States.

'It's called being a bit creative. Let me make a couple of phone calls, speak to my contacts and I'll give you a bell.'

'I think I've reached the point of being willing to do anything mate.'

Clifford had given up sitting down to breakfast; stood instead at the worktop holding his bowl of muesli, watching everyone else. He still massaged his face as he ate. Eating was still a struggle due to the Bells but he'd had some twitching in his cheek; the feeling was coming back making him wonder if it was starting to get better.

The family breakfasts had broken down. Nobody came down at the same time and everyone served themselves, selfishly taking the last of the milk or the last slice of bread arguing over crockery or which chair they sat in. There was a perfunctory 'morning' from each child, to acknowledge his presence - the baseline of civility. He was biding his time, considering all options.

Joss came down carrying a flask and said morning in an extra loud voice, then told Gina that the flask containing the soup he had made on Friday, at school had pinged open and ruined all his books in his school bag.

'Some bugs don't need oxygen to grow. Christ. You don't teach your kids anything. You shouldn't be left alone with them.'

'Left alone?' Gina swiveled to glare at him. He didn't like the glare. Even she had turned sulky in the mornings.

'I would have thought you would teach them about basic food hygiene.'

'He forgot to take it out of his bag. It's what kids do. Your problem?'

Clifford felt huge despair.

Carrie came into the kitchen with plaited hair, complaining about a wobbly tooth.

'Not going to say good morning then? Have you got dementia this morning?'

'She's got toothache. Give her a break Cliff.' Gina snapped.

'What's in my lunch box?' Carrie asked picking the lunch bag up and pulling at the zip.

'Don't open it. It's all wrapped in foil. Leave it please.' Gina said.

Carrie opened the zip further and started to unwrap the foil.

'Leave it.' Gina pulled it away, did the zip back up.

Then Carrie picked up Gina's car keys from the table and asked why she didn't have a picture key ring.

'Just put them down, hurry up and finish your cereal then we can do some spellings.'

Clifford was watching from behind the worktop. Thankfully he would be leaving for work before the dreaded spelling test began. He couldn't bear listening to the repetition of the same words over and over, words that she had been learning for months now.

It was hard to stand by and watch while all this went on.

'You horrible child. Why don't you just do as you're told? Why are you always doing what you're not supposed to be doing?' His eyes locked with the child's in a mind confrontation which replaced a thousand words she would have spoken with an adult vocabulary. The cold hard stare was back. The one that riled him, ensnarled his emotions. The stare she saved just for him. Goddam it. What was wrong with the kid? He was trying his best to provide.

'I was always told on parenting courses to concentrate on the positive things kids do, not the negative. If you praise the good things children will do more good things.'

He turned away. Carrie's stare had been replaced by a glint of triumph he didn't want to see. Gina was talking bollocks again but what was the point?

'Well that's where you're wrong. That kid doesn't improve,' he said instead avoiding looking at Carrie this time.

'She's trying very hard actually.' Gina shot him a warning look. Carrie picked up her fluffy blanket and started to cuddle Gina.

'Get away from your mother. We've got things to do. Go and sort your damn hair out.'

Carrie went upstairs to find her hairbrush. Her usual distraction when it came to spellings. Her feet thudded on each step, annoyed at having to find the brush herself.

Gina moved towards him, still standing by the worktop, now eating a banana. Clifford wondered what she was going to say. She looked menacing.

She crept feline towards him and in a whispered vicious voice said 'Do you know what? I'd really like to see you with a special needs kid. Someone with Downs or ADHD. I wonder how you would cope.'

She jabbed her finger on the wooden worktop to make her point.

'Is that what she has? I did wonder.' Clifford smirked.

'I think I'd have strangled her by now if she were my kid. *You* didn't have much intelligence to go with the moron in the first place and get pregnant.'

Gina's face suddenly darkened yet looked calm. He wondered what would happen next. Her hatred was like the wind outside. He knew it was real but couldn't see it.

In one swift action she jabbed him in the neck with a finger.

'Don't you fucking...' He was quick. He grabbed her finger, thrust it back at her chest and walked away.

Saria came down, said a robotic 'good morning,' quietly poured some milk over cereal and sat down next to Joss who was eating in silence.

'You're the most sickly annoying boy in the school you know.' Saria digged. Have you looked at your eczema lately? It's all disgusting and flaky. And if you see me in the corridor at school by the way don't say hello because I don't want my friends to know you're my brother.' She said viciously.

Clifford looked at Gina. Waited for her to say something. All she managed was a feeble 'shut up squabbling.' Things were never going to change. Clifford had reached rock bottom with it all.

'I know what I would do with your bitch of a sister, Joss,' he said, huffing. Saria and Joss said nothing as they always did. He thought it errie how they never hit back, acting in unison, never challenging him, docile, apathetic creatures. It was unnatural. What had made them so unresponsive he wondered?

The bitter chill of January of 2011 crept into February. The coldest winter since Met Office records began wasn't relenting.

It was Sunday morning. Snow had fallen heavily overnight. Clifford sat in bed talking to the owner of the northern factory on the phone.

'I'm not sure.' Clifford hesitated. 'It's dangerous and reckless.' His head thumped with the fear of what he was contemplating. He looked outside and noticed how still and fresh it was - a fairy tale world. Snow twinkled under the intense mid morning sun. The country weighed heavy under snow. His mind weighed heavy under the blanket of problems preying upon his mind. Just as the landscape crouched and cowered under the snow, his problems cowered in his mind.

'We all start out being law abiding. Circumstances change all that.'

'How much would it cost?'

'A grand. A grand to get your independence back.'

'And the penalty if I'm caught?'

'Again a grand. That's nothing compared to what you're earning.' The friend chuckled.

'I wonder what the risk is of being stopped.'

'Think of it this way... how many times have you been pulled over in all your years of driving?'

'Once, twice maybe.'

'Exactly. You've got nothing to lose. Just drive carefully and you won't get pulled over.'

He pondered the idea, running the risks through his mind. A little voice kept interjecting, pricking at his conscience. '*Don't do it.*' He tried to ignore it. But the other voice was winning through.

'The law may have decided I can't drive any more but I know I can. I'm perfectly capable.'

'There are so many people on the road who shouldn't be driving. You're not a boy racer or an old git with a walking stick. You're brain is still as sharp as a razor.'

'I'll think about it mate. Shit. Got to go Gina's coming up the stairs.'

She put a coffee on his bedside table and got back into bed.

'Who was that on the phone?' She asked.

'Just business.' He reached over started to massage her breasts with one hand while gripping his i phone with the other. He put the phone down and reached down to shove a finger into her very slippery vagina. He started kissing her back. She was his temporary comfort.

'I'm your antique. Have my name, my wallet', he whispered, nuzzling into her hair. 'Do you want to go back to the 'bring and buy sale'? You're not going to find a better man you know. I'm everything you want. I do it for you Gina. It's time to give up life as a prole.'

She turned and stared at him.

'Do you know how confusing you sound? After all the things you've been saying lately. I thought you wanted to end it. Now you're doing the sales pitch to the church aisle.'

'Maybe I do want to end it. My life I mean. I'd like to die on top of you, pumping away. It would be the perfect way to go.' He thrust his torso into her side and resumed fingering her fanny. Soon he was down between her thighs. He always felt as if he were in another world when her legs were muffs around his head and his tongue was inside her, lapping at the stickiness hearing her whimper. Her fanny was the place of refuge; it was like a perfect crimson red lobster, plump and fresh from Harrods, the finest there was. He would miss all this but what alternative was there? He knew she would never agree to him driving illegally. She wasn't going to insure a car registered in his name and watch him drive off every morning. She was law abiding. Part of him admired that. But part of him resented that. In time he would detest her. If the tables were turned how would she cope, he wondered? It was all too easy to be self righteous and claim you would never break the law but how did anyone know how they might react? Sometimes in life drastic action was called for. You needed to think outside the box to survive.

Soon he was inside her focusing on climbing the mountain; an insurmountable task, higher and higher, each thrust never reaching the summit. He imagined the summit and reaching that target; his boys arriving at destination ovary. He thought of her swelling belly, hard and heavy under the weight of his baby, her tender, engorged breasts suckling. He wanted that so much. It gave him reason to stay with her, a connection between them, greater than the thread of friendship, a purpose to his life and something good to come out of the mess of everything. Holding onto the vision of her naked, sitting cross legged on the bed feeding their baby turned him on in new ways he had never imagined. His cock grew harder, more determined and when he came there was a slight pain and then exhaustion took over.

He buried his head in her neck, panting. Her lemon perfume was still fresh and zesty, a fragrance he wouldn't forget.

'I did consider spunking all over your tits, your face - a kind of Creme Anglaise, or in my case a Creme Yid. But I want you up the duff. So I carried on. I'd like a positive pregnancy test or failing that some sticks of wood to make my coffin - for my birthday please.'

'You're cheerful. As ever,' she tutted.

He took a gulp of air. Braced himself. 'I asked Ben if he would insure a car so that I can drive again.'

Gina prised herself away from him. Their bodies were clammy and sticky and it felt like a Band Aid had been ripped from his body. She sat up, her mouth tight like a cat's backside, her face spread with a *what the fuck* look. She hesitated, making that mental adjustment to his news.

'You're thinking of driving again?'

'Selfish brat - the boy won't do it. After everything I've done for him. We were in a restaurant. He got up pushed his plate across the table and stormed out, leaving me to finish my meal alone and of course pick up the tab. I won't be humiliated by my own son.'

'I'm glad. I would have done the same. It would ruin his career. Bet you didn't think of that.'

'Exactly what he said. He's talking out of his backside. He doesn't want to do anything to help me.'

'Well yeah. It's illegal.'

'You know what? I don't care anymore. You don't get it do you?'

'Accept what's happened. I know it's hard. I can give you lifts, do the driving.'

'For fuck's sake it's not the same. I'm not a good passenger. I want the spontaneity back in my life. He paused. 'I know someone who could get me a false licence.' The sentence hung in the air, like a dirty fart.

He rubbed his clammy forehead. 'Bet you're shocked.'

He knew it was pointless question. He waited for her answer.

'What the hell are you thinking?' She sat up, shaking her head as she squeezed her cheeks and lips together with one hand.

'I can't believe you'd do that and risk going to prison.'

Clifford felt a rush of anger. The conversation and the relationship were slipping away into a place he didn't want to go, but it was like sitting on the edge of a cliff, everything from that point on was balancing towards the unknown.

He held his tongue, something he didn't do very often and waited for her to carry on.

'How do you think David Blunkett manages?'

'What the fuck Gina? Being born blind isn't the same.'

'Look at some of the people who suffered in the 7/7 attacks in London. Gill Hicks lost both her legs but she rose to the challenge. Positives can come out personal tragedy. If you change your outlook on life you'll see things differently. All the time you don't accept what is happening it's harder. You'll be destroyed.'

She wasn't convincing him.

'Have you quite finished?' He looked at her, noticed her lip quivering in the way it always did when she was upset. This time he didn't find it cute. It was irritating.

'I'm just trying to help.' Her voice wavered.

Clifford's voice became shrill.

'You're as much help as a cancer. That's my passing shot to you. You and your scummy kids.... get cancer.' He paused. Took a breath.

'See? I'm really not a very nice man. And I'm not Gill Hicks.'

'So what will you do? Buy a car? Who is going to insure it for you?'

'I won't be asking you. That's for sure.'

'Why would you want to risk killing an innocent pedestrian who you don't see crossing the road? It could be somebody's kid.'

'Do you know what? I don't care. If it's your bastard kid all the better.'

Clifford had never seen her snarl before. In the moments that followed she became feline, springing from the bed; a crazy cat. He didn't care. Her presence was almost surreal. He was a bulldozer and she was in the way. But he felt more like a bulldozer trying to catch a butterfly; everything in his life had that sense of impossibility. Life was flitting along, escaping from his grasp.

Gina

It was becoming harder to stay calm. But she had to. Didn't want a massive argument; him walking out, leaving her with the rent to pay.

Play the game she told herself. Anger bubbled and boiled inside her. His moods were swinging like a pendulum. She couldn't keep up. Couldn't trust anything he said anymore. He was totally consumed with his own problems in a childlike and vulnerable way.

Clifford

There was still no sign of a thaw in sight; for their relationship or the landscape outside. Silence hung all around. Life had ground to a halt. Clifford was determined to get to work. He needed to think, to carry on as normal. He set off with a bag containing his laptop and a few overnight bits in case he couldn't get back that day due to the weather conditions and trudged his way through the thick snow and biting wind to the station.

His team had called in, unable to get to work that day. Alone in the office he couldn't focus. He flipped between different porn sites, called the bank, venting his usual frustrations. Then he put his head on the desk, banged it several times, looked at some more porn, made a coffee, kicked the door a couple of times - just for the hell of it, then had a piss. Another coffee, a futile attempt to sell an advert. Then a dump which always cheered him up - for a while. The wonderful feeling of his sphincter muscles contracting was the most pleasurable feeling next to an orgasm.

The phone rang.

'Sorry mate but I can't get a licence any more. My contact's been caught.'

'Shit. I was relying on you. Gina won't insure me. Neither will Ben. What the fuck am I supposed to do now?'

He looked at the swamp of paper on his desk, couldn't bring himself to sort through it all. Invoices, files, bank statements, junk mail that hadn't been binned, sweet wrappers, orange peelings, dirty mugs. He had never experienced such a crushing feeling of futility, of being trapped on a dead end street. He got up. Even that was an effort. Stood at the window. It had snowed very lightly along the south coast. He watched a zimmer frame, a wheelchair, old people with crippled backs, people queuing in the post office.

The four walls around him seemed to be breathing, pressing inward. The patterns on the walls became Virginia Creeper, threatening to choke. Were his thoughts trapping him or was the world trapping him? He returned to the computer, could see the reflections of zimmer frames and hunched backs on his screen. There was no way out. No light at the end of the tunnel because the end ultimately meant darkness. All roads, all avenues led to the same thing.

Clifford had never known such crippling lethargy. It was starting to get dark outside. As the hours went by he became less concerned, giddy, blank, trancelike.

Through the malaise he typed into google the words 'suicide how to.' Various 'exit' sites sprung to his screen in the gloom of the unlit office. He didn't know what he felt. It wasn't distress or pity, simply a quiet resignation. Ideas were spinning round his head. This wasn't difficult. It was an easy route out. The only route. The more he pondered that the more excited he became. There was so much to read and many choices but lots of risks of it going wrong. All he really wanted to do was go to sleep; a deep and peaceful drug induced sleep and not to wake up the next morning. There was nothing to wake up for. His son didn't need him. Not really. And he had no ties to Gina. At times he felt like he was living on another planet and no one understood what he was going through. He felt as if he'd lost himself. Who was he?

He didn't want the effort of jumping in front of a train or over the cliff at Beachy Head or from the top of a multi storey car park. He didn't like heights. And he wasn't about to hang himself either. All of these methods involved pain and inconvenience and distress of some description and the inevitability of disability if it all went horribly wrong.

And then he stumbled across a promising idea. It was entitled the helium exit bag method. He was intrigued. Read on. 'Asphyxial suicide with helium and a plastic bag'. 'Inhalation of 100% pure helium causes rapid death due to oxygen deprivation'. As he flicked around some words grabbed his attention.

'The will to live is so strong that in all but the most exceptional cases it will prevail until the end. But if you regard your life as special (as it is), if you are the sort of person who likes to be in charge of their own life, then the final segment should be one of your own choosing.' He liked that. It was dignified, respectful and obvious.

He was in control. He wasn't being reckless but rational. Part of him was shocked at how calm he was. It seemed so easy and acceptable - judging by the dozens of blogs written about it and books explaining how to carry out the method. He clicked on one book, called 'How to make your own helium hood kit,' carried it to the shopping cart, then another 'Let me die before I wake.' Relief swept through him. He wasn't alone. Hundreds were living scared lives planning the same thing. He found this comforting. Resources were being pooled. With all this information he thought, it wasn't going to go wrong.

In no time at all he had purchased a large size helium tank. His secretary wouldn't ask any awkward questions. She'd just assume Gina needed it for party balloons. It was as easy as placing an order for dog food. On a scrap of paper he made a shopping list of everything else he needed. Three metres of hose would be sufficient and a jubilee clip to attach it to the tank and some very airtight, good quality cooking bags. It almost made him laugh that he had to buy a bulk of a hundred cooking bags because that was the minimum order. Next he ordered some elastic, toggles and micropore. He didn't want to waste time buying from a DIY shop. It was easier just to place the orders and get it all delivered quickly.

That evening he slumped down on the leather settee he kept at the far end of his office suite feeling light headed and slightly out of it after several gin and tonics at a grotty pub round the corner. Putting a cushion behind his head he tried to sleep but it was cold. Thoughts ran through his head, like wild horses. He suddenly remembered something G.K. Chesterton had once said. *'By killing yourself you insult every flower on earth.'* What tosh, Clifford thought. Why did people have to think so deeply into suicide? It was just a route out of a difficult life. And neither was he 'falling victim to suicide.' It was a life choice - a choice he wanted to take.

Ben called, breaking the silence asking him how he was with the snow. They chatted. After a few minutes he found himself blurting it all out. He didn't cry. There were no tears. No emotion. His head ruled. Everything was under control. His son was old enough to understand. He had his own life to lead. But Ben was alarmed and wanted to do something to help. He fired lots of questions, said he'd phone his mother and doctor. Five minutes later Roda called and he told her to piss off. He didn't want to discuss anything with her. He wished he hadn't mentioned it. He just wanted to quietly slip away.

A short while later a very irate Gina called. She said she'd called his doctor on the emergency out of hours number.

' Gina. Would you just shut up a minute and listen,' he shouted down the phone. His head pounded. He lay back, nursing his head and neck.

'Google it. It's the best option I have. I don't feel anything. I can see a way out. Christ you should see the sites. There are so many, all with really helpful advice. This helium idea would work. Read about it. Go on.'

'That's sick. Where's it arriving? Here or your office?'

'Hopefully it will get to the office by the end of the week.'

'Well that's ok then. I'll just tell your secretary to get rid of it when it arrives.'

'I'll be angry with you Gina if you do that. I've paid a lot of money for this equipment. I spent all evening on the internet. I'm only sorry I told you.'

'How bloody selfish you've become. I should have poisoned your sprouts at Christmas and be done with it. How do you think Ben would feel finding out his dad has topped himself?'

'He'll be qualified soon, making his own money, enjoying life. He'll understand.'

'And how's he supposed to carry on after you've gone? When you had him you took on a lifetime of responsibility. You shouldn't forget that. He'll always be your kid. And you'll always be his dad. He needs you.'

'You sound like a second world war poster. He doesn't need me. He's a complete cunt these days.'

Gina

Gina sat at Clifford's desk in the cottage making phone calls to friends, his doctor. Her friends had contempt for Clifford. '*Let him get on with it*' they said.

But panic had set in. How could she make him get help? She felt helpless, useless. Would he seek help? Why had he told her? Maybe he just wanted the attention, everybody running around in alarm. Her emotions flung from fear to irritation and back to fear. But at the end of the day he was an adult and adults could do as they pleased. She couldn't be there at every moment of his day to stop him.

26

Clifford

January 2011

He fell into a deep sleep waking at around three with a banging head. A sense of nothingness washed over him. Several texts had pinged in while he'd slept. He scrolled through. Didn't bother to read them properly. They were all from Gina and Ben asking how he was, suggesting he visit a doctor. Then he checked his inbox. Several emails needed his urgent response. He sat up, suddenly feeling charged with energy. This was a good opportunity to make a few calls to Beijing. Get on top of things, catch up with his Chinese contact. It was eleven in China. He went through to his office switched on the computer.

Yesterday seemed a long time ago. Had he really ordered helium and cooking bags? It now seemed surreal. He felt calmer. Was that because he knew, at the back of his mind he had plan B now in place in case it all got too much? Plan B would arrive in a few days. It could sit on the shelf for now and be taken off, assembled ready to go. And if and when that time came he'd have to work out where it was going to happen and what time of day. There was a grotty hotel with a peeling facade on the sea front. He didn't imagine they would have many visitors. Somebody he didn't know would find him; a Polish maid maybe.

By 9am he had connected with the outside world and written an article for the next issue. He sat back satisfied. Something had lifted from his shoulders. And as he made a mid morning coffee he thought again about how he would drive again. He stirred in the sugar, clinked the spoon on the side of the mug. Tapped it on the top. The action reminded him of someone.

The spoon was suspended mid air. He was taken back there; his mind reeling into the past, a series of stills. He could see her in the tiny kitchen 'brewing up' and the old dear in a chair by the fire, wrapped in a blanket asleep. He could hear her screechy voice almost whistle through her false teeth '*cup a tea love?*' She was always making tea. He used to tell her she'd drown in it - a horrible death. Tea was her answer to everything when words failed.

'You can't buy happiness' she'd say 'but you can buy tea.'

He could see them playing Scrabble round a chipped formica table as they waited for the old dear to go to bed. She never liked taking him upstairs in her employer's house, but talked herself into allowing ten minutes. She needed it, he needed it. He always left the house adjusting his flies, feeling as if he'd just used the toilet and she hastily rearranging the dead cat on top of her deeply scarred bare head. He shuddered, remembering the story of how her first husband had taken a coat hanger and ripped out chunks of her blonde hair.

He hadn't heard from her in a while. Wondered if the old dear was still alive. Poor cow didn't have a home of her own and at the age of 65 she was getting too old to be humping old dears in and out of baths and beds. He imagined she would work till she dropped. These days everyone did. Clifford threw the spoon in the sink, cupped the mug in both hands. An idea was taking shape. He placed the mug on his desk. Picked up his i phone. Scrolled down the contacts list. Her number was still there.

He returned to the cottage that evening his head buzzing with ideas. He was exhausted, ready for a good sleep in a proper bed. It had been a busy day he hadn't given the helium another thought. But as he turned the key in the door and went through to the kitchen Gina was waiting, poised for attack. They faced each other in limbo, balanced on the edge of an argument. She shrugged, a look of hurt in her eyes. He put his bag down. She was like a brazil nut. It wouldn't take much to crack open her fury. He could see it in her posture.

'Whatever you say I'll make sure you don't get the helium when it arrives.' It felt like they were in the boxing ring and he'd received the first blow; bigger would follow.

A tirade erupted.

'So you didn't think to call me to say you were ok?'

'And what were you going to do?' His eyes looked round searching for the gin.

'At least you would have stopped me worrying.' She reached for a glass, offered it to him.

'Why the hell did you tell Ben what you were planning?

'He'd understand.'

'Understand? What the hell? Once you have kids you stay on the planet. They exist because you exist. They aren't left on your doorstep. They don't come free in a cereal packet. You stick around. Right? It's the unwritten rule on parenting.'

She looked like she would burn with rage. He didn't care. She had no idea.

He yanked his tie, tossed it to the ground, poured a gin and went to his study slamming the door behind him. He wasn't going to be made to feel like a naughty schoolboy. If only people could wear mood indicators on their foreheads, he thought. *I've had enough,* his forehead would read.

The atmosphere in the cottage hadn't really improved a couple of evenings later.

The kids were upstairs when he got back. He'd long given up on them coming down to say hello. Gina was cleaning shelves, sorting out bottles of alcohol; throwing some out, dusting others. She gave him a dismissive look, went back to cleaning.

'You really have no idea how stressful life is until you run a business.' Clifford dumped his red leather case on the pine table.

'More problems?' She pulled out a chair, sat down.

'Running that place is like steering a ship through a storm. I never know what will happen from one day to the next.'

He took his glasses off, rubbed his eyes.

Gina gave a plastered smile of sympathy, handed him a glass of brandy, then poured herself one. 'Fancy finishing off this bottle?'

He looked at the row of bottles sitting on the table.

'There's a cocktail called 5 o clock in the morning. Brandy, rum, gin, vodka. Throw it all in. Grab a glass. I'll make you one.'

He began opening bottles, poured an inch from each while Gina gave a relaxed laugh. Soon they were light headed and making up names for all the different combinations they could think of. To hell with his diabetes.

Clifford was swigging a bloody Mary.

'I looked at you lot in that poky flat and wanted to rescue you. You were sharing water bath for Christ sake. But the truth is it would have taken me 20 years to sort you all out. But now *I* need rescuing. There's no reason you should saddle yourself with a defective product.'

'It shouldn't be like that. Not if two people truly loved each other.'

'What is love?' He took another swig. Flopped his head on the table. 'You'll get over it. Out of sight, out of mind.' He mumbled.

'Great. What's it all been about then?'

'God knows Gina. I feel like a case conference. There's a webcam on ice like a bear documentary. I'm remote. I'm merely an aberration of myself. I don't have a good relationship with your kids. Saria is developing sexual awareness, Carrie is struggling at school. I don't like the way this house is run. I don't fit in. I gave you lot a good Christmas, now I'll quietly slip away.'

'Why don't you poke your nose round their doors and say hello?'

'No point. Metaphorically they are so shut its like Fort Knox.'

'You only look at the negative.'

'That's right. Have a dig.'

They didn't hear Saria come down the stairs and creep up on them. Her eyes were red and Gina stood up with concern. Saria was wearing the same baggy pajama bottoms and cotton top she always wore around the house.

'I don't want to go to school tomorrow. I keep telling you I want to leave, go to a new school but you never listen.'

Her voice took on an irritating whine, rising to a fever pitch as the conversation began. Tears welled. Her long mousey hair hung in rag tails around her oval face. Clifford's head thumped. Christ he didn't need this.

'What's happened now?' Gina asked.

'A really popular boy on Facebook has got it in for me, saying nasty things and I might get beaten up. Oh my God.'

She started stomping round the kitchen, repeating the mantra 'oh my God' as if she was a Muslim walking round the Kaaba in Mecca.

' It'll blow over,' Gina said dismissively.

'90% of the kids at that school are chavs. In a virtual world everything's open to all. It's nasty, pernicious and far too powerful to be left in the hands of immature people. That's what you're up against,' Clifford sighed.

'But this boy is the most popular boy in the school. They will all believe him and side with him against me. Oh my God. I hate everyone.'

She was sobbing now, fighting back her tears, emotions spilling as she tried to control them.

'All I want is to change school and then I'll shut up and be timid and come off Tumbler and Facebook and be invisible. I can leave myself behind.'

'You'll always be up against different people, accused of different things.' Clifford thought back to Simon's death and his own childhood.

'You've got to learn to cope. Say FUCK YOU. Practice it in front of the mirror. Shout it. Let it roll on your tongue. Don't ever be scared to use the F word. Then turn up at his house or meet him head on in the corridor.'

'They're just teenagers. They'll soon forget'. Gina headed for the kettle.

'They think I'm pathetic. They'll think I'm a complete bitch if I swear at them.'

'You'll be out in a couple of years. You need to toughen up. We all have to. You're bright, good looking. Look at your strengths. Otherwise you may as well kill yourself.' Clifford said.

Gina looked away. There was a momentary silence.

'Can't I just get home taught?'

'No one can disappear. You're just passing through. School's soon over. Then real life begins. Use it, chew it then spit it out. Look at me. I'm 5 foot nothing, I'm a minor success. I put up with crap every day and I get through and I don't give a damn.'

'Concentrate on you.' Gina rubbed Saria's back.

'Then they will call me selfish. Oh my God.'

They were in bed. Clifford had his hand on Gina's pubic mound for warmth.

'Three kids is a lot. I don't have the energy. That business with the bullying - it was draining.'

'But you said all the right things. Relax.'

'You're up against a lot.'

Clifford closed his eyes, then placed his hand on her breast, wondering if he could find the effort to suck her nipple.

'You knew I had kids when you met me. I don't know what you expected.'

'Not this.'

'I don't know what to do. Neither do you.'

'I feel completely disinterested Gina if I'm honest. I don't have the will to do anything.'

'I used to think you had fight inside you, that you were going to make the world a better place for us.'

'Whatever made you think that?' He turned to look at her. Their heads were resting on a pillow. She looked young, innocent.

'You just always gave that impression. I remember you always saying trust your Clifford.'

'I'm defeated by it all.' He sighed, looked at the ceiling. ' Life. The long, hard struggle of it all. I just want to go to sleep and not wake up. A coma would be nice. Or amnesia.'

He paused. 'You know sometimes I imagine you standing at my funeral, crying.'

'You make it sound like an armed struggle, the struggle for black freedom, in South Africa. When did that struggle begin?'

'Oh I don't know.' He turned again, pulled at a lock of her hair.

'Gradually. Suddenly. The exhaustion never goes away.' He kissed her on the forehead.

27
Clifford

January 2011

They woke in an embrace, made love. Sometimes achieving an orgasm was so easy, like taking a stroll through the park. At other times it was like carrying a heavy load. The only way he could carry on, remain firm was to imagine her in pregnancy or cradling a baby; a massive turn on which sustained the energy and the blood flowing through his penis.

He flunked back onto the pillow as she swiped tissues from a box nearby, mopping up, then wriggling around to avoid lying on a wet patch before flopping towards him - her arm now slung across his belly. His mind was in turmoil. When he was pounding away inside her he knew he couldn't leave her. He still loved her. But he had to put himself first. He didn't want to 'dump' her back at the overcrowded, shabby flat on the council estate. But she wasn't at the end of the day his responsibility. Those arsehole dads should be doing more to help he kept reminding himself. They were the fathers, even though they behaved more like sperm donors. He felt like a robin reliant towing a caravan.

All sorts of feelings shot through him. Bitterness, anger, fear, regret but mostly just a dull pain that seemed to pervade every cell of his body. One of his rules was to ignore the heart, trust the mind and listen to what the gut was saying. Everything came from the gut. But sitting here now it felt as if his heart was divided into all sorts of different compartments, like a haberdashers.

'That was a lovely meal the kids made last night and the conversation was lively. Everybody was engaging. You can't say my kids are always aloof and quiet.' Her statement was more a question; seeking his reassurance that things had improved. He knew they hadn't. She was in denial. Everything was far from ok. He felt total disconnection from them all.

'Was it?' He responded limply.

'You're always negative. The enchiladas were really tasty and Saria made a lovely creamy pie. Key lime pie is really special in our family. It kind of brings us all together, a shared love. Rather like having a puppy or a baby.'

'It's you lot and me.' He gave a resigned sigh. 'I once read a quote I liked. Can't remember where. 'When the food runs out, the family reunion is over.' It's so true.'

'They were happy to wash up. You should have washed up with them. It's all part of it.'

'And I should have played on the wii at Christmas with them, I can hear you about to tell me for the millionth time.'

'You have to join in. Seize the opportunity if it's presented.'

Clifford was sitting up, poised to begin the day, when he heard a ringing. Neither moved.

'What's that?' He got up, disorientated.

'I think it's the landline.'

'Where is it?'

'How should I know? It's never rung before.'

'You must know where it is.'

He ran down stairs cursing about the lack of a line in the bedroom.

'I'm sick of this shithole,' he shouted, as Gina padded on behind him.

As he passed through the playroom towards the ringing phone he registered that Carrie was curled up on the settee in her nighty snuggling her blanket watching C Beebies. Every time he looked at the kid he found it hard to erase the visions he had in his mind of her conception with the untermench. He still couldn't work out what had been on Gina's mind. He wouldn't have handled his semen with a turkey baster if he were the last humanoid on the planet.

'Turn that bloody thing off,' he shrieked as he passed. She glared back. It was a glare that stirred something deep within.

The clock on the study windowsill read 7.20. When he heard Ben's voice alarm rose within.

'Why are calling on the landline?'

'You're phone was switched off.'

'Shit. Yes.'

He sensed something was wrong. He was confused. Ben's words spat out at machine gun speed, escaping from his mouth quicker than his brain could formulate the sentence. In one breath he told him he had imagined the police were coming to take him away. Then he jumped on in random fits. His friend had laced his food with hash and he could no longer trust the food in his fridge. Then he said something about seeing Phil Collins playing in his room late one night. Then he went on to explain that on a few occasions he'd been late into the veterinary hospital a few times and there were people wanting him out.

It was muddling and disjointed. The TV was distracting his thoughts, stopping him focusing. Stress mounted. He couldn't think what to say, what to do, how to help. Ben had already flunked two sets of exams and been put back a couple of years. This couldn't go on. He had to finish the course, gain the qualification and start work. It was taking an eternity. But he didn't see that it would happen. Maybe he'd been wrong to steer him into vet training. Maybe he'd put too much pressure on him. But if he gave up now what would he do? He wouldn't have a degree. He'd have to start all over again. And he - Clifford would be paying for it. That much was guaranteed. He longed for the day when his son would be financially independent. It seemed as if he'd been in education forever. He imagined still supporting his son in retirement.

As he puzzled Ben's mental state, the TV swelled in his head. Laughter, children's voices, music and Ben's confused words played a death dance in his head. He threw the phone down; could hear Ben still yabbering on. He flung the door back and flew like a raging bull towards the settee where Carrie was still curled up, her cheeks pink, damp bed hair matted across her flushed face, thumb in mouth, pulling pieces of fluff from her blanket to stuff up her nose and form a balcony across the rim of her lip. He couldn't process any rational thoughts for there were none.

He could hear Gina in the kitchen putting crockery away. He fleetingly registered Cameron's voice talking about cuts over the kitchen radio. Every day the list of services planned for cutbacks grew like a shopping list. The smell of fresh toast wafted through.

'Turn that thing off.' He shouted at Carrie.

She looked down. He wondered, as he always wondered what sort of a family this was and why they always cowered into silence. She curled her body tighter; a spider in a bath plug. He could see her knickers, tight across her opening. She pulled her legs together as he came closer, her arm tight around them. His eyes bored into her. He could see Wayne in her body outline. Suddenly he flew towards her. How dare the kid ignore him. She looked up now. He didn't like the look on her face – grabbed her arm, yanked it. And in a flash he saw into her mind and didn't like what he saw. In her eyes he could see pure contempt burrowed through to her soul. Defiance shone from those innocent blue eyes. He could see her as a baby in a cot, a blanket wrapped round her. He could almost see her Neanderthal father's face within those eyes and it was as if they were communicating words: 'you can't make me, I'm going to ignore you.'

Nobody ignored Clifford. Not since that day he'd shat his pants. He'd made sure of that. He couldn't exist, do the things he needed to do without a certain level of order, control and continuity.

'Get up,' he barked. 'Turn that racket off.'

She bent her face lower, like a petal curling in rain. He knew in that second he hated that kid and everything she represented. She was the miniature incarnation of her father. Everything from her sordid conception in the Micra in a Little Chef car park to the ugliness of Wayne, his loud monotone and dreadful south London accent, the poor grammar and how he reminded him so much of his dreadful ex brother in law. Ben would be waiting. He couldn't think, couldn't process. He needed to get back to the phone, find out what was going on. He grabbed her tiny arm, yanked her towards the TV. Still she said nothing. She was a stupid lifeless rag doll with a sewn on snarl across her face. The image of a rag doll had been etched into his mind for so long. An image he'd carried from eleven years old. He took a step nearer. The music from the TV swelled in his head, thudding, consuming his thinking space. He wanted to rip the blanket away, tear it up, burn it. That blanket represented everything.

And then Gina was in the middle, the referee and he was shouting at the pair of them, screaming for them both to give him some peace, some silence.

'Everybody trashes over my feelings in this place.'

He flew back to the study, banging the door behind him but Ben had gone and he was late for his train and had to get on.

He showered and dressed and came down for breakfast doing his buttons up. Carrie was asking what breakfast cereal she could have.

'Oh shut up. Sit down or you'll really have something to cry about. Where's your spellings anyway? You don't give a shit about your education.'

He walked towards the counter where Gina was pouring cereal.

'Have you stopped talking too? Christ this places gets worse.' Gina didn't speak. Her body was rigid at the worktop. He didn't remember her being this quiet. He looked at her face. Her upper lip was quivering again.

'So what did Ben want? What's happened?' she eventually asked in a timid tone.

'He's been late to the vet hospital a few times. There are people that want him out. I didn't really get the whole story. Your little shit here saw to that.'

His words drummed across the kitchen. He looked over at Carrie, the anger had subsided but was still simmering in the pot. He was aware that if Gina hadn't come in at that moment he would have flown the child through to the next week, a thought that didn't sit easy. He knew how the course of history could change in seconds.

'What? Chucked out of the vet hospital or off the course altogether?'

'You stupid bitch. Off the course. What do you think?'

They swam in a tense pool of silence for several minutes. He huffed, poured a coffee from the filter jug. She slammed a yogurt pot, with great force onto the worktop next to him. The bottom cracked. Thick pink creamy blobs spurted and squirted, reminding him of a decorating accident with Dulux.

'Don't you ever call me a stupid bitch again. Do you hear me?' Her face was stone in a foreboding graveyard.

'Well, you're very slow on the uptake at times.'

'You didn't need to shout at her. You could have just closed the study door. She had already turned down the volume.'

'You did nothing to help. So don't blame me. Next time it happens I might be forced to strangle her.'

Gina swept out of the kitchen, saying nothing, taking Carrie with her.

What a pathetic woman Clifford thought to himself. He half wanted her to snap. Maybe one day she would.

28
Gina

February 2011

Dreams and news scrambled in her transitional state of sleep and consciousness. Soldiers and rioters throwing tear gas, hand grenades and petrol bombs. A reporter from Al Jazeera talked of rioting in Tahir Square. The leader of Eqypt, Mubarrak had toppled from power.

'You have no idea how bad it's all going to get. An Arab Spring. And here; cuts and more cuts. Clifford offered his daily analysis.

When Gina went down to the kitchen Carrie was standing on a chair reaching for cereal on top of the fridge; blanket and fluffy camel pinned under one arm.

Gina grabbed the cereal and whispered into Carrie's ear.

'Don't forget to say good morning when he comes down.'

'I always do. Mummy you look scared.' She held Gina's hand. 'Why is your hand shaking?'

She was aware that her breaths were short and jagged. Her whole body hurt. Misery seemed to be closing in around her. She hated this way of life – treading carefully around Clifford. She glanced at the calendar on the wall. Absent mindedly counted the weeks until they could move back to her flat.

She chiseled into her thumb nail, still studying the calendar as she tracked each thud of his Hush Puppies descending the stairs.

'So you're finally learning to be civil now I'm about to leave you all.' Clifford had his back to her, took a bowl from the Welsh dresser as she dutifully gave him the loudest, politest good morning she could. He took out his i phone. Gina could see he was scrolling through properties on Rightmove.

She felt trapped in a cauldron of competing emotions, bubbling to the surface, one big toxic concoction and nowhere to escape.

He pushed the bowl away, got up, put his jacket on, complaining about stiff aching shoulders. Picking up his red leather laptop satchel he said 'When you're ready then dear.' Gina bristled. She hated to be called that. And hated her new and main role – that of taxi driver to the station. She sensed he was aware of how she felt.

Seeing the frosted windscreen Gina nipped back in to fill a kettle of tepid water to swish across the screen.

In the car she closed her eyes, flopped her head onto the dashboard and waited for him to get in. There was still two months remaining on the tenancy contract at the flat. *Keep calm*, her inner voice screamed.

Bizarrely though she still loved him. Would miss him. Hers was a conflicting bag of emotions: she feared loneliness but also craved the solitary experience.

In the past 24 hours she had kicked herself for an emotional response but none had come. What sort of mother would feel blank after a threat to their child's safety? Maybe deep down she saw a broken man full of hot air.

The passenger door clunked open, the woody aroma of his after shave filling the car. Joss' friends were gathering on the pavement, waiting to cross.

'What's wrong with *you* then? Living with me given you depression too then? What have you got to look so sullen about? I'm the one going blind.'

She ignored the missive but inside her head a storm was brewing, a change descending and engulfing. She looked at the boys as she reversed. Their ties were loose, hanging in big gaping knots half way down their shirts, none of which were tucked in and their hair was unkempt.

'I wish they'd learn to dress properly.' When she spoke it wasn't her it was a veneer.

'Bunch of scum. They should all be shot. And you want to stay in this area because of the school?'

She refused the spoon of provocation.

'Why did you use a kettle of water on the windscreen?' He digged.

'It's quicker to defrost.'

'What's your problem? I told you to buy some deicer.' His voice had risen.

'It corrodes the wipers.' Her reply was flat and to the point.

'You're talking bollocks again. Listen to yourself. Is this what I'm going to have to put up with? Things are going to have to change. You'll be driving me around for a long time to come. We wasted three minutes doing it *your way*.'

A red mist descended as swift as a storm cloud, a pressure cooker inside her head waiting to explode. In the moments that followed everything changed and was redefined. She inched up into the seat. Goddam it. She deserved so much better. *What am I doing?* Her inner voice screamed. *I don't need expensive hotels, travel, meals out. Happiness isn't for sale.*

She remembered an Ernest Hemingway quote she'd read somewhere, a long time ago that applied so much to Clifford. 'Happiness in intelligent people is the rarest thing I know.'

Every possible emotion thumped through her veins, settling in her stomach, a pool of acid.

She was trembling as uncontrollable anger ripped. The floodgates had opened and there was no stopping her. It was as if she were having a fit.

'You miserable, miserable, miserable cunt.'

She spat the words, enjoying the flavor, the texture, the explosion. She couldn't remember when she had ever used the 'C' word but it felt good – forbidden and vulgar. It's power washed through her like a stiff whiskey and she could sense Clifford shrink in his seat beside her.

'I'm sick of *your* problems, *your* misery, *your* nasty behaviour. How dare you? You're not getting away with it. I'm not a push over. It's all about you. You, you, you.' She banged the words out, thumping the steering wheel with each shot. 'You and all the D words in your life: divorce, driving, depression. You selfish, selfish man. You don't give a damn about anyone but yourself.'

She ranted on trembling and shivering as if she were in icy water. She thought she heard him call her a crazy lunatic. Her brain had frozen over. His words weren't registering.

By the time they pulled into the station forecourt she was pulling his collar. The car stalled, jolting forward behind a taxi. She tugged and pushed. The car was still running. He had morphed into a rag doll. And like throwing a rag doll across a room this seemed so easy. His glasses flew to the footwell. He crouched to retrieve them covering his head for protection. She carried on tugging and pushing and screaming.

She pushed him out, watching him crumple to the pavement in full view of gawping potential witnesses. She looked in the mirror. Her face was ashen. She was shaking. She lost her grip of the foot peddles. As she pulled away she saw him brushing himself down, adjusting his glasses, shell shocked, as if he'd just been mugged in a dark alley. Her heart tugged and in a flash she felt sorry for him. But she couldn't run after him. That would prove she was in the wrong and he in the right but what had she done? Maybe she was mad, as he had often told her. But part of her felt pleased; free and liberated like a chick hatched from a shell.

As soon as she got home she frantically began calling friends.

'I'm not at all surprised,' one friend said. 'He's been seeping away at your confidence for months. You've changed. When you're both calm you need to tell him it's not a healthy relationship for either of you.' And another friend said 'he's a controlling pig. You're best out of it. Let him get a rope and hang himself.'

She didn't know what to do. She made a cup of tea.

Half way through the morning she received a puzzling text from him. Her heart thumped.

'BITCH. You'll pay for this.'

And ten minutes later: 'You'll be sorry when the police come knocking.' She slammed the phone onto the pine table, cursing to herself. Was this the same man who had long complained about his ex wife calling the police at the slightest slap round the face or push against the fridge? And was this the same man who had utter contempt for the police referring to them as pigs. Was this pay back time for all the occasions Roda had called them?

She flunked down into a chair, knowing in her heart he wanted bitter revenge and above all to ruin her chances of returning to child minding. A bad mark on a CRB check would mean she couldn't work with children.

She buried her head in her arms and cried. He had complete control over her. And he was supposed to love her. She was supposed to love him. What had happened? It was hard to unpick the events of the past weeks. She had surprised herself in the car. She didn't know she had so much pent up anger welling inside. Venting off had made her feel better and briefly in control. But she now felt wretched, embarrassed and ashamed. He was right. She was neurotic, crazy. She had no future if she couldn't get a CRB. All the jobs she had ever done required one. She had given up child minding because as a registered child minder she would have to apply to Ofsted to child mind at the cottage and there were too many things that needed repairing to make it a safe place for children. But when she returned to the flat she would resume child minding and another idea was to work in an old peoples' home.

Her heart thudded. Another text. A picture filled the screen of her pink Nokia. A self portrait of red gashes across his cheek - about two inches long, quite deep. Her stomach fizzed with fear. *She had done this.* This was evidence. And yet it seemed that she couldn't possibly have done it. She didn't remember. She'd remember doing something like that. The gashes were too hideous, beyond her capability. Her memory was blank. Erased.

She had pushed him - could see her actions like a series of muddled shots. She remembered him picking his red glasses from the foot well. Mostly she remembered just ranting and swearing and shouting but at no point could she recall digging her nails into his face. It wasn't the sort of thing she would do. She was too squeamish.

Another text broke the silence of the kitchen.

'I'm on my way to the police station - your kids will end up in care. They're better off without you. Nick was right. You're not fit to be a mother. You should jump under a train.'

Gina got up. Grabbed the whiskey from the dresser. Poured a small glass. Warmth washed through her.

Her phone vibrated again. Lit up.

'BITCH. You of all people should know the ramifications of this. You're ruined.'

She poured another whiskey. Inside her it felt as if the sky was crashing down. She went to the bathroom, began picking blackheads under the bright light. She scratched her scalp, flicking dandruff into the basin. She had never been in trouble with the police before. He had. What was she supposed to do? She went to the kitchen, pulled a fork from the drawer and began to scratch her back furiously, then her arms as nerves marched like an army of ants up and down.

She walked up and down the kitchen scratching her back, thinking, focusing on facts. She'd be ok. She had no criminal record. She sat down, pressing her fingers hard against her forehead; smelling the pleasant grease on her finger tips. He was a bully, 'known' to the police. She remembered the story of his mother accusing him of stealing money from her wardrobe.

She had scratched him. He had proof. She rubbed her forehead harder. She would tell the truth. She didn't remember. It was as if dementia had set in – like the time she'd rolled the car and banged her head. This wasn't something she went around doing to everybody that aggravated her.

What if she was capable of much more but didn't know it? She scratched her ears, began digging for wax, smelling it, her mind wandering. What if she were capable of hurting a child or anyone, if driven to anger? How did any of us know what we were capable of?

She got up. Paced the kitchen. Tried to clamp the fear. *'Play it cool,'* she told herself. Play into his hands for a bit, bide your time. In just a few months this would be history.

'Go ahead. I'm not scared. Make those pigs work for their money. You pay your taxes you should get something back,' she replied to the text.

She waited for him to come home that evening. Kept glancing at the clock. He didn't return.

'I'm not coming back. It's unsafe. Next time it might be a knife.' He texted.

'I'm sorry. Please come back.' Her emotions were mixed bag of fear, shame, confusion, love and it was ridiculous but in a practical sense all she cared about was the unpaid rent and a roof over their heads until the tenants in her flat moved out.

'I'll look for a new rental.'

Everything she had hoped to achieve by her outburst in the car had been fruitless. Yet again he was in the right and he the victim – a vulnerable man who was going blind and she was the aggressor. The crazy woman.

Part of her wanted to make it up to him. But inside her head was a drum beating warning her of all the things that wouldn't improve.

'Come back. We can talk.'

'The police are dealing with it now.' He replied. 'It's out of my hands.' came the cold text answers.

She called the rental agency, pleaded for her tenants to vacate the flat so they could leave the cottage. She was stuck. That would be a breach of contract. She had to bide her time. What if he came back? Better that he did Gina thought. Keep him here, paying the bills.

She heard his key turn in the lock. Her heart thudded as she listened to his footsteps on the wood and the creaky door knob turn. Blood drained. She sat down, in shock. Heard his footsteps in the hall. Her body was rigid. Fear coursed through her.

'You're back?' She tried not to gasp. His face was worse than the picture he'd sent via text.

He dropped his bag. Didn't smile. 'I'm not staying.' His words were cold, matter of fact.

'Where will you go?'

'Back to the office.' His face showed no emotion.

Gina got up, tried to hug him. Touched his face. 'Stay... please.'

They stood in icy silence. After a several minutes he lifted his arm, put it over her shoulder, a limp half action.

'Sorry. I still love you.' She touched his face again.

'You're a crazy bitch.'

'Sorry. You were driving me mad.'

'I don't know where we go from here.' His eyes looked softer. His guard was melting.

'That's the problem.' Gina squeezed his shoulder. For a moment they gazed at each other as if trying to understand what each other was really thinking. In the depths of her stomach a voice screamed *let him go, let him go.*

'Would we end up killing each other?' He touched her hair, his words disconnected from his actions.

For a few days the atmosphere was charged but bizarrely there was a level of normality and even superficial hope. Gina played it cool.

The following evening he called the kids down. Everybody sat around the pine table in awkward silence, their bodies rooted to their chairs.

'So. Your mother attacked me. That's why I've been away. I'm a victim of domestic abuse.' He started to laugh at the enormity of the statement. Saria had a '*what a drama queen*' look on her face.

He was appealing to the sympathy card and they didn't react.

He raised a hand to his sore face and grimaced.

'It's a terrible thing to be attacked by a woman. I can't shave. That's why I'm all hairy. Your mother's depressed. That's why she attacked me. She needs to see a doctor; go on medication and she will.' He looked at Gina; a look which said *'you'll be better soon'* and put a hand on her hand, gave a reassuring squeeze.

'But she's depressed probably because I'm depressed. I have business issues to deal with and my health... that gets no better. I can't drive anymore.'

What a clever twister of facts Gina thought. Very Stepford Wifey.

'Then there's you lot.' She wondered when this would come.

He sighed as if describing the burden of tackling a heavily overgrown garden. A ghastly tiredness swept over her. He rubbed his forehead.

'Quite frankly *you* lot don't help.'

Here they were again, back on trampled ground, a place they had been a thousand times before.

Gina counted to five in her head while she tried not to react. Part of her felt strangely disconnected from the scene.

'I came into this wanting to change your lives. I've given you a lot, but I get nothing back and that doesn't make me feel great.' He sounded like a failed missionary in Libya.

'You're never here. You're always in your rooms. As soon as you've eaten you slope off. We have the disappearing routine every evening, then you're off to your dads. And woof... your life will be gone. This is like a flat share. The type of life you'll have at university. Everyone tolerates each other but that's as far as it goes. Tolerance isn't enough. And basically...' Clifford cradled the mug of coffee in front of him, as if it were his emotional prop. 'I'm not putting up with it anymore. It's not how it should be. It's abnormal. It's not a good quality of family life.' As if he knew what that was.

Clifford yet again was doing the talking.

'What if we move to America?' Joss had been dabbing his running nose with a tissue. His blue eyes were suddenly bright and electric. He was like a hamster that had suddenly woken.

'That's not going to solve anything. You'd sit in your room there instead.'

'No we wouldn't. We'd go to Mc Donalds. They're way cooler over there.'

'Or sunbathe in the desert. Pleeeeese can we move over there?' Saria's brown eyes were wide. She linked her arm into Gina's and squeezed Gina's hand pleading with her pleases and her whines.

'It's not dangerous in America mummy.' Joss continued.

'I didn't say it was. Apart from the gun laws.'

'If you're worried about tornadoes - well - per square mile its more dangerous in England.' Joss smiled. All at once Gina felt sad for his feather like vulnerability in the face of this huge thing she was attempting to erect – a modern stepfamily. She'd placed the first bricks on the cement. But the bricks were the wrong shape and the cement wasn't hardening.

'What if we move to Glasgow? I've seen a really cheap house on Rightmove with seven bedrooms. The bank would give you a small mortgage. We could have massive parties and go fishing.' Saria said.

'That's bad for fish.' Joss gave a smile not directed at anyone that really said *I can't think what to say, I feel awkward sitting here.*

A swift change came over Saria. She got up. Her arms were in mid air, her voice high pitched. She was an animal on stage at the Lion King.

'Well I'm very very sorry we're not the perfect kids for you Clifford. We do try talking to you but you go on and on and most teenagers prefer their bedrooms. Why would I want to sit down here all evening and talk to you two. Jesus Christ.'

'Saria! Don't say that.'

'That's fine. The kid's alive.'

'I don't want her swearing like you.'

'That's about average.' Joss shrugged, a glint in his eye.

Carrie sat snuggling her blanket, her head on the table.

'I think we should come up with a plan.' Gina sat up, painted on her best cheery face and switched into childminder/teacher mode. She rummaged in a drawer for paper and coloured pens. Returned to the table.

'Instead of all this moaning why don't we do a brain storm of ideas on how to improve things.'

She wasn't going to allow him to sink into negativity. The kids relaxed, a change came over them. They even looked excited. Saria handed out the pens. Carrie took the lids off testing them out. Gina felt proud of her kids. They were ok kids. Clifford looked whacked - as if he'd been running a therapy class. She wondered if he'd sneak an escape this time.

'Let's all come up with one suggestion each,' she instructed.

'Bacon sandwiches.' Joss offered.

'Popcorn and a film on a Saturday.' Saria added.

'No spelling tests.' Carrie mumbled from under her blanket.

'A family photo album.' Saria said, elaborating on what it might contain.

'Oh and a swear box.' She added and looked across at Clifford.

Soon the large blank paper was filled with ideas. Gina was impressed.

'Your turn.' She offered Clifford a pen. He was looking in a hand mirror, studying his wounds, dabbing them with moistened cotton wool. He waved the pen away as if it were a pesky fly.

'Ok.' She said, smothering his sulk in cheeriness. 'What do you all think the word family means? Let's brain storm that.' Gina felt as if she were back in the classroom.

Saria shrugged. 'How would I know? I don't remember it. I was only seven when you got divorced.'

Gina felt a stab of guilt.

'We moved on my fifth birthday. I never had a party. That flat was so poky.' Joss said.

'Do you really want to go back to that poky flat? Wouldn't you rather have this lifestyle? A big bedroom each? Never short of money? You don't want to rely on Government help. That's no way to live. I can buy you what you need. It really does depend on *you* lot though. If you play the game your old Clifford will see you're ok.'

'Not if it's like the other morning when Carrie was eating a bacon butty and you got all annoyed and called her a stupid little brat because she wanted it cut into squares with the crusts cut off.' Saria was quick. Her words were fired like a machine gun. 'What would the game consist of? You shouting at us?'

'In Iraq the Sunnis and the Shiites have to get on. Otherwise it's game up. You get what I'm saying?' But he'd lost them.

Carrie started to tear corners from the brain storming paper, licking her finger then twisting the pieces into balls. Gina noticed the child shoot an evil look at Clifford.

Saria was sketching a house with a neat little path and roses in the garden. Joss looked at his watch then at the door, calculating his escape.

'I'm going to bed. I'll leave you lot to finish. My face is killing me.' Clifford got up, nursing his face with one hand. He was the focus anymore, Gina thought and clearly didn't like that.

He closed the door behind him and the children immediately looked more relaxed.

'He's a complete prick.' Saria spat.

'My daddy doesn't like him.' Carrie chirruped.

'He's cool when he's not moaning.' Joss shrugged.

'Clifford the family therapist rescues broken family!' He sang as he tossed his underpants across the room and tugged off his socks. He'd claimed the trophy.

It was like tiptoeing around glass in this game of cat and mouse. Maybe he hadn't reported the gashes to the police. Perhaps he'd been bluffing? She didn't want to ask. Were they two parties in a legal case, unable to exchange any conversation about the incident?

A couple of days later Gina was in for a shock. She was shouting from the bottom of the stairs for the kids to hurry for school. There was a loud, decisive knock at the door. Two tall black solemn figures stood behind the frosted glass. She invited them in, remained calm while inside her heart was banging. This was the ultimate in humiliation that any man could throw at her. Instantly she was reduced to the status of a widow in Nepal, labeled a 'bokshi.' The power that he held felt so intense, it was almost suffocating. How had he made her feel like this? What did he hope to achieve?

The following morning all would be revealed.

29

Gina

February 2011

Gina watched him undress; toss his socks and underpants to one side, place his folded trousers on the wicker chair. He sang in a Bob Marley voice 'it's time for a urination across the nation' as he peed into the porcelain and his wince as he took the daily insulin shot.

He devoured an orange in the pool of light from the street outside, tossing the peel across the white floor boards, as he did each night. They were the facade of a couple; their naked bodies inches apart, body odour and dead skin cells mingling under the sheets. Their clothes hung side by side in the wardrobe; their damp bath towels together on the heated bath rail. But they were two bodies lying in limbo. Unspoken though the issue was they both knew that in a matter of weeks it would be like a bereavement: two people joined together, sharing their lives for a while - about to become strangers once again. The brief time they had spent together would be a blot on the landscape of their lives yet they would carry the scars of their short time together.

She thought of all the foreign trips; glossy Thomson brochure memories now torn to shreds burning on a massive funeral pyre. She saw them in a gondola in Venice; sipping cocktails at the top of the Burj Khalifa; she saw them side stepping the bluebells in Scotland - beautiful memories each one. Had it all really happened? She'd thought the good times would go on forever. But the truth was they were long over. Still she struggled to admit that to herself.

She listened to him sleeping in the midst of the phoney war they had created. Did he know the police had visited her? It was the elephant in the room and both were carefully side stepping around it. And that was totally out of character for him for a man who normally played bull in a china shop.

God damn it. What was he doing back here? And in the same bed? She wanted to scream. Pretending everything was semi normal when really all he wanted was to see her charged and any chance of re building her career in tatters. She turned over in bed sighing dramatically, spectacularly tugging the duvet away from him in annoyance. She was cornered. And he knew it. This was spite. She tugged again at the duvet almost willing him to wake.

His whispered voice broke the silence. She almost jerked in surprise. 'Have the police been in touch yet?'

'What a bastard you are. What are you trying to do? Ruin my future? You're enjoying this.' She steadied the tremor in her voice like a seasoned opera singer.

'Not heard anything. Don't expect they are that interested in a minor domestic. Bigger fish to fry.'

'They're a bunch of tossers.' His spital hit. ' It's been several days now. They don't give a shit. They're a joke. It seems you... fucking women can do anything to me and get away with it.'

'You nasty bastard' the silent voice continued. The calm voice said 'It's probably way down their list of priorities I imagine.'

'I'll have to ring in the morning. Find out what's going on.' He tugged the duvet, inched further from her.

Gina thought her pounding heart would rip through her chest. She curled her body into a foetal position, butterflies dancing the tango in her stomach.

When daylight flooded through the curtains Clifford reached over to touch her breasts. Maybe from habit. She didn't know. He worked his fingers around a nipple. Warmth crept across her thighs seeping deep inside. Part of her wanted to respond but she remained still, refusing to react remembering what lay ahead.

His hand wandered down the side of her body resting on her pubic area. *'You've reported me to the goddam police and you must know they are interviewing me this morning. Taking my DNA, my fingerprints and you think you can get away with slipping a finger inside me.'* The silent voice screamed. She gritted her teeth. Lay rigid.

'I feel close to you yet distant. We're the scene in Titanic when they're shivering in the icy water. They're over but waiting till death consumes them.'

'How cheerful.'

'We're all waiting to plunge into Cameron's hell.'

He touched her breasts again.

'I'm not in the mood.' She inched away.

'You're slowly turning into my ex. Maybe it's the menopause.'

He cleared his throat.

'Ladies and gentlemen this is your captain speaking. The weather is heavy at London Gatwick. We now begin the descent to menopause. Please stow your tampons, plug in your seat belts. The cabin crew will be coming to collect all tampons, pads, belts, pins, sanitary ware.'

She was looking down upon someone else's life; watching the scene from the ceiling, like an episode of Eastenders. Detached from her body she could see a copper and a woman in a wet raincoat and hat.

Of all the nasty things Clifford was capable of. Now this.

The only bad thing she had ever done in her entire life was kill a toad in the garden. All it had taken was for him to pull the release valve that held her patience together.

One moment of justifiable anger and now she was about to be handed a police record and be placed on List 99. She felt dirty, toxic.

The officer went through some paper work and explained that he would be taking a DNA swab and fingerprints later on. Pleasantries filled the void while they waited for the duty solicitor, held up in traffic.

'Do you know what ABH is?'

'Standing for?'

'Actual Bodily Harm. That's what you are accused of.'

She felt her body shrink. 'Does he know I'm here - Clifford?' His name was gristle in her mouth.

'Yes he knows you're making a statement this morning.'

'Bastard' her inner voice screamed. Her hands tightened to fists in her pockets.

'Be very careful what you say to the solicitor. Just to warn you. If you tell him you intend to lie I don't think he is able to represent you.'

The solicitor arrived, dressed in a black suit and looked more like an undertaker. He was flustered, brushed the rain from his jacket complaining about the weather and the traffic. He shook her hand.

They were left alone.

'You were provoked then?' The solicitor scribbled notes, listened intently as the story came tumbling out: Clifford's general attitude to the kids, the toilet argument, how she had felt that morning; a pressure cooker about to explode. At times her voice splintered, but soon she was on a roll. She repeated the same story as she had to her doctor and friends.

He hesitated. Gina sensed his calculation. An adjustment. He inhaled. Sat up in his chair. He didn't immediately speak.

'He's hit you before you say?' He rubbed his chin. ' And his wife?' Gina couldn't believe how much background she'd vomited in such a short space of time.

'Yes.' She hoped this would work in her favour.

'So you thought it might happen again?' He looked straight at her. She frowned. A haze descended.

'No, not really. I'm not afraid of him. And I don't remember scratching him. I really don't. It's as if my memory has been erased. It's odd though because the scratches were on his left side. That would have been harder for me to do but I must have done it because the evidence is there. He has the photo.'

'Maybe you *were* scared? If he'd hit you before.' He leaned forward.

'No. If anything he was probably scared of me at that moment. He said he was scared to come home; thought I might knife him.' Gina scrunched her face, closed her eyes tight, trying to summon a clear picture. 'I pushed him. Pulled his jacket. It's all vague. He covered his head with an arm when he bent to pick his glasses up from the footwell. Must have thought I was going to attack. He was scared. Not me.'

The solicitor sighed again. 'You can admit this. Or deny it. Or state that it was in self defence.'

'My work depends on a clean CRB check.'

The solicitor studied her face for a moment, rubbing his chin as he thought. She stared at the floor.

Then he sat up. 'Oh come on. You lashed out because you were scared. He provoked you. He'd hit you before. He had that look on his face. He raised his arm, like this.' His points thudded across like bullets.

'And *you* thought he was going to strike you. I would say, categorically that you were acting in self defense.' His voice had passion. She imagined him in court. She wasn't sure if he was playing through all the possible scenarios or trying to redefine what actually happened.

'I'm not telling you to lie. It just depends on how you see the truth.' He added.

Gina was puzzled - more confused than ever. She bit her thumbnail wondering what she should do.

The tape was on. She glanced at the solicitor. He nodded. Half smiled. Then the penny tinkled and dropped.

She turned to the machine. It was as if she had been drowning in a pool of porridge, slowly giving up the fight. But now she was swimming - hard to the surface.

'He'd hit me before. His hand was raised and I thought he was going to hit me. I don't remember what next, just of being terrified.'

The officer presented pictures of the wounds. She stifled the shock. Tears began to well.

'Can you explain these cuts?'

'I don't know. How could I have done that? It was on the left side of his face. I pushed him. I was scared he was going to hit me. Maybe his zip caught his face. He was wearing a jacket with a zip.'

Faced with the pictures she was struggling.

'So you deny doing it?'

'Yes.' But it was one of those yeses that could have easily been a no.

'And if I did do it I don't remember doing it, it was in self defense.'

'Thank you.' The machine clunked. The officer removed the tape and allowed her time with the solicitor alone before taking DNA samples.

She saw the solicitor's visible relief. 'Well done. That was great. I really don't know how they will charge you now. All we can do is wait.'

Gina didn't feel his optimism though.

Doubts niggled in her mind. That evening Clifford again asked if the police had been in touch.

'What are they doing?' he moaned. She stayed quiet. Why was he asking when he already knew the answer? He seemed to be enjoying stoking the fear, watching her go through this nightmare.

The phone call came on the Sunday evening. She looked at Clifford across the table. Relief washed over her. 'Thank God. Thank you.'

'What was that about?' he asked.

'Nothing important. Something actually quite trivial.' She smiled at him.

'You're beaming. Can't be trivial.'

'The CPS have dropped the case. They aren't even giving me a caution.'

Clifford got up. Stepped towards her. He could look as menacing as he wanted she thought. She felt nothing but triumph.

Soon she would be free.

'And how did you get away with that?'

'No comment.'

30
Clifford

August 2011

'Look at these rioters.'

'Wha' about 'em?'

' A primary school teacher, a father stealing nappies for his kid and even a millionaire's daughter. If these people can get away with it so can I. Fuck the law.' Clifford put one finger up as David Cameron told the nation 'the fight back has now begun.'

He tutted in Penny's direction, but her eyes were locked once more on the Danielle Steele she was reading.

He was on an imaginary podium shaking his head at the TV, watching shop windows being pelted, news of three dead, London ablaze. He cheered as bricks were thrown at a bank. He'd long wanted to do the same.

Cameron's Etonian plum grated. What had he ever done with his life, apart from sending more fodder to the sweltering heat of Afganistan only to return in body bags? Had he ever been a soldier? Had he ever got his hands greasy under a car bonnet or shoved his cock up a prostitute? Did he understand the daily struggle of living in Tottenham? The only boisterous male experience he understood was the Bullingdon Club.

'Gordon Brown said we were fighting terrorism to make the streets of Britain safer. Look at the streets now.' Clifford laughed.

'Kids smashing shop windows bored, frustrated, out of control.'

'Now what 'ave I done?' He'd momentarily forgotten the screechy, witch like voice that now occupied his living space. She reminded him of the irritating voice in the seat behind at the cinema.

'You've done nothing. Don't jump every time I swear or shout. You're like a scared weasel.'

There had been several occasions, during the past few weeks when Clifford had really lost his rag and it had been on the tip of his tongue to turn round and yell: *'I'm beginning to see why your ex husband took a coat hanger to your head.'* But she was a sweet, harmless soul – and reminded him of those emaciated, shivering mongrels that were handed in at Battersea.

'Bother you. I'm going to make a pot of tea love and make your sandwiches for tomorrow, let Squeaker out for a wee and lay up for the morning. Will you want the same breakfast again or shall I put out Cornflakes for a change?' Clifford tried to drown out her wittering, gyrating voice boring into his soul. He curled his fists into two stress balls -the only way he could contain himself.

'Maybe I'll wait till after the weather forecast. Might be a good washing day tomorrow. I'll take off my make up so I'm all ready for bed. I might finish this book later. Only one chapter left. How can you keep watching that? It's so depressing.'

He sighed. How had his life come to this? Where was this written in his star signs? Was this how he was going to end his days?

'Don't take your wig off down here. I can't cope with the dead cat.'

He had seen her once, without her wig on and she'd reminded him of a wild gosling with no feathers.

'Jesus,' he sighed. It was like living with a corpse. With make up on she was just about bearable to sit opposite in the mornings, as she slurped her tea having stirred in 5 sugars.

From behind and at a distance she looked ok: curly blonde wig, a curvy waistline, long slender legs. But not on closer inspection. Heads didn't turn, stomachs turned instead. Her witch life profile and deep wrinkles looked like the valleys of Afganistan.

'I could drive a truck through those wrinkles,' he would joke to Ben. In the shower as he sponged his saggy belly and turkey neck he'd sing: 'She's an old

old bag. Her tits hang down and her fanny's all dry. She's an old old granny with a very dry fanny.' His life had reached a new low.

'The downstairs toilet could do with a bleach love.'

'What are you trying to do? Intoxicate me?'

'And there's a pile of ironing for me in the morning, love.'

'You're like one of those Stepford wives. One day I'll come home and find you've ironed the dead cat wig and the dog. I'll find the make up outside going for a wee and the cereal in the dog bowl.'

'Sorry I haven't found any time for hovering this week.'

'*Love.*' He mimicked. 'I'm not expecting Mary Poppins perfection. You don't need to prepare my bed at night or make animals out of the bath towels or iron the dishcloths. And get rid of the vases. I can't stand flowers. This isn't a hotel lobby, or a funeral parlour. You're here for one thing and one thing only. Don't forget it.' He screamed.

She cowered. 'But I have to live here too love.'

She plumped the cushions as she got up from the settee, slipping her feet into pink feathered slippers heading for the kitchenette.

Gina
May 2011

Gina thought it ironic that they should be eating their 'last supper' in her favourite restaurant, Carluccios where she had wanted to eat on their first date two years ago. She loved the atmosphere, the delicatessen counter and the rows of neatly stacked pesto and packets of ciabatta on display. But on that first date Clifford had swept her past the entrance – determined she would prefer the sushi bar a few paces along. She hadn't liked the Sushi experience; it had been like watching a mini conveyor belt at Heathrow airport. Even the food tasted luggagey.

The atmosphere was tense between them, like a first date but without any of the hope. It had been weeks since they'd parted.

'Your Bells Palsy seems to have gone now. Face looks loads better.'

Clifford gave a full Cheshire cat half moon smile. His cheeks had tone and his eye no longer drooped.

'I've been having weekly facials. It's virtually recovered but gets painful when I'm very tired and my eye starts stinging when I've been on a long haul flight. Bells is rarely permanent. I knew it would eventually get better.'

'And Ben? How is he?' Gina drummed the questions. It was easier to keep him talking. She felt less awkward that way.

'Oh God. You've no idea. So much has happened. Where to bloody begin. They're treating him for bi polar. He's on lithium. All the indicators were there. Can't believe I hadn't seen it. He's not been the same in a long time.'

'Shit.' She tried to digest these headlines. Clifford's life was one big road crash. 'It kind of makes sense. His behaviour...'

He filled her in with all the ghastly events leading to the diagnosis and the worry of him being chucked off the vet course. She wondered if Clifford had caused it all but kept her thoughts to herself. They fell quiet for a time. She waited for his apology for everything he'd put her through.

'So. Let's just get this over shall we?' Gina pushed the last of the woodland fruit around the dish. The meal had been disappointing.

'What is it you needed to tell me that couldn't have been said in a text? I haven't heard from you in weeks. Why now?' When Gina had received his text asking to meet up because he had something important to tell her she imagined he was going to say sorry. She longed to hear those words; a final acknowledgement that he was wrong and shouldn't have treated her or the kids so appallingly.

'I just wanted you to hear it direct from the horse's mouth.'

'Hear what? And how is that very likely? Our worlds don't mix.' Gina thumped her drink down,' flushed with irritation.

'Leaving you wasn't easy.' He rubbed his forehead, finished his cheesecake. He was still eating desserts, she tutted to herself. It was no longer her problem.

She remembered watching him standing on the pavement outside the cottage as his removal van pulled away; a pained look on his face.

'Signing a new tenancy agreement was like throwing mud on my brother's coffin. I couldn't quite believe it was happening. The pen hovered over the document for what seemed like an eternity, before I finally entered my squiggle.' Clifford pursed his lips, in that pained way he always did. His eyes were translucent, tiny pools.

'It didn't take you long to get a rental sorted. You're quick and decisive when you want to be. Making plans that suit you. Fail to plan, plan to fail as you always said. Anyway. What's the new place like?' It seemed polite to ask but she didn't want the answer.

'It's just another rental. What can I say?' Clifford shrugged. The harsh lighting in the restaurant made him look sickly. ' I'll probably never buy again. It's a bungalow. It reminds me of those kids' toys, Transformers. Joss probably has a few. When you die they transform into coffins.'

He sighed. 'Look Gina. I'm going blind. I can't drive anymore. I can't sell the business. I'm finished. I'm not a great catch anymore. I'm staring down the barrel of old age and it doesn't look great. You were looking for a surrogate parent for your kids. What you got was a dying man to fill the vacancy of those drift away, fade out loser dads and quite frankly if we were getting back together you'd have to eat your dull kids first.'

She looked down at the woodland fruit she'd been eating. An icy chill shot through her blood. She thought of the kids at home, three in one small room. Resentment curdled. She had to find a way to get him back. He just didn't get it. As far as he was concerned he was always in the right. And she had imagined he would apologise!

He carried on. 'It was like somebody put an old gramophone on but they'd paid their money and the vinyl was scratched. That's basically my life in a nutshell. I feel impudent and useless, chained and doomed and sick and washed out. It was all of it Gina. What were we looking forward to together? We weren't going to have kids. We weren't even going to grow vegetables in the back garden. It was all one delusion. One big lie. My biggest problem is me. You'll have no problem pulling. Until they discover the three kids, two dads that is.'

The waiter came over and asked if they were finished. 'Oh we're most certainly finished. That I *do* know.'

The waiter returned with the slip of paper that Clifford always called an invoice rather than a bill.

'Can you pass on my comments to the management that the meal was pretty shit? The portions were tiny.'

'Can I get you a coffee, on the house?'

'No. Like I said we're finished. Tell the management they're cunts.'

'There's no need for that sort of behaviour sir.'

The waiter looked as if he'd been punched. He took the silver dish containing the signed bill and swiftly moved away.

She shook her head, watched the man disappear into the kitchen; a fresh waft of garlic and basil filling the restaurant as the door flung open.

'That's despicable. Using the 'C' word in public. It's vulgar. Unnecessary. Nasty.'

'Well that sums me up Gina. A vulgar nasty little man. You're best out of it.'

So..?' It was time to find out why he wanted to speak to her.

'Penny's living with me.'

'What? The woman you slept with before you met me? I thought you'd lost touch with her. I don't believe it. It didn't take you long to get fixed up.'

She clasped her hands to stop them shaking. On top of everything else that had happened he just had to get the last kick in. Suddenly it felt as if a truck had driven over her stomach. Did she really need to know all this? How dare he insist they meet to deliver this final blow.

'It's nothing like that. She's got her own room. I'm paying her.'

'You're paying her? How very nice.' She smiled her best Chelsea grin and picked up a napkin rolling it tight into a cigar, then pressed it with the heel of her hand.

'While I have to manage on cleaning jobs because I can't find work you're paying some bitch to live with you. For what reason exactly? It can't be for sex. Your stools were always bigger than your tool, last time you failed to flush the toilet properly.'

She was internally seething, but held on to the one crumb of comfort that she had managed to save £10,000 in the six months she had lived with him – through renting her flat and some of the housekeeping money he had given her. That money would help in buying a bigger property. And of course the children were happier and that, after all was the most important thing of all.

'That's right. Get the cattiness in. I'm going blind. I'm going to need a carer at some point and she needed a job.'

'How very cosy. So you were still in contact with her?' She curled the napkin tighter.

'I still had her number. I need her to do what you would never in a million years agree to do.'

' I wondered when it was going to be my fault in some way.'

'She's a kind soul and would do anything for me.'

'I bet she would. Probably grip your limp dick if required.'

Gina sat up leaned back on the red leather seating, sniffed deeply.

' I needed a name on the car insurance documents. She's got a clean licence. I needed a driver.'

'You're paying an ex, someone who slept with you to be a live in driver?' Gina flicked the napkin across the table and it fluttered to the floor.

'That's unbelievable. So I wasn't good enough as your taxi driver. You needed to employ someone. You bastard.'

Heads were starting to turn as Gina raised her voice with mounting anger. 'Un-bel-ievable.'

'She picks me up from work everyday. And when I can't see my arse any more she'll be wiping it.'

Gina ignored the latter comment.

'You can't take the train? Way beneath you I guess. Or move nearer to work?'

'I brought the car tonight. She's away. Thought I'd drive here. Bit of a test really. It's the first time I've driven since I lost the licence.'

She shrugged, shook her head. 'You shouldn't think about driving again. End of. I don't care about your life but what about the lives of other, innocent people - pedestrians crossing the road, little children?'

'Well that told me. I didn't think you, of all people would understand.'

'You're not above the law.'

'It's a ridiculous law imposed by Europe. I've done the research. The law shouldn't have been changed.'

' The law is the law. You've been told by professionals that it's not safe to drive.'

'And I know I am safe. It's my passport to freedom and my independence. Anyway, like I say tonight is just a test. I don't feel great about it. She's done all the driving so far.'

'You sound like America at war. Do what you like. I hope one day they catch you. But maybe they never will. And if they did I bet the fine is so small it wouldn't even burn a hole in your pocket. The money you earn.'

'You always were jealous of what I earned.'

'Oh pleeeese.' Gina snorted. 'There are plenty of people on the road that shouldn't be driving. People over the limit, or too tired or old and dithery. They're the real danger. You see them all the time.'

Nothing she said could convince him. Not even a Bosch to the skull. She sighed.

'Look I didn't expect you to understand which is why we aren't together any longer but I just needed you to know about Penny that's all.'

'Why? It's not exactly made me feel better. I was completely insignificant to you.'

'You meant everything to me, Gina. I still love you, you daft cow. But you need a man not a mouse and this blind man's looking for a farmer's wife.'

'Oh please.' She twisted her nose. 'You don't know what love is. Empty words Clifford.'

'Love's just a psychosis.'

'Let's go. I don't want to hear anymore. You've always been somebody that's convinced that you're right and everyone else is wrong. I'm not going to change that.'

They stood up briefly facing each other, eyes momentarily locked. Gina wondered if he was going to wrap his arms around her, but he didn't. He frowned, pain ingrained into his face.

'It was never going to work.' He sighed. She wondered if he was going to touch her face, but he didn't.

'If you knew that why did we bother?'

'Step families don't work. Everyone warned me. People think they can buy into the dream but the dream doesn't exist. Blended families, step families whatever you want to call them, they're a complete mess. It's like bringing together the cast of a film knowing the characters are wrong for the set. I was never Mr. Step Family Man. I was Mr. Steptoe and I had to step away.'

He headed for the door. She knew he was right.

'Look I've got some stuff you left behind.' She called after him. 'Give me your address and I'll drop it over sometime.'

Gina had an ulterior motive. In a flash she felt the knife of revenge descend. People had always told her she was a typical Gemini – someone whose personality could turn in an instant. And she had also heard the expression love and hate are just two sides of the same coin. And in that split second the coin had flipped to hate. She smiled quietly to herself.

Clifford pulled out his keys tossing them from hand to hand.

'You don't need to. Dump it at the tip.'

' I don't mind. Give me the address. I'm sure I'll be passing in the next week.'

She tried to prevent her voice descending into a desperate plea.

'We were crash on impact Gina. The plane trundling down the runway. When it reaches V2 it has to be committed to lift. It needs to commit at V1. We didn't reach V1, we couldn't commit.'

' It wasn't all bad.'

'Look.'

He tugged at her coat, his lip twisting the way it always did when he wasn't sure.

He sighed. ' I'm Clifford the shit, Clifford the nasty, Clifford take a chancer. Nothing will change. That's me. The Conservatives have taken over and everything has been privatized and sub contracted out, commissioned out to different services.'

'And I lost the tender.'

'You won the entertainment budget.'

'Great. That's all I was to you?' She looked down, saddened but with hope for a fresh new beginning for herself and the children. She'd sacrificed her family, her heart and her dignity. Never again. She'd come close to losing their respect and damaging them forever. Now it was time to put them first. Their future was in her hands. And no one else really mattered. There would be happy evenings ahead with Popcorn and the X Factor, curry on Fridays and cuddles on the sofa. Life was on the up. She had her dream. The three children were the dream.

They reached the multi storey and as she watched him unlock the car door surreptitiously slipped her phone out of her pocket - took a few shots from an angle to show the number plate. As she walked off she made a fist and banged her other hand.

'Gotya, you bastard.' Revenge was a sweet in the mouth and a spring in the step. She punched the air.

She turned a couple of minutes later to see his car thundering down the ramp. And that was the last she ever saw of him.

Clifford
February 2011

Clifford staggered up the steps to the platform dazed after Gina's tirade. He stopped. Leant against the wall of the station taking stock of all that had happened. He felt like a cat after a scrap, disheveled and dazed. He straightened his collar and feeling chilly partly through nerves zipped his jacket; the important buyers meeting ahead gone from his mind.

Each step felt heavy, pained. He checked the digital boards for his train, headed to the toilets feeling feverish and looked in the mottled mirror. The reflection that stared back wasn't his. Hadn't felt his in a long time. They were two different people occupying two dimensions.

'Bitch,' he told the reflection. He splashed cold water across his cheek, pieces of pavement grit swirled towards the plug, icy water stung. It had been years since he'd clumsily fallen to the ground, smacked the pavement, face into clumps of fresh peppermint gum and discarded butts, the searing sensation of flesh tearing against the hard surface.

He cursed.

Don't let her get away with this. Do something about it. His reflection screamed back.

He stared hard at the broken flesh, feeling hypnotic. Blood pricked to the surface. He removed another piece of grit. Since the Bells Palsy and his glaucoma he'd likened his face to those of old broken bears in kids stories; eyes missing or replaced with black buttons, wonky stitched mouths and stuffing escaping from the cheeks. The tone in his face since the Palsy had improved quite a bit but eating was still hard and when he was tired or stressed the affected side of his face began to hurt. Taking a deep breath he clasped his cheeks and with a swift strike dug his nails deep into the flesh and tore across the cheek. His face burned. Four raw gashes cried in anger, tiny rivulets of blood coursed towards his mouth. He stood back, admired his artwork.

'She'll pay,' he told the reflection.

He pulled out his i phone and took several shots of the side of his face. Then he went to the basin and washed his finger nails with soap, carefully removing the evidence before heading to the taxi rank and off to the police station.

31
Clifford

December 2011

He'd long agonised about whether to visit his mother. But before long it was too late.

Following a nasty fall she was rushed to hospital where the doctors discovered she was at end stage kidney failure.

He had visited the care home only once and had been shocked by the extent of her decline. He couldn't put himself through it again. Dementia had slowly stripped away the very essence of her being. She was a shell of the former person - almost ghostlike. He remembered the haunted faraway look in her eyes, the uncoordinated speech, the vacant way she walked, oblivious to all around her. She'd changed so much. The ultimate relief was death. Part of him envied her reaching that end, the bitter sweet release of pain, the letting go, the warmth of nirvana.

And yet through his relief and sense of peace and closure her impending death gave him came a nagging guilt pricking his conscience. He thought of all the other families stoically visiting their loved ones, in care homes up and down the country, taking in flowers and chocolates. But this whole routine, this false charade wasn't Clifford; the way he operated. He wasn't about keeping up appearances, doing all the things he ought to do, should do. He did things his way. Life was tough. Shit was shit but you didn't have to wade your way through it if you didn't have to.

A couple of days later she returned from hospital to the care home effectively to die although nobody seemed to acknowledge that or use the word 'dying' or 'death.'

A Nigerian care worker over the phone described her condition as 'comfortable.' What the fuck did that mean? It reminded him of an old Jewish joke about a Jewish guy knocked down by a car. Helpers put a pillow under his head and asked if he was comfortable.

He phoned again and spoke to a Greek care worker who kept saying 'what a lovely lady your mother is.' He wanted to hit back: *how would you know? You know nothing about her. You've seen her at the end of her life, a life now clouded by the ravages of dementia, her brain slowly rotting away. She pisses and shits all day. What is so lovely about that?*

As far as Clifford was concerned his mother had died the day she had reported him to the police. If only he had seen her mental decline coming. If only the medical profession had seen it all coming too, but there had been too many people coming and going, no sharing of information, no coordination and God knows he hadn't been around to oversee what was going on.

The woman she was had slowly crept away, vanishing piece by piece. His father's sudden death, when he was just 20 had come as a bitter blow to her; a grief she carried around, a heavy weight in her pocket. Her daily misery was about her suffering and loss. The suffering and the thinking about the suffering had spread to every vein of her body; she had gradually turned into a tormented soul. It was almost as if his death had left her in a permanent state of fear and suspense, transforming the rooted life she once had into a terrifying experience which was slowly eating away at her. Her grief took a cyclical pattern starting with Yom Yippur getting worse each year around December at the anniversary of his death. Then there was a slight revival of spirit each Spring, around Passover as she attempted to restart her life.

She had channeled all her energies into her grandson in an attempt to rebuild her life. She had loved looking after him, providing childcare, taking him to the beach, the park, the duck pond, doing the school run but her grief remained. The second half of her life had been a tragedy, wasted years of sorrow. The day his father had suffered a massive heart attack had changed her world. All he saw from that day on was a dull sorrowful look in her eyes. But did the source of her pain, a pain that seemed so tangible within her very being, begin even way before his father's death?

When he looked back upon his childhood for answers there seemed to be something missing. He couldn't quite put his finger on what it was. The aura of something in that household that should have been there wasn't. When he closed his eyes, tried to recapture the atmosphere, the scene from all those years ago all he could feel was a cold numbness. He remembered sitting in his bedroom making model aeroplanes, setting up different experiments with gadgets he'd constructed, staring out for hours just looking at the rooftops and the metal smoke stacks of the Metal Box Company and those of the Co-op Diary and laundry, a huge edifice occupying several acres. To his child's eye they looked like the funnels of two ocean going liners.

But his overriding memory was of looking out on a Saturday afternoon onto their cherry tree lined road and seeing other parents teaching their children to ride a bike. He'd felt trapped within his four walls, as he now felt trapped without the freedom to drive a car. He'd seen children toppling over on the grass verges, their mothers or their fathers rushing to their rescue. He'd heard the laughter and the screams when he'd opened the window and leant out to watch. And he'd been filled with the most intense envy he had ever experienced. How he'd longed to ride a bike; to feel the rush of wind on his face. He'd dreamt of where those wheels could take him and how far he might be able to travel in one day, resting by the verge when the chain came off, feeling the greasy cogs in his hands.

And as he grew older he'd watched clusters of teenagers leaning against bar handles in the road below or wheeling round in circles, messing around enjoying each other's company. But he wasn't part of their culture. He'd been desperate to wear the hat of belonging. Nobody had listened to him when he asked for a bike. Nobody had had time to teach him. And now he felt that same sense of exclusion at not being able to drive.

And most of all when he swiveled back in time he felt a tingling sensation of fear but didn't know where the origin of that fear was. Fear of being in the bathroom alone with the scary plumbing noises; the hot water tank that made banging noises when the system got too hot, the gurgling when the taps were turned on. Fear in the front room. The baby grand piano he was never allowed to touch. The wall mounted electric fire that had sparked and arced when it was switched on, reminding him of an electric chair from a US jail. And fear of being alone with his grandmother who frequently shouted and cursed at him for being in the way.

His mother's life had seemed so hard – all drudgery and caring, few pleasures. He could see her frying fish at the stove and boiling cauldrons of clothes and the long washing line of steaming clothes in the front room. The house was like a railway terminus before the end of the age of steam.

He could remember the fear of diabetes from a young age, having watched both his grandmother and his mother testing their blood glucose in the kitchen and the terror that one day he might inherit the condition. The constant testing both intrigued and scared him. At a young age he saw them pee in a cup, then mix two drops of the urine and ten drops of water into a test tube. Then they added a blue pill. The pill reacted violently with water, so when they dropped the pill in the test tube it would immediately bubble and boil, heating the liquid to about 200 degrees F. The liquid would change color. If it was blue they were negative. If it was green, they were spilling a small amount of glucose into their urine. If it turned bright orange, they were most likely peeing honey. Diabetes was ingrained into the very fabric of his family and so when he received his own diagnosis he wasn't at all surprised. He knew then it would spell his death knell.

He was shocked at the change in her as he pushed open her bedroom door in the care home he likened to a bland looking Travel Lodge. The nurse had shown him the blood and biochemistry numbers, presenting the whole picture. It wouldn't be long. He made it clear to the staff at the outset – no more hospital, no antibiotics if she got a chest infection and no resuscitation if her heart stopped. There was a DNR in place. He wanted a swift end.

She was thrashing around like a wounded animal. A dog's end, he thought was more dignified. But then a nurse came to increase her sedation and her body became still. He rested his hand on her forehead, stroking her increasingly dehydrated arm, hour after hour, perhaps making up for the lost two years he hadn't visited. He listened to the changing breathing patterns; a rapid, hyperventilating rattle. Then it would grow shallower and shallower until it almost fell away and he would feel a momentary panic. Then it would start up again, like a banger on the London to Brighton struggling to life.

He sat on an armchair next to her, one arm rested over the bed bars, his emotions in free fall. One minute he felt huge relief. At last he could move on, mentally and physically. He'd be able to buy a house. And the next minute he felt a tangled web of pain. He didn't quite understand why he was here. Was it for him? Was it for her? Was it to finally plug up that void that had always existed between them. Those unspoken moments when they could have talked about Simon over the years but hadn't. He got up opened a fresh lemon moistened cotton bud to dab around her dry lips. Caring for the dying was a futile exercise. It was about retaining dignity in dying. But what exactly was dignity? Did she appreciate a pad change? A tiny dab of water on the lips? Did she hear him whisper that soon she would be reunited with the man she never stopped loving and the baby she had lost all those years ago?

He removed the blanket that covered her feet. Looking at it made his eyes well. He folded it, placed it under the bed. He leaned in towards her ear, whispering 'sorry' over and over. What did sorry mean? He wasn't sure. Then he picked the blanket up again, hugged it to his face, brushed the soft fibres against his cheek, breathing in rose water and old dinner. He closed his eyes, breathed deeper, wheeling back in time; to the sickly smells of the past; milk and talc and vomit. All at once he was back there; could hear the cries, the thump of feet on the wooden steps, the heavy hand of his father pushing him aside.

He brushed his eyes, tucked the blanket away where he couldn't see it and be reminded, then thought about his parents - two weak willed panicky adults who couldn't cope with the basics of life, like changing a light bulb or fixing a broken toaster. At times Clifford had loathed their stupidity and ignorance. He'd always wanted a better life for himself.

Her breathing shallowed and her head turned a fraction towards him. He thought he imagined it. Her eyes flickered. He wanted to believe this was her way of forgiving him for what he'd done or what he hadn't done.

The light in the room was fading. Shadows bounced across the bare walls. A candle burned from a tea light on the windowsill for it was the Sabbath. Soft carols gently filled the room, from an old radio in the corner reminding him of his confused childhood – a mixture of half religions. A pungent sweet smell grew each hour that passed, growing heavier, more cloying, signifying her body was slowly shutting down, cells were no longer dividing, the release of toxins - the end in sight. He tried to think of what the smell was like. He sniffed the air, frowned. Was it a mixture of menthol and rubber and roses? Or was it the not unpleasant sweet smell of menstrual blood on a fragranced sanitary towel? God knows that was a smell he knew too well. Anger still bubbled; the memory of Roda bleeding and bleeding for weeks, for months on end; her fanny a giant jam doughnut, refusing to go to the doctor, plugging herself up with massive Havana cigar style tampons and the hysterectomy he insisted was done privately – one of the only things she had paid for herself. He had always imagined a yellow skip taking away all her bits; the fallopian tubes were big rusty pipes from a building site. Nature was cruel. Women were just a badly designed machine; cars with leaking sumps; a whole region with so many potential plumbing issues; everything coming out of different pipes.

He recalled the picture of Roda's fanny he had taken on an old Ericson back in 2003; his first phone with a camera. He remembered its' ugly crooked sneer. Even her fanny had contempt for him. And bizarrely he thought of Jack The Ripper arranging Whitechapel prostitute's bits and pieces on a table.

He was transported back to that painful time, which was in effect the beginning of the end of their sexual relationship and ultimately the end of their relationship itself. How ironic it had been that she had paid back the costs of the hysterectomy but later racked up so much crippling debt. Red letter reminders plopping onto the doormat daily, coiling round their daily life, suffocating the future, destroying everything. He still wondered where the money had all gone.

He snapped back to the present; studied his mother's translucent bruised skin. Microbiology had always intrigued him. Death both repelled and drew him in. He wanted to consume every moment fascinated by the hourly minute by minute changes. She had lost so much weight, looked much older. Watching her skin was like watching the light fade in the night sky, the colour subtly changing. One moment he thought her skin looked more yellow. Then he would look away to his father's baby grand piano which took up a large part of the room studying its wonderful polished veneer. He looked back at his mother; noticed her skin was greyer – like the photo that had sat for as long as he could remember on the corner of the baby grand of his parents beaming proud faces looking down upon the baby Simon. As a teenager he had stood for ages looking at the picture; trying to imagine Simon at different ages and stages, wondering who he would have become and what they would have been like as brothers. When people asked who he was and it was explained to them they said they were sorry. Clifford had never understood why they had always said sorry. It didn't feel like a loss. It felt as if Simon had never gone away; a presence remaining, never to die as long as his mother lived.

He stood up, walked over to take a closer look. The garment Simon was wearing had hung on the side of his mother's wardrobe for many years, yellowing and crusting with time. The central picture on the piano celebrated the pinnacle of his father's career. He was wearing a black tie and big beaming smile as he received a music award in Vienna. Clifford gently wiped his finger along the sheen of the piano wood, feeling its beauty under his touch and the prickle of sadness deep in his chest. He turned back towards her, scanned the room. He wondered if she had ever asked the nurses about him or had she completely forgotten her own son.

He sat down. Tiredness washed over him. Suddenly he felt a cold chill creep swiftly through his body. He looked at the cushion beside him. It was as if there was a presence on the armchair beside him. He could feel it so intensely, so eerily; it was as if Simon was sitting next to him -the brother that should have lived, the brother that should have been there to support him through all the hard and painful times. He'd spent the best part of 40 odd years cycling back in time, revisiting the memory. He heard again the pounding of feet on the bare wooden stairs outside the baby's room, like Nazis arriving at Anne Frank's hideaway. They swept the baby up, pinching his cheeks. He could still hear his mother wailing. The baby whisked away, wrapped in a white sheet, never to be seen again. He'd felt like an Antarctic explorer who sees his ship disappear over the horizon.

He leaned in again, stroking strands of grey hair from around her ear and whispered 'Love you mum.' He brushed the salty tears welling up with the back of his hand. But the same words that had continually echoed round and round in his head all these years came back to haunt him: bitter sharp words of his father to him as they'd carried Simon away.

Happy now? The words were louder now. Ringing round and round. *Happy now?* And yet the only sound in the room was the rattle of her breath and the lilt of 'Silent Night' and call bells ringing intermittently along the corridor.

He lifted up the sheet covering her body and touched her heavily swollen ankles, rock solid feet. Her legs were growing colder, even her arms were starting to chill. The circulation was slowing. Time seemed to be slowing. Soon she would be carried away in a body bag. He found himself imagining a tiny baby coffin. His heart thudded at the revulsion of the reality of death but also the mystique and beauty of death.

And then the last breath came. Either that or the next breath didn't come. He called for the nurse to take her pulse. And then without warning sobs hit flooding up from his chest, spilling out. A heat of shock and crushing feeling of loss swept his body. His whole family had gone: one person now remained - a son he no longer knew.

32
Clifford

December 2011

The rabbi instructed Clifford to go home and light a pillar shaped candle for his mother. Strangely he found himself taking comfort from the rituals of the faith he was born into.

The burial took place two days later on a Sunday and he and Ben arrived at the gates of an Essex Jewish Cemetery. Clifford asked the taxi driver to wait. They wouldn't be long.

They stood for a moment in the biting wind and he thought how like the entrance to Aushwitz Berkenau the cemetery looked with its long approach to the archway of death and a building that looked like the low, long red building that met the victims and the whole de humanizing experience of Auschwitz. How ironic, he considered. He wanted desperately to understand the suffering of his race but he couldn't crawl inside the reality.

He thought about the generations of his family who had lived before him and all that they had suffered. Maybe suffering was deep within the blood of each and every one of them, carried from generation to generation. All he knew was the deeply entrenched mentality to succeed that had always existed within his family and other Jewish families he'd met along the way and the need to turn suffering around with a dry humour. The words of an uncle a long time ago had always returned to haunt him driving him on through every business challenge he'd ever faced.

You've been put on this earth to make money Clifford.

Either side of the road the headstones were densely crammed in, like rows of vegetables. After a short service which was heavy on ritual but of no comfort whatsoever the basic wooden box containing his mother was carried on a cart to the plot and lowered into the precarious hole. He put his arm around his son. The fallout from the divorce had very nearly torn their relationship apart but as they stood against the biting wind the bond between father and son could never be broken, for the love was too strong and blood ties meant everything.

He'd never stop worrying about Ben; he didn't want to admit that actually he was completely terrified of Ben's future, much more than his own future as a blind man terrified him. The desperate uncertainty of the state of Ben's mental health and where things might lead nagged away in the pit of his stomach. He was all too aware of the tragic nature of mental conditions and didn't want to confront the worst imaginable fears. Why did the worries of life never ease? When one thing was resolved why did more problems simply follow along?

He'd never forgive his wife for everything she'd done, everything she'd taken and destroyed. He'd wish her cancer for as long as he lived - a slow, painful and agonizing death. He was sick of reminding his son how lousy she'd been and what an insincere scum bag she still was.

He just didn't get it. He'd begged and begged Ben to disown her, to cut her adrift. At times he'd hated him for his lethargic attitude, his smugness. The way he sat on the sidelines thinking he had nothing to do with the divorce when he, as their son had everything to do with it. He'd threatened time and again to cut off his student maintenance if he didn't put pressure on his mother to drop her claims. He'd called him a scumbag in restaurants, he'd spat across the table 'you're no son of mine.' He'd given up counting the number of occasions Ben had walked out before the end of a meal.

Looking down and throwing a single red rose as the box was lowered he knew at that moment that nothing much really mattered in life and that life really was so short. The writing had been on the wall for him years back, when he had received the diabetes diagnosis. He'd ignored the warning lights, he'd made some changes to his lifestyle, but what the heck? It would beat him in the end, as it had beaten his mother.

While the bitterness of the divorce never really subsided the healing hands of time seemed to ease the pain, dull the sting of the memory, for Clifford began to notice he talked of the divorce far less these days, the loss of all the money and his beautiful home, high up on the Downs.

33
Clifford

December 2011

He returned to the care home a couple of days later to collect her belongings and arrange for a removal firm to deliver the piano to a storage firm. It personified his father's career as a very talented pianist and it represented the very essence of his childhood. There were very few belongings in the room where she had spent her dying days: a drawer containing neatly ironed nighties and knickers, a hair net, a pot containing her false teeth, a pair of reading glasses, a set of dirty hearing aids and a poetry book. He held up a pair of the large white knickers and thought about how women's bodies were like fruit left too long out of the fridge; their pelvic floors collapsing under the strain of childbirth and life. He thought again of Roda and how her body had become over the years a dangerous structure marked WARNING: FOR DEMOLITION.

He grabbed his mother's pink dressing gown from the bathroom door, her crimson velvet slippers, a bottle of Nina Ricci and slung it all into a black sack taking it to the outside bins. It was all part of the exit process from life; every part of which was ghastly; a necessary part of the departure bureaucracy. In the end it was about waste; an environmental issue and no other.

Sitting at the baby grand he opened the mahogany lid - swept a finger across the keys -all the time transfixed on the black and white photo of his parents holding baby Simon. After all these years he couldn't grasp the concept of such a young death. Birth and death rolled into one. He pressed a single key. Then another.

He looked outside. The sky was foreboding. The grass sodden. Splats of rain thudded onto a brick pathway like handfuls of nails. Even the natural world seemed angry. The sky was poised in anticipation. His stomach too felt full of nails, digging, turning. He focused on each bubble of water as it hit the ground and one moment imagined they were tiny UFOs; the next they were silvery fish coursing along in ripples.

He'd never know the truth about what had happened to Simon. And all the time his mother had sat, rotting in the care home he could have visited, could have asked but hadn't and now it was too late. He'd spend the rest of his life searching for the truth, wondering - the same questions thudding round and round his head.

The sky outside was black and ominous, as if a big confession was waiting to tumble down

He looked at the photo again. Suddenly his parents were strangers. Behind the smiles were lies and evil. The secret danced within the grains of the photo.

He began to laugh. He banged the keys of the piano with his fists and laughed from the pit of his belly. His laughter became quiet tears, escaping from the ducts.

He looked at his mother again in the picture. He looked behind the curled smile; saw ugliness, pain, dishonesty, sadness, but not beauty. The beauty within the photo had been stripped away. He couldn't take a trip inside her soul. The secret took on a deadly power of its' own with each passing minute. His thoughts settled on what his father had repeatedly said to him after Simon was gone.

Happy now?' The words sounded like a melody played on his piano.

That night he scarcely slept. The exhaustion had drained out of him like anaesthetic. It felt as if a great tide had hurled him onto a beach on a deserted island, leaving him to fend for himself.

He had no sense of time, history, or family. They were concepts that no longer existed. He would never know the truth. Where was he going to find that truth? In the pads, the knickers, the perfume, the dressing gown, the slippers he'd thrown out? The truth only existed in the minds and the hearts of those who had died.

34

Clifford

September 2011

'STOP!'

'Wha'?'

'Stop the fucking car. NOW.'

The brakes screeched and locked. They were flung forward. The seat beats clunked. He thought her wig would escape from her head and fly to the dashboard.

'Jesus fucking Christ.' Clifford gripped the door handle. Wiped his brow.

'Wha'?'

'Get out.'

Diligently she got out. He shuffled to the driver's seat. Pulled the seat forward. Adjusted the mirror, still cursing.

She opened the passenger door and got in, wafting heavy perfume and immediately took advantage of the opportunity to apply more lipstick. Bloody women, he thought.

'It's a wonder you ever passed your driving test. You're in fourth gear when you should be in first gear and first gear when you should be in fourth gear.'

'We didn't have an accident love.'

'We soon fucking will. Stalling at traffic lights or in the middle of roundabouts, braking too late, grating the gears, not indicating.'

'*You* shouldn't drive love.'

'From now on I most certainly will. I only need your name on the documents.'

'Look love.'

'I'm not your love.'

'I'm not having the police come knocking.'

'Fuck 'em. I write articles for Goodyear and Dunlop on tread depths, aquaplaning, efficient grips. How can I do that without actually driving? I'm not prepared to be passenger to a crazy witch in my new sixty grand Mercedes. How do you think I feel? A handcuffed kid in a candy store. I want to drive myself to work.'

'Don't be 'orrible love. Otherwise I'll look for a new job.'

Repeating in his head the mantra mirror, signal, manoeuvre he pulled away from the kerb like a seventeen year old driver preparing for their test.

Breaking the law didn't sit easily on his conscience but what choice did he have? In the weeks and months that followed he got on with it, brushed the nagging guilt to the back of his mind, focusing on the road ahead and around. It wasn't easy with compromised vision.

Weeks and months went by. His confidence was back. He had freedom again. Could go where he liked, when he liked. As long as Penny's name was on the documents everything was fine.

Driving wasn't easy though. He might be driving along and suddenly the clouds would part, he'd be driving into the glare of the sun, dazzled and head-achy. Or grey clouds would gather and the light would drop dramatically and he'd strain to see. He wasn't going to be defeated. He came to realise that there were no perfect weather conditions for driving. You just had to expect and accept whatever was out there and take the risk.

The financial risk wasn't a particularly big one. He'd been surprised about that. In the scheme of things it was a morning's work, water off a duck's back.

He made small allowances for the problems he faced. Driving slower and sticking to the roads he knew, trying to re train his brain by concentrating on other senses – like hearing. He noticed over time that his hearing had become more alert, more receptive, almost compensating for the loss of sight. He scanned his mirrors diligently, driving as if he'd just passed his test, looking up and down the streets warily for police cars. He began to track the regular places they sat and he avoided those roads. He turned the radio off, didn't dare answer his mobile and held the steering wheel in a firm 'ten to two' grip.

And then on a Sunday afternoon in June ten months after taking the wheel from Penny everything was to change. That wonderful complacency that had kept him going, the feeling of control and independence in his life was suddenly all stripped away, in an instant.

It had become a regular event on a Sunday to drive out with Penny to a garden centre, taking tea and scones on the sunny veranda and a pleasant stroll around the plants, remembering his old garden from all those years ago or a wander around the garden furniture, dreaming of sizzling barbecues and summer evening parties with friends he didn't have.

As usual he was careful. The roads weren't busy. It was the weekend. He wasn't in any rush. This was a pleasant ride out. A trip he'd done many times. As he drove back he felt slightly drowsy. Penny had begged to take the wheel.

'There's no point in you risking it without a licence. Let me drive for once.'

He couldn't admit defeat or risk her smashing his expensive car. The journey was barely 5 miles.

Penny never plugged her point. Hers was a cushy number. She didn't have to wipe his arse, put him to bed, deal with toileting accidents. When he was at work the day was virtually her own. He told her it was in her interests just to keep her cackling mouth shut.

He parked the car, in its usual place next to the house and went to lie down for a while. Just as he was drifting off there was a loud, firm knock at the door.

35
Clifford

June 2012

Who was it?

Nobody ever called. Neither of them had any friends.

He got up, walked towards the door; relaxed but sleepy, the weight of the scones and heavy cream sitting in his belly.

Two dark figures stood behind the frosted glass. He knew who'd grassed. The chances of the police catching him had only ever been slim. In all his years of driving how many times had he actually been randomly stopped? Possibly only once.

'Good afternoon Mr Chancer. I think you know why we're here.' Their bodies were rigid, faces expressionless.

'And I bet I can guess who grassed me up. Fucking typical.'

'Your car keys please? We're going to arrange for the car to be impounded. You'll know more in about a week.'

36
Clifford

January 2012

Clifford closed the office door, minimized the porn to the corner of his screen, took a deep preparatory intake of breath then returned to the call.

Ben had placed the tanks on the lawn.

'Your mother disowned you. What does that say Dad? Grandma obviously changed her mind, wanted me to have her money.'

Clifford could taste the venom in Ben's voice.

He cleared his throat.

'Ben.' It wasn't the affectionate honey sweet tone of long ago, when things were so different and Ben was just an innocent sweet boy. This was lemon sharp. Clifford mentally loaded his incendiary device.

'I'm going to say this once more because I don't think you're quite understanding me.' He took a sharp intake of breath.

' You're a spoilt little shit, a greedy little fucker and clearly a chip off your mother's block. Now *you* listen to me. I'm issuing a challenge to Grandma's will and it's your responsibility as executor to obtain all the medical records.'

' Dad you're not thinking rationally. If you object to her solicitors assisting Grandma in changing the will you're not fighting them, you're actually fighting *me*. Do you not see that? I've been advised that if you take this to trial it could cost me £4000 in legal advice. Look. I suggest we split the money 50/50. I can have the will re written with words to that effect. That would be fair.... probably.' His voice faltered. 'I don't see why I should, mind.'

'That's big of you. I'm not relying on your charity or sense of fair play to come to the only logical conclusion - because, quite frankly I don't think you have any. You have enough background to the events. The date of the new will is pertinent and the documents you sent me weren't even witnessed. Now that's gross negligence. You know, as well as I know those solicitors should never have allowed Grandma to revoke the previous will. No doctor correctly certified testamentary capacity. There's no doctor's signature. I've been reading quite a lot these past days about the Mental Capacity Act 2005 and it's clearly a shitty piece of legislation which seems to put science and medical opinion to one side in favour of human rights crap. It's no wonder judges get gunned down in revolutions. She should never have been allowed to revoke it. She was a dozy old lady who had turned into a confused mess in just a couple of months.'

Clifford thought back to the hours he'd spent at her dying bedside and the tears he'd shed, completely unaware at that point that she had changed her will.

'How can anyone make a new will when they're suffering from dementia?' he carried on. A mentally incompetent woman was allowed to cut out her next of kin because she believed as a consequence of delusions she experienced in relation to her illness that her son had assaulted and robbed her. One can only assume the lawyers believed her delusions, even though the Crown Prosecution at the time did not.'

'You don't need the money Dad. You earn enough. I've still got a few years of study to get through.'

In a whining voice he added 'Grandma obviously wanted her grandson to have it.'

That night he went to bed with a headache.

'I'm engaging in a legal confrontation with my own flesh and blood,' he said to the mirror as he cleaned his teeth.

'A legal battle with my little boy,' he muttered into his pillow that night.

He couldn't quite believe it. It didn't seem possible.

The next morning Penny was unsympathetic. 'Maybe he does need it more than you love?'

'Oh fuck off you dozy bitch.' He didn't need her opinion or anyone else's.

'He's never took into account my feelings, especially all the stuff that happened back in 2007. It still reverberates around my mind. He's a selfish little bastard.' He rammed the toaster down.

This was no longer about the money, but God knows he could have done with the money. This was about principles.

'Watching it all disappear is like watching sand gently drain through a sieve.' He opened the marmalade.

This was about the bitter raw feelings left behind, after the death of a loved one, like tide marks on the beach when someone you always thought you trusted, always thought cared about you, didn't in fact care at all. It was about the authorities taking control, making decisions over your head not listening or examining the facts correctly. When he reflected back upon his life so much of it had been about injustice. He'd been excluded from seeing his own mother and then the big fuss when the power of attorney went to the solicitors and the very next time he'd seen his mother she no longer knew who he was.

She'd gone to her grave thinking the worst of him. The tapestry of their interwoven lives had unraveled and it had happened so quickly the stitches couldn't be gathered up again and rewoven.

Clifford's energy levels and general mood always soared when he saw a fight on the horizon. He was prepared to fight anyone, even his son. The thought of fighting his mother's solicitors gaining an admittance of negligence drove him along in the coming days.

'As attorneys to the will the solicitors would have had the power to re draft the will if they considered it right and proper.' His solicitor told him over the phone.

'There is some argument,' the solicitor continued, 'that given the allegations made against you, spurious allegations I know, they simply took that your mother would not want you to benefit.'

The fight was over. It hadn't even begun. Were they about to get away with negligence?

'So this has all been a waste of time?' Clifford asked flatly.

'I think all we can do is take what Ben is now proposing. Make a Deed of Arrangement, split the money 50/50 between you both but that will involve legal costs too, so what I would propose is a private arrangement whereby he transfers your share over to you on completion. I think that would be far easier.'

'*Whatever*.' Disappointment came crashing down.

He felt completely deflated, a saggy cushion. He was sick of fighting, sick of principles and most of all felt bitter that his son wasn't going to concede and hand over the entire inheritance - the money that *was*, after all rightfully his. Inheritance didn't bypass a generation. It went to the next generation. That was the natural order of things. He'd always stood on his own feet, he'd worked his guts out, struggled to keep the business going but this money was his, not his sons. The private education they had struggled to provide for Ben had ruined them financially and it had all been a waste of money costing their home and a whole lot more.

But he hadn't realized that actually things were about to take a turn for the worst as events unfolded and far worse than he could ever have possibly imagined.

The money hit Ben's account. He called Clifford to ask for his bank account details for the transfer of half the money.

Clifford waited. Five days later he wondered what had happened. Maybe there'd been a banking error. He called the bank. No error. Each day he flicked between different icons on his screen: the company's database, the company's bank account, Ben Dover's black beauties and his private bank account. Occasionally he jotted down figures on a scrap of paper working out the size property he could now afford. He browsed Rightmove and Zoopla and earmarked several cottages. He flicked through several pages of newer model cars. He thought about a holiday to Australia. Life was going to be better. The pressure to sell the business was now off. Even with half the inheritance the pressure was off. There had been a few prospective buyers for the business over the months but no firm offer on the table.

He desperately needed a property. One day the lights would go out. There was no way of knowing when that would be. And in addition to his sight problems diabetes was a complicated disease. He'd had one heart attack. At the moment he was ok. He could still earn. All the time he was earning he could afford to rent. But renting wasn't a secure future. Inheritance was the straw he now clutched on to.

He didn't want to call Ben to ask why the money hadn't been transferred, giving the little shit the delight of thinking he was desperate. But on the fifth day his blood ran hot and cold like petrol beneath the skin. He suddenly had that 'hit by a truck' feeling. Disappointment burned a scar into his soul. Children, more than anyone else in life had the power to seriously disappoint. For every smile there was pain.

Finally he called. To begin with he couldn't process. It was like listening to words in his sleep.

'Sorry Dad.'

Ben was matter of fact, like a waiter who couldn't offer the crème brulee but could offer cheese and biscuits instead.

'I changed my mind. I'm not handing it over. You don't need the money. It was Grandma's final wish that I should have it.'

Clifford sat back on his bed. He felt dizzy. It was as if he'd just heard a sentence constructed of jumbled words and he had to deconstruct and reconstruct what had been said.

And then slowly the bile rose from his chest, slithering through him like a snake, coiling around his chest, as reality hit. It didn't take him long to fire the next and final missive.

'You know what? I've done my very best for you over the years and I've helped you appeal against the university's decision to put you back a year, after the bi polar diagnosis and all the shit you went through but this really takes the piss. This isn't the bi polar talking now. This is you. The real you. This isn't you being impulsive, acting on a whim in one of your manic episodes. You've made a cold calculated and very nasty decision right from your head. I shall never forgive you now. Through the whole divorce I never had your solid support. You're nothing but a shit. One of life's takers.'

'You've never stopped banging on about the divorce, blaming me for not taking your side. What sort of a father would do that?'

'You're no son of mine. In fact I wish you'd never been born. And I mean that. I truly do.'

'You always did know how to hurt. You're a pretty crap all rounder really dad.' Ben sounded casual now and slightly smug.

'Well that told me. You won't be needing my contribution any more. Not now you've stolen my inheritance. You're on your own. Don't expect any more money. And don't expect to hear from me again after this.'

'The money will buy a house and a car. I still need maintenance. You're committed now. What sort of a father would go back on their promise to support their son?' Ben pleaded.

'Ive done my very best to support you over the years, through private education and university. Swindling me out of this money is the pits. It was bad enough when you're mother fought me in the courts and I fought her to the end over the spousal maintenance and won. I can't call you my son let alone carry on supporting you. Now what precisely don't you understand about the two words fuck off?'

'Grandma wanted me to have it. She made that decision. You got greedy and wanted the decision turned around.'

There was a long pause. Clifford was about to end the call.

' Watch your back. Don't expect to get away with what your doing.'

Clifford knew what he was referring to. He wasn't going to fall for blackmail.

'Fuck off Ben.'

'When you can't think of anything to say it's always the F word Dad. Swearing is running away. The coward's way.'

'The F word is pretty harmless. But pick any D word and look at how it destroys lives: divorce, dementia, diabetes, depression, dysfunctional families. The 'D' word is what my life has been about.'

Clifford hit the red button to end the call.

For the next half hour he focused on a plan taking shape in his mind; a plan which had begun a few weeks back when he had last visited China and made a new business contact with a man called Chiang.

This time next year he planned to be living and working mainly in China on a Mandarin version of the tyre magazine. The Chinese wanted to be more than just the factory of the world. They wanted to move up the value chain.

Through his knowledge he'd help them to become innovators; be more than a beg, borrow, steal culture. This was exciting. This dream was the new D.

Living costs were cheaper; he didn't need a mortgage. The obsessive desire for a mortgage to rebuild his dream had only shackled him to the past and the future. Bankers had handed them out like candy at a fair. Then taken them away in equal measure. Why give them that power? He'd followed the wrong dream. He'd find happiness in the east. His eastern promise. And maybe - in time his relationship with Ben would be restored. He'd always go on forgiving the boy no matter the pain he caused. Blood was thicker than water afterall.

Where there was despair there was desire, where there was distrust there was delight. It was around the corner; a long corner in another time zone.

And the best thing of all about living in China was that he stood a better chance of managing his diabetes. He had always had better blood sugar readings when he stayed in China.

And the women were fresh unchartered territory.

The End

36685160R00150

Made in the USA
Charleston, SC
10 December 2014